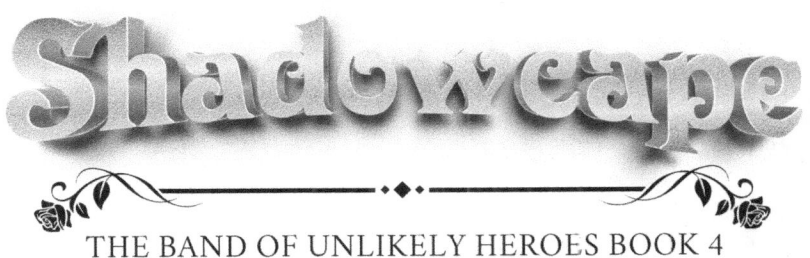

THE BAND OF UNLIKELY HEROES BOOK 4

DAWN FORD

To my dedicated readers.
You make all the hard work worth it.

CHAPTER I

~Horra~

Troll Queen Bearer Horra Fyd flipped a page in the large tome open in front of her. Golden sunlight poured through the floor-to-ceiling glass windows in Oddar's Grand Library, highlighting her study of bug critters' habits and defenses.

A full week had passed since the Erlking, her devious elven enemy, had cursed the fairy queen and disappeared on his kelpie to return to his elusive hiding place, leaving Horra's kingdom of Oddar adrift in uncertainty. To ease her desire to do something, Horra had thrown herself into research.

Rowan, her woodgoblin druid companion, shifted in the wooden chair beside her, his branchy crown snagging her curly red hair. His theory book on music magic, the favored tool of the evil elf, lay open before him.

Frowning, Horra untangled her hair from Rowan's limby head and smoothed the strands back into place.

He ignored her silent suffering.

"Bah, this is so boring," bellowed Fairy Princess Glory Toppenbottom.

Horra jumped at the sudden tirade.

Glory, the third of their study group, slammed her book shut. Her wings buzzed as they fluttered, then stilled.

Rowan sent the fairy a reproachful frown, but she kept her attention on the ceiling.

Glory heaved a heavy, put-upon groan. "It's been over a week, and we're no closer to taking him down."

Horra fought the urge to admonish the girl. Her protests would've been more believable had she been in the library for more than half an hour. Though she knew the fairy princess yearned for her mother's healing after the queen had suffered terribly under the Erlking's care, her moodiness was more likely due to her sister's demanding personality and the tedium of sitting at her mother's bedside. So much for Glory changing her ways. "Go take a break, then," Horra muttered as she scanned the Critterology book.

After Glory had confirmed the Erlking utilized bugs and small animals for his nefarious schemes, they started searching for ways to inhibit his influence. Which meant a lot of investigation and time spent reading—not the fairy princess's favorite activity.

At Glory's loud sigh, Horra ground her tusks into her top lip.

"I already took three breaks today. There's nothing to do in this forsaken place." Glory stood, her plethora of skirts swishing with her movement. Though Horra preferred the dresses to the tattered cloak she had worn before Grendel had reversed the Erlking's hexes, she was no fan of her gauzy replacements. Glory's heels clacked on the library's stone floor as she paced, her wings rigid at her back.

Each footfall against the cobbled floor was a nail hammered into Horra's brain.

Rowan cleared his throat—a despicable clackity racket that forced Glory's shoulders to her ears. "Perhaps you should join Grendel in the lab?" he suggested. "She was testing out a new device meant to catch sound on different wavelengths."

"Yeah, because that's so much more interesting," the fairy grumbled under her breath.

Glory stopped beside Horra's chair, her flowing brown hair gleaming in the full afternoon light. Though not as beautiful as she once was, the spells and potions Grendel had used to heal her had returned a portion of her beauty and allowed her some use of her semi-restored wings. Not as ethereal as she once was, the fairy now possessed a more natural attractiveness, which Horra preferred over the normal sparkling perkiness.

If only Grendel could've replaced the fairy's temperamental personality as well. Horra would've paid to witness that feat. Only yesterday, she'd shot a sparkling spell at Rowan after he'd settled in to lecture her. Glitter lingered in the cracks even after the hogboblins had scrubbed it clean.

"You know Grendel's experiments are way above Glory's understanding, Rowan." Horra had found that the one thing the fairy despised was to be seen or thought of as a lesser creature. So far, the fairy hadn't caught on to Horra's manipulations, and she would take advantage of her ignorance to the fullest degree in order to save her sanity.

An ugly scoff slipped from Glory's lips. "As if. Fairies are far superior to giants in every way." Her heel scratched on the floor as she spun and headed for the doorway. "Later, losers." The echoes of her footsteps faded after she left the room.

Rowan blinked at the empty doorway before turning back to his research. He'd grown large enough that his crown shadowed his face even in the brightness of a clear Springtide day.

Horra's stomach burbled. Unlike the druid, she had to eat regularly. Being that her head was also now aching thanks to the fairy, she needed a break as well. "Lunchtime. I'm going to head to the dining room."

"Hmm," Rowan mumbled. His branchy noggin was bent over a large informapedia. "Right, yes."

She shook her head as she strode from the library into the hallway. The smoky scent of grilled musk ox steaks tantalized her taste buds. A grin tugged at her lips.

Crash!

Bang!

Roar!

Glory let out a high-pitched squeal a second before a furry orange form burst through the lab, breaking the door.

Horra halted, her eyes wide.

Grendel Largeness, more beast than girl at the moment, snarled. Spit flew from her fanged mouth as it stretched into a more animalistic maw. Attached to her ears was something that looked like insect antennae. As Horra watched, Grendel grew larger.

Heart thudding in her chest, she ran toward the giantess. "Out! We've got to get you out of here." She caught Grendel by the arm, and her troll strength allowed her to yank the girl through the Hall of Monstrosity and into the throne room to the double-door castle entry.

Destroyed by Fairy Princess Misty Toppenbottom after the Erlking's last attack, the doorway remained a gaping hole, open and unimpeded. Horra shoved the giantess toward the crumbling opening.

Grendel growled and whined, the arm beneath Horra's claw bulging enough for the seams of her tunic to split apart.

They reached the doorway before Grendel grew too large. Her head struck the tall doorjamb, loosening some remaining blocks. Debris rained upon on them both.

The giant girl wrenched her arm free. Wild-eyed, she ran toward the trees, the strange gadgets in her ears still humming. In a few strides, the giant girl entered the forest on the side of the castle's northern edge before disappearing from sight. Trees trembled with the girl's movement as she tore through the expanse. In moments, silence fell again.

Horra stood staring after her, panting. It was difficult to drag a giant around, and the effort had cost her. Her claws trembled, both from shock and from the energy she'd spent.

Glory rushed to her side, her petite mouth hanging open. Her wings flitted in agitated jerks.

Horra turned to face the fairy. "What did you do to her?"

Shock crossed the fairy's face, and her wings stilled. "*Me?* I didn't do anything. I just walked into the lab and found her acting strange—quivering and mumbling." She gestured toward the space where the giant girl disappeared into the foliage. "Then she smashed everything. I'm fine, by the way."

Horra glared, still stunned by what had happened.

Rowan glided up beside them. "Master Knurl spoke to me. He said there's been a shift in the ether."

Horra took a deep, cleansing breath. "A good shift, or a bad one?"

The druid studied the tree line, furrowing his woody brows. "He didn't say."

"Well, isn't that helpful?" Glory spun and strode back to the castle. "That monstrous thing destroyed your lab, just so you know," she grumbled over her shoulder. "So don't blame that on me too."

"Was that Grendel?" Concern creased the bark on either side of Rowan's mahogany-specked eyes.

"Yeah. She—I don't know. Changed back to a giant. I rushed to get her outside. Otherwise—" Horra mimicked an explosive motion with her claws.

He turned to face Horra. "We need to go after her." His voice was low.

Horra shook her head. "She's huge now. One of her steps would take us a dozen to compensate. She could be who knows where already." She ran her claws through her frizzy hair and squeezed, easing the ache in her skull. "If what disturbed her was something minor, she'll come back."

"What if it isn't?"

Horra's heart sank for the druid. He'd grown close to Grendel. They'd shared much time together, working on the link between the Erlking and the critters the evil elf used to do his bidding. Her absence would be hard for him. "She's a big girl and can take care of herself. She'd been doing it for quite some time before we found her."

His eyes darkened and his body fell slack. "But the Erlking."

She knew what he was thinking. The last time they'd faced off, the Erlking had dispatched a dryad and had critically injured Glory's mother, the fairy queen. Stella Toppenbottom remained with the other princess, Misty, in one of the guest rooms. So far, their ministrations weren't successful in waking the woman from her magic-induced coma.

"Grendel's smart. The smartest creature I know besides you. If she's not back by morning, we'll track her down. Just like we did Glory. We'll find her."

Rowan lowered his head, his branches hiding his expression. He loped toward the castle.

Horra glanced skyward and prayed silently to the Creature God to supply her with strength and grant them knowledge of what caused Grendel to change back to her giant self. The

Erlking was obviously up to something. And that was never good news.

~Grendel~

THE TREES BLURRED as Grendel ran, and the noise inside her brain made it hard to concentrate. More than once, stinging from scratches pricked her consciousness. She fell several times but ignored the pain. All she craved was to stop the racket. Even her pounding heart couldn't drown out the discordance bombarding her. And so she ran, on and on in oblivion.

CHAPTER 2

~Rowan~

Rowan entered the laboratory minutes later, only to find chaos. Overturned tables and splintered chairs greeted him. Glass equipment lay shattered in pieces on the stone floor. Because the broken glass wouldn't hurt his roots, he stepped inside, determined to figure out what had caused his newest friend to lose control.

He sensed a presence behind him. "What was she doing before this happened?" he asked the fairy princess.

"You said it yourself. Researching airwaves or something." Glory kicked a glass shard, and it skittered across the smooth floor before colliding with a wall. Her wings drooped.

Rowan's experience with the princess proved she wasn't as dense as she sometimes acted. If she hadn't been curious herself, she wouldn't have returned to the laboratory. "Sound waves," he said, correcting her. He grabbed a tangled piece of wire and inspected it. His trunk pinched tight around his core. Perhaps he should've paused his research and joined Grendel.

Then he might've known what happened to her and could've created a plan to fix the issue.

"Whatever." Glory's dismissive tone was at odds with her snooping. She lifted an object, studied it, then set it back down.

"What are you looking for?" he asked. "Is there something you know that you aren't telling us?"

Her face scrunched, betraying her annoyance. Glory used the expression with Queen Bearer Fyd often. "No. I gave my word I wouldn't keep things from everyone anymore, and I haven't."

Rowan pivoted to face her fully. "Then what is your motive for staying here?"

Queen Bearer Horra strode into the room carrying a broom and dustpan. "She can't help herself. This is the most drama we've had in days, and she's like a glimmerfly to a flame." The queen bearer placed the dustpan on an undisturbed table and began sweeping the floor. The stiff bristles created a scritch-scritch noise in a rhythmic, uniform pattern. The sound pricked something in Rowan's brain stem.

He held out his arm, stopping her for a moment.

Princess Glory grimaced, splitting her displeasure between him and the grating of the glass across the stone floor.

The queen bearer hesitated, then drew back. "What is it?"

"I don't know." At her dubious glance, he continued. "The sound is triggering something in my memory, but I can't place my finger on what."

"O-kay." She stared his way. "Should I keep going, or—?"

"Yes. But in the same pattern, if you would."

Her next swipes were less vigorous, so he signaled for her to keep going, and she fell into the same rhythm as before. Images of the Riven—the graveyard forest, to be exact—danced across his mind. But why?

The queen bearer continued across the lab, sweeping and

collecting the pieces. Something nagged at his memory, but he couldn't parse out what. The laboratory wasn't big, and overturned tables hampered the queen bearer's progress. Without being asked, she traveled back to the open space. A piece of debris stuck in the bristles maintained the same sharp scratch across the stones.

He shook his head and dropped his arm. "My apologies, Queen Bearer. The answer is there in my mind somewhere, but it's elusive."

The queen bearer stopped sweeping and laid a claw on his forearm. "It's okay. Your confusion could be information Woodsly left in your seed, and it will take some prying to open up. Sometimes I do something else—take my mind off of it— then whatever was nagging me comes easier."

Rowan didn't glance her way. She was trying to be helpful, but information was his specialty. He rarely had a lapse in retrieving it. "Thank you. Maybe I'll go to the Conservatory and discuss this with Master Knurl. He may shed some light on my befuddlement."

"Or you could help us restore the lab." The princess lifted a table and set it back down, crunching glass beneath the legs.

"Isn't that what magic is for?" Queen Bearer Horra's voice held an edge.

Princess Glory narrowed her eyes at the queen bearer, and her wings twitched. "I don't have enough magic to whisk this ... mess back into shape." She pinched her lips together as she moved to the next table.

"That's too bad. The old-fashioned way of actual labor is far superior, anyway."

Rowan turned and left the squabbling duo behind. Their sparring held undertones he didn't understand, and he did not relish being boxed between the two again.

He passed the portraits in the Hall of Monstrosity. Though

he looked at the paintings, he kept his focus on what had triggered him with the scritching sound. Hobgoblins moved in the background, unintrusive to him or any of the other royals who wandered the castle and its grounds. Everything was normal except for the pounding in his heartwood. His sap sped through his fibers at an alarming rate.

Past the great Hall, another passage led to the Conservatory. Though unlit, he knew the way now, so the darkness didn't bother him like the Erlking's mountain had. His memories of that desolate trek still sent shivers across his bark. Outside the double doors, he lifted the key to unlock them. Pidge squealed from inside, alerted to his arrival. The surety of her presence and that of their resident rood, Master Knurl, settled him enough to be able to open the door without his hands shaking.

Before the pudge wudgie could sneak through the door, Rowan reached in his pocket and brought out a wrapped chunk of vapid viper flesh. Murly, one of their stable hands, had found the poisonous snake by the barns and killed the viper before it could attack their horses. He'd saved the skin for Rowan to test out the specialized toxins it held. After he and Grendel had extracted the glands, he dissected the snake specially for Pidge.

Rowan tossed the chunk in the air and left the parchment wrapping in the disposal crate so the poison wouldn't affect anything living. The pudge wudgie would have no trouble digesting any toxins left behind.

Pidge darted—a bright flash of ebony feathers—and caught her treat before it landed on the ground. She chirruped in delight.

He meandered to the central Yew tree and rested next to the aging trunk. Its leaves spread above him in a grand canopy. If Rowan tried, he could almost imagine he was back in the Weald.

He shook his head at such folly. It wasn't like him to be so reflective.

A creak sounded, and Master Knurl's face appeared in the bark. "Why are you troubled, young druid? What is on your mind?"

"Two things." Rowan dropped his head to study his branchy hands. "Grendel lost control and changed back to her giant form. I'm unsure what happened to her. Then, when we were cleaning the destruction she left behind, a sound pricked my memory. But no matter how hard I try to figure it out, I don't know what about it is bothering me."

Bark snapped as the rood frowned. "Another shift surged in the castle. Because the change was by air, I couldn't grasp what it was or why it happened. As for the sound, is it a remnant from your forebearer?"

Rowan pondered the rood's declaration before answering. "Grendel was researching sound waves. Perhaps something she heard triggered her change, then." He rubbed at the thinning moss on his face. Springtide ushered in warmer weather, and the foliage was receding, its cover and warmth not needed as much as during Wintertide. "As for your question, I'm not sure. Whatever the blockage is, it's beyond my perception."

"In my years of experience, I have found that the information will come, usually unheeded, when your mind strays to other topics. Often, it's a vague memory of something more concrete. What was the trigger, and what impression did it leave you with?"

Rowan explained what happened and spoke of his memory of the Riven.

Master Knurl remained silent for a few seconds before responding. "Since the giant girl was working on sound waves, and you mentioned the sound of the broom, could it have something to do with the music the Erlking uses?"

He was going to disagree with the old rood that the noise of the sweeping had anything to do with the evil elf's magic, when he recalled the chitterbugs. Their "music" was the ebb and flow of their mating calls. More than obnoxious, the sound was much like the screeching sound the glass made against the stone floor. "Thank you, Master Knurl. You've been very helpful." Rowan rushed out of the Conservatory, Pidge's dismayed screeches following him down the dark hallway.

~Horra~

SEVERAL MINUTES LATER, Horra and Glory were arranging the last of the chairs around the lab tables when Rowan burst back into the room, startling them both. "Rowan! What in the name of snake skin are you trying to do? Scare us to death?"

He raised a finger. "Chitterbugs. That's the sound your sweeping reminded me of."

Horra propped the broom against the wall and faced him, unsure what the connection was. When she turned, the druid was only a step away from her. "Space, Rowan." She pushed him away as his eyes grew wide and his brow lifted as if waiting for her to understand. She motioned with her claw for him to keep going. "And?"

He steepled his fingers, and Horra's shoulders slumped, knowing she was in for a lecture. "In the Riven, I caught the sound of the chitterbugs for a moment. The noise was loud, but it held a particular cadence. I rushed to block the racket, and that's probably why the significance didn't automatically come to me. What I'm deducing is that the Erlking uses his critters for more than just spying. Either he's enhancing their "songs," or they're enhancing his music magic."

Glory snickered and crossed her arms. Her muted lilac dress, which matched the hue of her wings puckered in the center, scrunching the colorful embroidered flowers she'd magicked across the bodice section. "So? What's so important about that?"

Horra bumped her arm, a silent reminder to be nice to the druid, as she climbed into a tall chair along the far wall. "It means if we can stop the bugs, we can weaken the Erlking." She turned back toward Rowan. "How do we do that, though?"

Rowan dropped his hands. "I haven't figured that part out yet."

Glory tsked, then scoffed. "Not more research! You guys are the most boring group of creatures I've ever had the displeasure of spending so much time with." She swiveled and left through the doors on the opposite side of the lab.

Horra waited for her to leave before addressing Rowan again. "She's not wrong." A long breath escaped her. "So, we concoct a plan to destroy all the bugs across the Wilden Lands. What about the frogs and the rodents? The Erlking uses ignored or unappreciated critters. If we targeted them all, the results would wreck the balance of nature everywhere."

Rowan's bark quirked into a rare grin. "Not if we do it right."

CHAPTER 3

~Grendel~

Some time later

Grendel woke to find herself on the ground and surrounded by a thicket of weeds. Her head ached, as did her body. "What happened?" She sat up. Bugs darted about in the overgrown area, and she swatted the nuisances away. Her sight was dim and her head swam. Swiping a hand across her face, she groaned. ' Where am I?"

The last thing she remembered was testing out her soundometers in the troll castle's lab. She slapped her palms over her ears. The devices were gone. Her heart thundered in her chest.

Those were her prototypes, the only pair she'd built so far. Grendel struggled to recall what happened, how she'd ended up outside the castle, but her mind wouldn't cooperate. Moaning against the dizziness, she gathered herself and stood. Blood rushed to her head, and she stumbled to her knees.

The last time she felt this way was when the Erlking had

changed her the first time. Her eyes snapped open. "This is so not good." A glance at her shredded clothes was the only proof she needed.

After that first change, she'd lost almost a day and felt woozy upon waking miles from home. The memories returned slowly. She swiveled and sat to wait for her foggy brain to clear.

Minutes ticked by. Her mind wrestled with the possibilities of what had happened. Had anyone in the castle seen her change and run off? Would they come looking for her? When some of the murkiness cleared from her brain, she dared a glance at the sky to gauge the time of day.

Grendel was no stargazer. She concentrated on what little she knew of the constellations. "The Shepherd's Star is the brightest, revealing itself during the day. This star points due north, past the Giant Lands. Below it are the sacred Seven Stars, which are visible on any cloudless day," she muttered as she glanced across the sky, avoiding looking directly into the sun. "And since Springtide is in full swing now, that means the Seven Stars sits below the Shepherd's Star. There." She laughed, pointing at the faint formations. The rush of blood in her veins was from glee this time, not magic.

Standing carefully, she oriented herself. Beyond her resting place, a path appeared. "Oi," she muttered. Crushed grass and broken foliage in the overgrown area detailed her harried movements. Though not straight, the trail was an arrow pointing back to where she'd come from, clearer than any sign. She'd follow it until she reached the rockier areas where growth was sparser and her footsteps sure to be less clear.

Slowly, she headed south, determination overruling her many aches and pains from dashing about. Her frantic trek was an experience she didn't long to repeat. Freed from having to navigate every step, she turned her focus to figuring out what caused her to change back so it would never happen to her again.

AFTER WHAT SEEMED like hours later, Grendel found one of her test antennae among the rubble along the edge of the northern Iron Mountain range. Her reflective tape among the gray stones winked in the light, catching her attention. She rushed to the piece and bent to pick it up. Somehow, she'd snapped it in half. Loose wires stood out like bristles, and she ran a pad of her forefinger across them. "Oh, bother." The broken item was much too small now to rest snugly inside her ear even if it hadn't been half destroyed. The base that amplified the waves, though, was still intact and usable. She could work with that.

Without a pocket to settle the segment in, she opted to carry it. Small as it was, it wasn't hard to do. Shadows lengthened as the sun moved lower in the cloudless sky. Her legs ached, but at least her head had fully cleared. She recalled the immediate audio racket she'd experienced after donning her antennae. So many sounds and whispers.

Whispers? Was that what she'd heard? Grendel shook her head. She didn't remember any words. Her footsteps faltered, and she stopped to contemplate. Rocks skittered with her sudden movement, but she paid them no heed. Like with her experiments, she went back to the beginning and worked her way through what was tangible and what was conceptual. Real and not real.

She sifted through the information but found nothing of substance that pointed to voices. Her mind and her gut warred with each other. The pragmatic, scientific part of her consciousness agreed with no whispers. Her nervous system, however, blared inside her, a fear that spread from her core and rippled along her limbs. The signal was an instinctual warning, telling her to not believe everything she heard.

Dilemmas such as these rarely plagued Grendel. One and one always equaled two. Giants approached magic as a tool, a means by which to enhance and enrich life. Giant society relied upon their serums for all manner of things, from beauty treatments to extending life. This knowledge allowed her to heal the fairy princess after the multitude of hexes she'd suffered. Their secret elixirs and restoratives were beneficial.

Grendel was top of her class and well-read. Nothing she'd learned had prepared her for the Erlking's unique brand of magic. His sorcery made no sense to her keen mind. The notion of hexes wasn't new or unheard of. Old giants' tales of the Witching Wars and elves' magical manipulations were told and retold over fires. They grew from partial truths to harrowing tales meant to scare the hearers. They hadn't been real to her. Then the Erlking hexed her and all those notions flew out the door.

Grendel walked on, her focus more on her thoughts than her surroundings. The hex turning her into a monster was a punch to the gut of her scientific mind. She dug a fisted hand into the blossoming ache in her chest to ease the harsh memory.

Giants had strict regulations pertaining to magical experiments. Children as young as Galumph used benign potions and elixirs on critters in their formative biology classes. They were harmless and informative to young minds, shaping them into the scientific mold her society deemed worthy.

But nothing about the Erlking followed any rule book. Grendel swallowed hard, her dry throat sticking with the effort. The Erlking had no boundaries with which to keep him in check. He placed no value on life or creature freedoms. Not that she hadn't known this. But another level of understanding settled across her mind.

In order to fight the Erlking, they would have to surrender their preconceived notions about how to fight him. They'd have to throw their guides out and create new ones. Changing tactics was the only way they'd win.

~Glory~

LATER THAT AFTERNOON, Glory reluctantly returned to the guest hallway before the evening meal. She didn't relish facing her comatose mother and her indignant sister again. The sweet smell of her sister's magic permeated the air in front of their suite at the end of the hallway. She glanced longingly at the door of the room the trolls had originally assigned her.

After the Erlking injured their mother, her sister, Misty, had insisted they all room in the larger suite for their mother's benefit. Being together would help heal the queen, so she'd said.

So far, that hadn't been the case.

With a hefty sigh, Glory turned the handle and entered the large room. Clouds of sparkling magic hazed the sitting area. The cloud was thickest by the bedroom in the back of the suite.

"Good. You're back. Your turn to sit vigil." Misty donned a silk robe over her silver chiffon dress. Slits in the back allowed her diaphanous wings to slip through easily.

Glory longed to have her normal wings back. Though the giantess had restored them a little, they were stiff and easily fatigued. She eyed her sister—from the top of her coifed head to her crystal heels. The only thing absent was the royal scepter.

And that, along with their royal carriage, was missing. "What royal duties are you dressed for?"

Her sister huffed, striding past her to the door. "If you were around more, you'd already know. The giantess has done all she can to heal Mother. It's time to return to our Shining Kingdom. While you watch over the queen, pack and prepare to leave."

Glory's chest tightened. She didn't desire to go home for the same reasons she'd escaped her mother after being cursed. Though she still yearned to have her beauty back, she no longer wished to trade the Erlking for the favor of it. His wickedness, she knew now, was beyond repair. He'd used and abused her affections in the most atrocious way. If only she'd realized her quest for gaining back her beauty wasn't worth the effort, her mother would not be in the shattered state she was currently in. That was on her. "Wait!" she cried out to her sister before the door shut.

Misty stood with her back rigid and her delicate hand clenched tight to the handle. "What is it this time?" Her voice bore thin restraint, something rarely seen with her sister's temperament.

Glory needed to approach her carefully or lose any chance of freedom. She took a steadying breath. "I'd like to stay, help in the fight to bring the Erlking to justice for his crimes."

Her sister's wings drew together as her shoulders pinched.

She hurried on. "It's not—" She stopped and restarted. "I'm not staying for selfish reasons. I pinky swear."

Misty turned to side-eye her at that promise, which was their childhood oath they'd always held to.

Glory walked to her sister and took her free hand in her chilled ones. "I've made too many mistakes for you to trust me, I know. There's nothing I can do to prove my intentions except to do better going forward. But someone has to hold him accountable."

"Say his name," Misty growled through clenched jaws.

Glory frowned but rallied. Her sister knew how to pierce her heart to create the biggest wound. She deserved Misty's ire, but that didn't make it any easier. "The name he used is fake and doesn't matter. He is the elven Erlking, second coming of the greatest enemy of our state, and the evil fiend who gravely wounded our mother and queen. I have no delusions of him now." She dropped her sister's hand and held out her pinky. "I swear to you I will avenge her and our kingdom."

Misty stood motionless for longer than Glory was comfortable with, but she didn't rush her sister. Misty's keening must be growing, for she felt the pinpricks of the other fairy's magic testing her truthfulness. After a few more moments, she nodded. "Fine. But you realize that leaves me the as Official Fairy Ruler. Once done, I cannot undo it until mother recovers, or in the event of my death."

Glory knew. Their training had ensured they understood. Only one could bear the royal title at a time. Her mother had bound them against each other since their birth. Twins were rare, and only the strongest would gain the throne. The battle for her mother's favor had always been like an ill-fitted dress. That struggle was partly why she'd rebelled and fallen into the Erlking's trap. "I've never desired the crown. The crystal throne was always going to be yours."

She endured more of Misty's probing truth-seeking. She knew her sister would become a wonderful queen. Much better than she would've ever been.

With a sigh, Misty hooked her pinky with Glory's. "Fine. Though you know I've never been comfortable with a leadership role, either. We were going to rule together, remember?" She unhooked her finger. "You owe me big time for having to care for Mother alone. Don't think I will let that go unpaid."

Glory grinned. "I am in your debt."

"I must speak to the queen bearer and the king before I depart. Just don't—" A sob caught in her sister's throat and she coughed, blinking back the wetness flooding her forest-green eyes. "Don't leave me alone to bear the crown. Not forever."

Glory shook her head. "You are much stronger than you believe yourself to be. Much stronger than I ever was or could hope to be. However, I promise to do all I can to return to you and Mother. I will be there for you when this is over, I promise."

Though not an oath, magic zinged between them, sealing her words. Misty left, shutting the door quietly.

Glory wrapped her arms around herself. She prayed she would survive facing the Erlking again, but she was no fool. Or she wasn't any longer. Defeating the evil elf was going to take a miracle.

CHAPTER 4

~Horra~

Around dinnertime on the same day, the ground beneath Horra rumbled, making dust fall from the rafters in the barn. Nimble shied and let out a guttural belch. Smoke curled from the gulgoyle's mouth. Horra finished pouring the water into her pet's trough and petted his neck to reassure him. "It's okay. Nothing to worry about." Good thing animals couldn't tell when she was fibbing.

She set the bucket aside and headed toward the door to see what the noise was when she heard her name being called. "Grendel?" Horra rushed outside.

"Queen Bearer!" The voice was distant, but since Grendel had returned to her regular giantess size, it carried like a tolling bell.

Princess Misty Toppenbottom exited the kitchen doorway that opened onto the back courtyard. Her official-looking silver dress betrayed her thin body structure. Her wings fluttered lightly behind her back. "What is that racket?"

Sageel darted around the princess's shimmering skirt, wringing her gnarled hands in front of her.

Before Horra could explain, Grendel's furry orange head appeared through the trees. Dozens of birds scattered from the limbs, the sound of their caws echoing in their wake.

Grendel's footsteps rattled the grounds as she clomped her way to the castle's front courtyard. Horra, Misty, and Sageel all approached the giantess. Other hobgoblin servant's faces popped into the windows as they moved around the side to the front.

"Goodness! She's so big," Sageel muttered before she stopped next to Horra.

"You're not kidding," Princess Misty said beneath her breath, her wings whirring as they beat erratically.

Grendel bent over and lay down, taking up a large corner of the courtyard where the Erlking had faced off with them a few short days ago. She groaned between heavy breaths. Tangles knotted her fur as other patches of bare spots revealed the skin beneath. Tears marred her clothes and debris littered her wispy hair as if she'd been rolling around on the ground. Perhaps she had been.

"Grendel," Horra started, breaking the silence, "we're so glad you've returned. Are you well? Can we bring you anything?"

Grendel shifted to sit up, moaning with the effort. "I would most appreciate a drink, Queen Bearer."

Sageel rushed off to collect it.

"I am sorry for rushing out like I did." She coughed and cleared her throat. Murly, the stable hand, brought a wooden bucket full of clear water and handed it to the giantess. "Thank you." She drank it all in a couple of gulps. "More, if you would."

Sageel ran over with another bucket as Murly took the first

back to refill it. Grendel drank the new bucket and returned it. "Thank you, Sageel." She gave Horra an uncertain smile. "My experiment went wrong." She dropped the antennae Horra had seen dangling from her ears before. "All the noise." She waved her paw-like hand to encompass the air. "It bombarded me."

Murly returned with another bucket of water, which she drank. "Thank you. My throat was dry."

Rowan glided over to the group, graceful like Horra's former instructor Woodsly had been. The druid's gaze was intent on Grendel's face. "Ah, good. You've returned."

Grendel bowed her head. "An experiment gone wrong, I'm afraid. The antennae worked too well. The music I heard must have triggered something from the Erlking's hex to turn me so quickly. All I remember is pain and cacophony. Noises. Voices." Her voice drifted off.

Sageel appeared with another bucket, but the giantess's attention was not on them. She stared into the distance, a troubled expression on her furry face.

"Leave that with us and prepare some food for her, please, Sageel," Horra told her favorite maid. "I'm sure she's famished as well."

After Sageel left, Horra sat on the ground. There was no way Grendel was going to fit inside the castle now. "What happened after you fled? Were you injured?"

Grendel reluctantly turned back to the group in front of her. "Nothing that needs attention, no." She ran a hand through her delicate red hair. It was different than the orange fur that matched the color of her skin and covered her body. The colorful jewels, which every giant had embedded in their scalp, lay hidden beneath thick wooly hair—a gift of the Erlking's curse.

She took a shuddering breath and continued. "I recall little after that initial barrage of sound. The clamor pierced my brain, and I couldn't make it stop. I vaguely recall you ushering me from the castle, Queen Bearer, but then only flashes of the trees and bushes as I ran through. How long have I been gone?"

"Six hours, forty-three minutes, and thirteen seconds," Rowan said dryly.

Horra opened her mouth wide and stared at the druid. It figured the woodgoblin would know down to the second. "You've been gone most of the day. It's dinnertime now."

Grendel twisted her face in thought. "So that means I ran for two hours, lay unconscious for an hour, and walked back for three hours. That sounds about right."

Rowan lifted the antennae and began a discussion with the giantess about the distance and how she came to that conclusion.

Princess Misty touched Horra's arm, startling her. She'd forgotten the princess was with them. "Queen Bearer, I hate to intrude, but I need to speak with you in private. Possibly together with your father?"

Horra glanced at the other two, who were discussing speed ratios and distances over differing terrains such as trees and the rocky mountain ravines. "Gladly. Let's check the dining room first since it's almost mealtime."

They headed back to the castle, entering through the broken front doors. Panic at seeing the castle so vulnerable rose inside her, but she gulped it down. What would her foremothers think? She shook off the terrible thought.

"The doors remain in this state?" the princess asked, shock clear in her tone.

"These stone doors are a special order from the dwarves, who seem to have gone missing. We're trying to contact the forest ogres now." The ogres were renowned for their excellent woodworking skills. Their prices matched their abilities, so most creatures only dreamed of owning an ogre-made piece.

Horra shrugged. "I'll have the knights gather logs to block the entry."

Misty's laugh tinkled, setting Horra on edge. She remembered the glee both fairy princesses had displayed when destroying all the plants in the Conservatory.

Oblivious to Horra's thoughts, the fairy smiled. "I remember when we first arrived. Or I should say, I vaguely recall it. You were holding court when we interrupted." Her voice drifted off for an instant, then she pointed a dainty finger at Horra. "You looked as bored as anyone I've ever seen."

Indignation pricked her gut, but the fairy was right. Petty grievances filled their weekly court schedule that day, making the time inside the assembly unbearable. Everything that day plotted to work against Horra in the most intolerable way. She recalled the endless complaints, the redhatter's prickly powder in her collar, and her numb backside. She giggled. "Goblin Courts are the worst. The shopkeepers were nattering on for hours about a rat infestation. Then your prancing guards danced in with you and your sister, dressed in the most awful matching pink dresses. Your visit was the horseradish on top of an impossibly long day. Nothing will ever top your spontaneous arrival."

They both snickered at the memory.

Horra sobered quickly, though. "Now we know it was the Erlking's handiwork."

Princess Misty's smile vanished, and she lowered her wings. "Yes." She glanced at the door again. "Let me fix this for you. I owe you for your efforts to save the queen from harm." She lifted a hand, and a small spark of light grew into a ball. The princess whispered into the sphere and threw it at the rubble of the stone doors. They shuddered and lifted, knitting themselves back together, rock by rock. "I apologize for my failure to notice. My focus has been solely on Mother's recovery."

Horra placed a gentle claw on her arm. Tears stung her eyes. "I'm so sorry we failed to protect her."

The fairy shook her head, the reddish light of the evening sun reflecting off her blonde hair and silver outfit, setting her aglow. "We failed the trolls first. Taking my sister's actions into consideration, I'd say there's enough fault to go around."

Horra moaned. "No one escapes his influence, not even me. He's like a force of nature."

"A dangerous, unexpected power," Misty agreed.

The door, now whole and sound, creaked closed, shutting out the outside light. It closed easier than it had previously. Flickers of fairy magic glimmered in the sunlight like millions of tiny gold flecks. The light around the princess dimmed until only a faint halo remained. At one time, the ability of fairies to enchant the essence of light with their presence would've annoyed her. Horra had come a long way since then.

"Thank you, Your Majesty." Horra offered her a fairy salute. "You honor us with your generosity."

Princess Misty thumped a hand on her chest, returning Horra's gesture with a troll tribute. "It's the least I can do. Now, let's find your father. I have news to share with you both."

MINUTES LATER, they found the king in the dining room, scrolls and books in disorderly piles around him. Hobgoblins raced around the room, readying the tables for the next meal. One of the younger maids set a pitcher at an awkward angle, almost tipping the liquid onto the parchments. The king deftly caught the jug and righted it before any damage was done.

Horra grimaced. "We need to place a desk for you in the throne room."

"Our kingdom has a suite of office rooms tucked away from any prying eyes," Misty said.

Though her tone held no vitriol, her implication that trolls weren't careful enough with their royal correspondence stung.

King Fyd grunted. "Hobgoblins cannot read." He shuffled the parchments in an orderly fashion—a feat, considering the disorganized pile. When he finished clearing the space, he stacked the books on top of each other and signaled to the gulpy herald standing along the wall. "Take these to my room and place them on my table."

The gulpy bobbed his head back and forth as he hefted the tomes and toddled through the doorway. The hobgoblins disappeared back into the kitchen.

Horra didn't correct her father. Woodsly, her late instructor, had taught the hobgoblins on his off time. Sageel had confided to her that Woodsly had shared many of Horra's old instruction books with their staff. Since then, Horra had found that most of the hobgoblins in the castle could read basic words. Woodsly apparently never informed the king of his covert mission to train the lesser creatures in the royal household. After consideration, Horra had done the same, sharing books and simple training manuals with them.

King Divitri waited for the creatures to leave before continuing. "Now, what can I do for you both?"

Misty bent her head in deference. "I need to inform you that I am taking the queen back to our Shining Kingdom for further treatment. Glory has insisted on staying behind to help with the Erlking." She raised a hand when the king opened his mouth to speak. "She has caused much trouble to your household, I know. But I believe she has changed. I would not leave her here otherwise. Our kind would do better with peace between our kingdoms."

The king rested back in his tall wooden chair. He glanced at Horra, who stared at them both dumbfounded before she schooled her expression. "Fine, as long as she doesn't undermine this kingdom or our efforts to capture and end the Erlking's evil plans."

Misty bowed her head again, accepting his assessment.

"When do you depart?" he asked.

"We leave at sunrise on the morrow. If my sister becomes ... troublesome, please send a messenger immediately. I will react swiftly. Will you please send a tray to our suite? I'd like to spend as much time with her as I can before we leave."

The king glanced at Horra and signaled for her to answer, reminding her she was Queen Bearer. Frustration that he didn't allow her to answer about Glory staying flickered, then died. He knew well the animosity between the two of them. And he knew she might reject the princess's offer.

Instead, and having learned her lesson on civility and diplomacy, Horra settled her courteous face into place and answered Misty. "Of course, Your Majesty. Please let us know if you require anything else before you go. May your trip home be uneventful." Horra signaled with the fairy salute again.

Misty bowed her head elegantly, then swept out of the room.

Horra turned to help her father gather the scrolls and parchments. His claw on her arm stopped her.

"You handled that well. I didn't even see a twitch on your face when you spoke." He hissed out a breath as if in pain. "You've grown so much in the past year. I'm not prepared for it." He shook his head, a lock of green hair falling across his forehead. "Your mother would be so proud. I am so proud." A dimple flickered across his left cheek. She'd seen the indentation so seldom since her mother died. He rarely offered a genuine smile.

Horra didn't mention the wetness glimmering in his dark eyes. She fought the prick of tears as well. His praise was all she ever hoped for—acknowledging her as a warrior worth her foremother's legacy. "Thank you, Father. That means more than you know."

Hobgoblins, surely sensing the fairy's absence, burst through the doorway and bustled around, setting the tables for the meal. The commotion broke the intimate moment, but Horra didn't complain. She'd earned her father's praise at last.

CHAPTER 5

~Rowan~

Rowan dug his roots into the front courtyard soil as Grendel ate. The amount of food looked meager in her hands, but several trolls, including two strong door trolls, led a procession of numerous platters from the kitchen to the giantess.

Grendel wiped her mouth with a bath towel. "I need to assemble a batch of contracting candy so I'm not stuck out here all night." Her eyes darted around, surveying the edges of the forest. For what, he wasn't sure. "I don't enjoy sleeping in the open."

Rowan disengaged his roots from the ground. "Allow me to assist you in making your contracting compound. What do you need?"

Grendel hesitated. "I'm not allowed to share giant's trade secrets. It's one of our kingdom's greatest classified recipes. If I tell you, you cannot tell another."

Rowan's limbs shook with a rush of wind, the air cooler

than normal. His roots detected a storm coming before morning. "I cannot make any promises, as I am beholden to the troll kingdom for mentoring me outside the Weald. If circumstances in our war against the Erlking demand it, I might have to break my word to you."

She folded the towel into a neat square, a furry furrow between her hazel eyes. "My training is in healing and experimentation. They raised me to never divulge certain secrets, even in the event of an emergency. My fears are not more important than my kingdom's need for confidentiality."

Rowan steepled his hands in front of his trunk. "Merrow taught me that circumstances can eclipse traditions or even rules. When the queen bearer trekked across the Wilden Lands with my seed, she found herself in some dangerous situations. Once, she traveled through a poisoned forest that tainted my seed. Then, when she was busy saving her kingdom from the marriage between her father and the fairy queen, I suffered the effects of a magical curse. She arrived at the Weald just in time for my seed to be viable. But the journey damaged it."

He gestured toward her. "Queen Bearer Fyd had stolen some of the contracting candies and expanding pastries while escaping your house, thinking they were merely sustenance. Not only did she utilize them on her trek, but she allowed Merrow to apply them to help sustain my seed. That magic helped me sprout. Without it, I might still be a dormant seedling, waiting to unroot and start my battle against the Erlking."

Grendel shifted to a different sitting position. "So, what does that have to do with my kingdom's secrecy concerning the configuration of the candies?"

Rowan approached the subject from a different angle. "What is the purpose of the candies and pastries?"

Her face fell slack. When she spoke, it was through gritted teeth. "That's confidential."

"But I've been told you trade it. Balk, a mercenary friend of the queen bearer, has used them before. If the purpose is classified, why share it with other creatures who could then take the candies, break them down to their ingredient forms, then recreate the whole?"

She fidgeted, her lips pressed together into a hard line.

"Have you been tongue-tied?" He referred to the magical spell he'd thought the Erlking employed not so long ago when his ailment turned out to be a grubby worm infestation instead. She certainly looked afflicted at that moment.

Grendel shook her head.

"Then I fail to understand the necessity of the contracting candies. You told me once that giants are spell-crafters who create antidotes and spells that do incredible things. I believe you claim scientific calculations and intentional purpose formed the basis for the contracting candy. What purpose is that?" He narrowed his eyes as a suspicion raced through his brain stem. "Unless giants don't employ them for beneficial reasons."

Grendel pursed her lips, fiddling with shreds of her shirt hem.

Rowan watched her closely. He'd assumed that since they'd discovered her outside the Erlking's lair, scared and alone, she'd been truthful. He'd witnessed her generosity and charity firsthand with the fairy princess and her mother. They'd held in-depth discussions about experimentation. For the first time since Merrow's death, he'd found another intelligent soul he could connect with on a deep level. He had so little experience with others, he was quick to trust her. Had he been wrong to do so?

She closed her eyes. When she opened them again, they

revealed a glimmer of tears. "There are far-reaching implications that were drilled into my head from the time I could speak. The configuration would be dangerous in the wrong hands." Wind parted the tuft of hair on the top of her head.

Her implication was clear. Rowan stiffened. "And you think I would exploit your confidence?"

Her mouth dropped open. "No! That's not—I mean ..." Her voice died off. "I don't know what I mean." Grendel shifted around once more, showing her unease at their conversation.

Rowan had never seen her so nervous, not even when they'd first found her and she'd been terrified after watching the Erlking hex the fairy princess. "What is your reluctance to share such information?"

She stared at her thumbs, which she twiddled in an annoying manner. "You don't understand. It's not only a secret. It's like the giant army's confidential information. You'd die to protect it."

"And this is worth dying for?"

Whispers from trees waking from their winter hibernation traveled with the wind. They murmured news about the strength of a coming downpour. Rowan glanced at the darkening sky, where clouds created a wall of rain in the distance. He'd missed the voices of the forest.

"Storm's coming." Grendel's voice held a note of alarm.

"Yes. I bid you good evening—"

"Rowan," she started, then stopped. "Please don't go. I'll tell you about the contracting candies if you promise to only tell the queen bearer and no one else, and only if she forces you to tell her."

He thought about that. Technically, Queen Bearer Fyd was the only one he answered to, as she was his mentor. Her father could ask, but from what he understood of troll politics, only Horra's death would bring King Fyd back into power. "As long as she lives," he promised.

Grendel narrowed her eyes. "Fine." She held out her hand.

Merrow had versed him on oath rituals, so he took her hand and magic entwined them, the air growing heavy. In the blink of his eyes, it was done, the magic sealing their agreement.

Grendel dipped her head, her voice low enough to not carry above the wind. "I need large amounts of these ingredients."

An hour later, Rowan and Grendel spread out in the corral behind the stables, where he could have an open fire without attracting too much attention. In a large cooking pot Sageel had snuck out to him, he added the last ingredients to the contracting-candy mixture. The sweet scent whipped around in the wind.

A twig snapped. "Well, well. What are you two up to out here all on your own?" Glory's voice rose above the gusts.

Grendel's shoulders tightened. "Rowan is making me a dessert. I don't fit inside the castle, remember?"

"Oh, I remember. However, this doesn't smell so much like sugar as it does chemicals. And I do pride myself on my ability to scent a sweet treat. So, I ask again, what're you up to?" She moved over to the pit where Rowan had placed a metal frame to hang the pot over the flames.

The concoction inside the pot bubbled and hissed as the liquid splashed against the hot exterior of the metal. Grendel told him the mixture had to cool before it gained its full strength. The formula was almost complete. They only needed to add sour puckerberry. Rowan had struggled to find that ingredient since it was out of season. But Sageel had some in her personal stock, which she claimed helped ease the arthritis in her gnarled hands. He'd traded with her for some bee's nettle honey he believed would help her more than the puckerberry.

He measured carefully, ignoring the fairy.

"Huh. Both of you chitty chatters are silent." She bent over the fire, far enough away that her filmy dress didn't catch flame, her wings spread wide. "Is it prickly powder? I heard Horra is desperate for more to be added to her laundry."

Grendel hefted the fairy in her arms and placed her down beside the barn. "I realize sneaking around and spying on people is one of your favorite things, but this is none of your concern."

Glory's eyes grew wide, and her wings slashed back and forth angrily. "We'll see about that."

Rowan stirred the boiling brew. He waited for the fairy to stomp across the cobbled courtyard before speaking. "What do we do if she goes and tattles on us?"

Grendel shrugged. "Who's she going to tell? Horra? The king? Neither of them like her snooping around."

"You didn't finish telling me what the candies are for." Rowan waved at the giantess to continue.

She moved so she could watch the kitchen door. "It's not the candies that we keep quiet about. It's the expanding pastries," Grendel whispered. "When giants moved into the northlands, they found a rare bird we call a bloomer. Only found in the northern regions, this bird grows to twice its size when threatened. One of their primary food sources is the stinkhorn mushrooms that grow abundantly in our forests. Anyway, my forebearers had growth spurts after they ate the birds. The increase wasn't much for the first generation, but the ones after that grew enormous."

Rowan stepped back from the fire, though it was the only

thing keeping him warm as the temperature dipped. It wouldn't be long now before the rain began, then they'd both be out of luck.

Grendel continued. "Thorough search concluded it was how the stinkhorn worked with the bird's glands that enabled it and us to grow." She lowered her head. "My forebearers slaughtered them to extinction. One scientist, however, kept a small kettle of them. He surgically removed the glands of two of the largest birds. With the information he gleaned from his research, giants distilled the compound and, together with the stinkhorn, recreated it through artificial means. Now every baby across the giant lands receives a shot of that extract when they're born. It's helped us to grow into the largest nation the Wilden Lands has ever known."

"And your kindred believe if others figure this out, they will manipulate it to challenge the giants?"

She lifted her head, a hard expression on her round face. "Or kill us for it. We've received threats before."

"I see." Rowan blinked. He studied her voice inflection and body language. Having dealt with both Horra's and Glory's ever-changing moods, he could now decipher nuances of emotions. Fear and concern were the most obvious ones he detected in the giantess now. "Are not the giants big enough to overcome any other creature who might dare to intimidate them?"

"You've seen the damage one evil elf can do. Our magic is minimal and doesn't expand as we grow. Only our strength can keep things in check."

"So how do the candies work, then?" Rowan asked, curious.

"In contrast to the stinkhorn, we also found that the sour puckerberries temporarily reverse the effects of the expanding pastries. Therefore, we can shrink when needed, but only for brief periods of time." Grendel sniffed the air, then motioned to the pot. "The scent is right. It's ready to cool. And just in time. I sense rain."

Rowan took the pot off the dying fire and snuffed out the flames with a bucket of water from the well. The rain would take care of any remaining embers. "To the barn," he said as the first spit of rain touched his bark.

CHAPTER 6

~Horra~

After her evening meal, Horra entered the Conservatory with a pocket full of treats and a jar of torentula eggs at the ready. She shut the door behind her, making sure it latched before turning to find her pet pudge wudgie.

Pidge rose from her nest in the central Yew tree. With a loud screech, she darted directly toward Horra. She landed lightly on the stair platform, clucking as she normally did when she was extra hungry.

"You poor thing. Hasn't Rowan fed you yet?" Horra tossed her two of the pickled eggs, the juice filling the air with a pungent aroma. Then she took a stick of dried skeeze jerky and threw chunks of it into the bushes for the bird to hunt.

The door behind her opened, and Rowan and a newly shrunken Grendel entered. "There you are," Rowan stated, gliding over to her. "We've been looking all over for you."

Pidge popped her head above the foliage after finishing her

treats to chatter at Rowan. The ebony bird fluffed her feathers and returned to her hunt.

Horra ignored the frustrated tone in Rowan's wooden voice and bit back a comment about how she'd been sitting in the dining room only minutes before and anyone could have found her. "I think Pidge's annoyed that you didn't feed her according to your schedule." Horra smirked at the woodgoblin. He'd given her such a hard time over Pidge's exercise regimen, which coincided with his feeding times, that she had to poke fun at him.

She finished tossing tidbits to the pudge wudgie and turned to Grendel. "Good to see you back to your smaller size." Knowing about the contracting candies, Horra didn't inquire about how the girl shrank. "Are you hungry? The maids are cleaning up, but I'm sure they can throw something together."

"Thank you, Queen Bearer. I had my fill of vegetable soup earlier."

Horra narrowed her eyes. "Is it the lighting, or is your"—she hesitated, holding back the word "fur" for something less insulting—"skin growing darker?"

Grendel glanced at a fur-covered arm and frowned. "It rained on us. Perhaps that's what you're noticing."

Horra clapped the crumbs from her claws, then brushed them across her tunic to wipe the grease off. For such small creatures, skeezes were inordinately oily. "So, what is so dire that you were searching *everywhere* for me?"

"Do you know where the music book went? It's not where we last left it," Rowan said, his branchy hands twitching.

Horra gaped. She and Glory had cleaned the laboratory together after Grendel's tirade. She hadn't seen it there, and she hadn't returned to the library since Grendel's incident. "Where's the last place you recall leaving it?"

Rowan and Grendel glanced at each other.

Grendel fidgeted with the fabric on a dress Horra hadn't seen her wear before. She recalled Sageel telling her that the maids were fashioning some new clothes for the girl since she'd only had one change of clothing and Grendel ruined them when she'd returned to her giant size. "It was in the laboratory," Grendel said. "I'm so sorry. I promised to keep the book safe, and I've lost it."

Though her stomach plunged, knowing the consequences if the fairy took possession of the book, she tried not to let her anxiety show. "I'll go check with Glory and see if she has it."

"What if she took it?" Rowan clacked. His branches rattled, marking his unease. "She might not tell you the truth."

Horra stretched her neck, her shoulders growing tight. "She promised she was changing her ways. This will be a fine test of that claim."

HORRA LEFT them and wandered to the guest rooms, her father's praise still on her mind. What would she do if Glory returned to her petulant behavior? She'd thought the girl had changed her mind about obtaining her former beauty. What if it was all a ruse like Rowan had insinuated?

She'd arrived at the large guest suite's doorway before she could devise a diplomatic answer to that problem. One thing Horra was sure of: She preferred to face Glory in front of her sister than on her own.

She knocked on the door and waited.

Princess Misty opened the door. She wore a more casual dress the color of turnip ends—pearl with a purple tint. "Queen Bearer. Is something amiss?"

Horra dipped her head in a formal greeting. "Not at all, Your Majesty. I'm sorry to intrude, but I need to ask your sister a question."

Glory stepped to Misty's side, who glided back so Horra could enter. The sitting room was larger than her father's. Its purpose was to house royalty and their retinue. Largest among the personal bedrooms, the suite could comfortably house six fairies.

"Does this have anything to do with the giant girl and wood boy brewing something mysterious in the barnyard?" Glory asked, a haughty tilt to her head.

"No." Horra wasn't going to broach the subject of giants' fascination with contracting candies with the fairies. She took a deep breath and charged in. "The Erlking's musical spellbook has gone missing in the confusion of Grendel's change. Have you seen the book anywhere, by chance?" She worked to keep her words light, not accusatory.

Glory's lips pinched, then eased. "I have not. You were with me when we tidied the laboratory."

Misty studied her sister from beneath lowered lashes. Then she glanced at Horra with wide, innocent eyes. "Where was the book left? Perhaps if you retraced your steps?"

Horra had to admit the blonde fairy had become an accomplished diplomat since her mother had gone missing. Or maybe her sudden maturity was because circumstances had never warranted Horra to become exposed to this side of the princess. "I believe Grendel and Rowan have done so, yes. They came to me thinking I may have taken it. I, too, have not seen it lately." She glanced at Glory again, trying to gauge the girl's honesty.

Glory placed a dainty hand over her heart. Her wings remained steady, unfluttering. "I promise I am not hiding anything from you. Sister, can you perform a location spell for the book? If the rats had anything to do with the book going missing, it will come back to us," she reassured Horra.

Rats? Horra blanched.

"Of course." Misty pushed her tight sleeves up. The material was stretchy and soft-looking. She murmured a few words and threw her hands out. Sparkling magic flickered, traveling through cracks in the windows and through the still-open suite door. In an instant, the cloud disappeared. "There. It will either fly back to us or, if it's in a confined space, the book will chime to help you locate it."

Horra bowed her head to the princess. "I am grateful for your generous assistance."

They all stood and waited. Nothing happened.

Misty tsked. "The spell is quite simple. Even a fairy child can operate it successfully," she explained, breaking the silence. "Something must be restricting the book's movements. If it liberates itself and follows my magic here, I'll send it your way immediately. Now, if you don't mind, I need my beauty sleep."

Beside the princess, Glory stiffened. Misty didn't seem to notice her sister's discomfort. It only took a moment for her to regain her composure, then Glory forced a friendly smile. "I'll see you in the morning?" she asked tightly.

Pity bloomed inside Horra at the royal's careless words. Glory was still sensitive over losing her fairy beauty. And though she looked nothing like the disfigured piggish monster the Erlking had first turned her into, no amount of giants' potions would return her to her original elegance. Not having a sibling, Horra was never quite at ease when situations such as these arose. She swallowed back her sympathy, knowing the fairy wouldn't appreciate it, at least not in front of her shining sister. "Yes. See you then."

Horra turned and strode from the suite, glad to be an only child.

Two hours later, Horra, Rowan, and Grendel finished searching the castle with no luck. They sat at a table in the Grand Library while rain lashed against the floor-to-ceiling glass windows. Sageel sent a young maid in with a tray of drinks. Horra took them and handed them out: a sustaining sap for Rowan, beet juice for Grendel, and spruce juice for her. "Thank you," she told the girl, who blushed and raced away, holding the tray to her chest.

"She's new?" Grendel asked.

"We've been recruiting new staff." Horra didn't tell them that her father had found it difficult since the Erlking started kidnapping children to find new staff to replace the ones who'd left. All creatures were skittish now, and with the imps and redcappers protesting against Horra's and her father's rule in every town across the Wilden Lands, few fancied being harassed when they were out and about.

"Where do we look next?" Rowan asked, his sap finished in one gulp.

"We wait for the rain to stop and search the grounds." Horra sipped her juice, intent on searching the hidden passageway next. Impatience to return there and start looking for the book nipped at her gut, but she stifled it. No one could know about the secret paths inside the castle walls. Not even her father knew about them. Because male trolls had not supported the females when her foremothers built the castle, they missed out on their Creature God's blessing. The secrets of the passageway were a tradition handed down from matriarchs to the next generation.

"Queen Bearer?" Rowan clacked. "Have you heard a word we've said?"

Horra jumped, knocking herself from her musings. "I'm sorry. What were you asking?"

"Grendel and I have called the search off until the storm passes. Is that acceptable to you?"

Her heart skipped a beat. She was more than ready to slink away from them, back into the passages. "Yes. Of course. Good idea." She rose and gathered all three of the empty mugs. It took all her control to walk slower than she desired, trying not to show her eagerness to return to the real search. "I'll see you in the morning, then," she called over her shoulder.

Horra hurried to the kitchen. She could've gone to her room, but she couldn't chance becoming sidelined by anything else. And she only kept certain doors unlocked: her room, the stables, the dungeon, and the kitchen. The stables were out of the question with the rain. The dungeon was too dark and brought to mind too many uncomfortable memories from when the fairy queen had imprisoned her there. That left the kitchen.

Only one maid cleaning the floors remained. Horra nodded at the woman and placed the mugs in the sink. Rain hammered against the small window above the preparation area. She waited, staring at the window. The wet floor gleamed in the dull lantern light, all but the last corner by the stove and hearth area. Despite the cool air escaping around the outer door's frame, the kitchen remained warm from the evening meal preparations. Horra twitched with impatience

When the maid moved out to the preparation area, Horra rushed into the pantry and flipped the switch. The door opened without a sound. She hurried in, flipped the other handle, and didn't wait for the barrier to close before she hurried into the passages.

Her night sight kicked in, allowing her to see outlines in the darkness. Familiar with the layout, she moved toward the center of the passages.

She rushed on, stopping in the center—a space between the library on her right and the dining hall to her left. Blood rushed through her veins as she listened.

Over the sound of her heartbeat, a faint high-pitched chime echoed in the distance.

CHAPTER 7

~Horra~

T he scritch-scratching of claws darting about the passageway echoed in the empty space. Horra frowned. They hadn't had vermin since Pidge gobbled them down when she'd concocted the mesmerization antidote. Even when the princess mentioned them, Horra hadn't fully believed rats could be behind the book's disappearance.

Why now? And did it have anything to do with Grendel's change? Was her use of the soundometers at the same time a coincidence?

Horra didn't hesitate. She rushed through the passageway, searching. Rats hissed in the distance. The chime echoed from different places all at once. What in the Wilden Lands did it mean?

One particularly aggressive rat rose on its haunches in front of her. Startled, she swung her claw and walloped it square in the jaw. Pain exploded along her knuckles as the little beastie squealed and darted away. "Ow, ow, ow." She shook her claw. "That's right. Run away, you disgusting critter."

She needed Pidge. Her pet wasn't afraid of these vermin. They'd regret the moment they returned to the castle, that was for sure.

She was closest to her bedroom, so she headed that way, holding her throbbing claw to her chest.

More scuffling echoed in the outskirts of the passage. How many of the rats were sneaking around? Were they all as combative as the other one? She needed to hurry. Without a weapon, she was vulnerable. Her heart drummed inside her chest, making her claw ache more. She used her uninjured claw to open her bedroom door, a task that proved more difficult than she liked to admit, since she was shaking from her encounter.

The stone barrier moved slower than she desired, and she bounced on her feet until it opened enough for her to blast through and punch the buttons that would close it. She hoped none of the critters would follow her into her room. For an instant, she wished she could lock it from her side. Unfortunately, she couldn't. The best she could do was retrieve Pidge and sneak back into the passages to deal with the unwanted pests.

The stone shut so slowly—too slowly for her liking. When it finally closed, she rushed across the dirty clothes littering the floor, shoving some aside in her haste. Then she flung her door wide, hurried out, and ran right into Grendel and Glory. Grendel squeaked in surprise, and Horra's door slammed shut. Why were they in the royal corridor?

Glory slapped a hand to her chest. "Sparkles and glitter, you scared us. What in the Wilden Lands are you doing?"

Grendel narrowed her eyes. "I thought you went to the

kitchen. I didn't see you pass me. We've been out here talking since I came upstairs."

Horra's chest heaved, and she worked to calm her body, but her claw still throbbed and her instinct was to run and collect Pidge. She forced herself to act casual. "Um, I don't know. You weren't here when I came to my room." Her voice wasn't as confident as it would be if she were telling the truth.

A confused look crossed the giantess's face.

Glory, however, seemed unconvinced. "No. I would've seen you. I've been out here for the past hour, pacing back and forth. What are you up to?"

Gah! How was she supposed to explain what she was doing without telling them about the passages? "Couldn't sleep. I thought I'd visit Pidge for a while." Horra pushed her way between the two girls and darted for the stairs.

They followed her. "Vinegar," Horra muttered beneath her breath. She didn't have time for this. She stopped at the bottom of the stairs and spun on them. "Listen. I don't have time to explain. I have something important to do, and neither of you can follow me. Just go back to your rooms and I'll fill you in on the details in the morning."

Grendel's face crumpled. For such a large creature, she could be so sensitive.

Glory slammed her arms across her chest in a defiant stance. "Oh no you don't. If this has something to do with the book, let us know. It's only fair. We're in this together, right? You said so yourself."

"Not now." Horra spoke through gritted teeth as sweat coated her claws. Well, at least her uninjured claw. The other one was still partially numb from the hit. "Don't force me to order you to your rooms."

"What's with all this commotion?" King Fyd's voice boomed, startling all three of them.

Horra whipped around to face her father. Seconds ticked by with each heartbeat in her chest. She was running out of time. "I have official business to attend to, and they won't leave me to it."

Her father gave her a one-eyed glare. "I'm unaware of any official business. Explain."

No, no, no! This was not happening. "I—" Horra started.

"It has something to do with the Erlking's missing music book. She won't let us help with it," Glory accused. "And you call me self-serving."

The king ignored the princess's insult. "The music book? That's the one with the spells he uses, isn't it? How is it missing?" The king planted himself in front of Horra, his stance wide and unmovable.

Horra was sunk. He would demand an explanation, and she couldn't admit the truth. At least not the full truth. Her mind raced. She settled on a partial truth. "I thought I saw a rat in my room. I hoped to go gather Pidge so I could dispatch it. Okay?" Her eyes darted back and forth between the three, praying silently that they would believe her, maybe leave her to do what she was itching to do—get to Pidge and return to the passageway.

Her father waited for a long moment before he eased back, his shoulders loosening. "That's what we get for leaving the front doors open. Carry on."

"Why can't we follow you?" Glory persisted, her wings humming as they beat. She was like a pesky gnat.

Horra blasted out a breath, wishing for a big bug swatter. She stretched her aching claw, trying to ease the throb. "Because my room is a mess. I don't like others seeing it in its current shape."

"Pshaw! I've seen the deplorable state of your room more than once." Glory's laughter edged on the tinkling sound it used to be. The ridicule grated on Horra's nerves like nails against a hard surface.

Grendel stayed quiet, watching the exchange with a curious tilt to her eyebrows. Though Horra knew it wasn't a good sign for the giantess to be so attentive, now wasn't the time to question it.

"Yes. Be that as it may, I'd like to catch the rat before it disappears and finds its way to your suite." She'd added that last part hoping to dissuade the princess from following her around.

It worked.

Glory's face paled. "Fine. I've seen enough of those creatures to last me a lifetime."

"Can I come with you to the Conservatory? I'd like to speak with Rowan, and I don't see in the dark as well as you do," Grendel said.

Woodsly's lessons on etiquette battled with her yearning to sneak away. Her training won. "Yes, of course. But quickly, if you please." She rushed past her father without looking back at the fairy princess or checking to see if Grendel followed. She was a giant, after all, even in her shrunken size.

"I realize you are in a hurry," Grendel puffed behind her. "But can we slow down a bit? The contracting candies tire me out."

Horra remembered how the giant's sweet treats had pulled her into a deep slumber. Reluctantly, she slowed her steps, her lips stretched tight across her tusks. Sweat dampened her neckline by the time they reached the glass double doors. The key was not outside the Conservatory, and Horra almost growled in frustration.

She pounded on the door, forgetting she'd just smacked a rat with that fist. Pain bloomed again, and she cradled it carefully. Horra took a deep breath. "Rowan, open up."

Pidge's screech leaked through the barrier. Horra danced from foot to foot.

"Is everything all right, Queen Bearer?" Grendel asked quietly. "You seem quite agitated."

The door opened, and Horra rushed past Rowan, only to realize she had no snacks to entice her pet to her room. In her impromptu plan to take Pidge into the passages, she'd forgotten that minor detail. "Rowan, do you have any jerky or treats for Pidge?"

His face showed no emotion. "She is a master huntress. She would sniff out a morsel from a hundred feet away."

"So you're saying no?" Horra tittered to her pet. "Here, Pidge. C'mon, girl. We're going on a hunting adventure."

Rowan cleared his throat, irritating Horra further. "May I ask what this is all about, Queen Bearer?"

"No," Horra snapped the same moment Grendel said, "She has a rat in her room."

Horra slumped, defeated. Having so many creatures in her castle was cramping her ability to move about as she pleased.

The bark between Rowan's eyes crinkled. "Will someone please tell me what's going on?"

Abandoning her ruse, Horra wandered over to the Yew tree. She touched the solid trunk, grounding herself. "I heard the chime Princess Misty placed on the book, yes. But I couldn't reach it. I needed Pidge to help me. Now it's too late."

"Why wouldn't you tell us? We could've helped you look for it," Grendel said, her mouth twisted with concern and accusation lacing her voice.

"Because—"

"Because there are hidden spaces in the castle?" Rowan's gaze remained steady on Horra, and his comment was anything but a question.

Grendel gasped.

All the breath left Horra. She was sure her heart stopped beating for a moment. Then she, too, gasped. "What? How did you know?"

Rowan tsked. "It was obvious the second time you appeared in the Conservatory without using the known entrances. Why all the secrecy?"

Pidge scree'd from her nest, curious, but not enough to emerge without the enticement of a treat. Leaves rattled, and a few swirled to the ground around them.

"Spoiled bird," Horra growled, then flung her arms out in surrender. "Fine, yes. There are secret places in the castle. But I'm sworn to secrecy."

"By whom?" he asked. He tilted his head as if examining her.

Horra dropped her head into her claws. She couldn't face them. She'd failed her mother. The hidden passages would no longer be confidential within the royal lineage. "Mother. And her mother before her. And her mother before her, back to Oddar's first ruler, Queen Calcy. It's not only a secret. It's privileged information only the heirs to Oddar's throne have access to."

"Oh," Grendel said.

When no one spoke, Horra lifted her head to see what they were doing. Rowan stood relaxed, staring at her. Grendel's lips were pursed as if she were thinking hard about something.

Finally, Grendel spoke. "Giants have secrets too—things no other creatures should find out about. It's a security matter. Is it something like that?"

"Yes. And no." She sighed, her chest pinching with disappointment in herself. "It involves a pact my foremothers made with the Creature God. If I tell anyone, or if anyone else besides those of the royal line finds out about it, our blessing will be void. Oddar will be no more."

Rowan held up a finger. "Is it a pact agreed to with or without a magical object? As I understand it, without magic, trolls cannot fashion binding agreements with any other creature, even a sovereign one. Did the Creature God appear before your ancestors and seal the blessing? Or did they wield the gold sword to seal it? How did this blessing come to be?"

Horra opened her mouth to answer but stopped. She recalled her mother's story about how the female warrior trolls had secured the castle after defeating the elves. This was not a story her foremothers presented in any of their history books, but a tale passed on from generation to generation for royal ears alone.

But for the first time, she wasn't so sure. "Mother told me the first troll warriors were female. They built this castle from the mountain. They mined the gems they found and created Oddar. The kingdom developed and prospered shortly after that. My foremothers believed the Creature God blessed them for their hard work and bounty. They formed blood-oath promises using sacred vows to keep the royal line pure."

Rowan steepled his fingers. "But where is the blood oath sigil for the hidden places? Why is no one else allowed to know about them?"

"Because the male trolls doubted the God of all creatures, my ancestors forbade them entry onto what they believed was sacred ground. Mother told me the passages were a special gift for royal trolls only." Horra scoured her memories, the stories her mother would tell her about Oddar's history. Rowan's questions had her reexamining what she knew to be true.

"Wouldn't kings be considered royalty?" Grendel asked timidly, as if not wanting to cross Horra.

Horra sighed, unsure how to make them understand. She recalled her mother's words vividly. *"Our passageways are the brightest gem in our crown, daughter. Our God created trolls with the ability to do and build, but only warrior trolls believed in the Almighty. He blessed us for that, and we promised in blood oaths and with sacred vows we'd keep our line pure. We built a mighty kingdom, even defeating the elves to keep it. Because the male trolls doubted the God of all creatures, they are not allowed to step onto this sacred ground. Remember, the best things in life come from hard work and sweat."*

Because of those words, Horra realized the blood oaths and sacred vows were to keep their royal line pure.

Rowan bent his head as if listening. Possibly the Conservatory's rood was communicating with him. "Was there no actual blessing spoken over the hidden spaces? No blood shed or spread over the stones to keep the space holy?" Rowan glided over and sat next to her beside the tree.

The tree behind them creaked and popped. Master Knurl's face formed on the trunk. He coughed, a sound like sticks rubbing together. "Queen Bearer, allow me to shed some light on your predicament. I was here when the first of the troll Fyd clan formed Oddar decades ago. Wanderers at heart, the clan happened upon the Iron Mountains during the great Exodus of the Elves."

"Exodus of the Elves?" Horra's thoughts turned from her mother's declaration to what the old rood said. Then realization dawned. "Wait. You were alive when my foremothers established Oddar?"

Hers wasn't the only mouth hanging open.

CHAPTER 8

~Horra~

L ight sizzled across the sky, and thunder rolled beneath
them. Master Knurl, his face in the Yew tree fading
and reforming in the blink of an eye, nodded at Horra's
question. "I, an oread healer, was here before the Great Exodus
when the elves ruled the Wilden Lands, yes." He lowered his
branches and pointed to the trunk. "This tree has been my
sanctuary since shortly after the establishment of Oddar. Many
creatures roamed freely here then, before the establishment of
villages as you know them." Sadness tinted his gravelly voice, as
if he missed those days.

He was an oread, the male version of a dryad? Horra's head
spun at the information. "That's ... incredible. What do you
know about the pact my foremothers undertook with the
Creature God?" Horra shook off her surprise.

"There was no formal pact. The elves started the passages
when they mined the mountain, before the Exodus. Your

foremothers were at odds with the elves long before the Witching Wars when they came upon the elves in the Iron Mountains. Trolls were nonviolent creatures then, and they had suffered at the hands of both the elves and the witches. Their mistreatment forced them to become warriors."

"But if there was no pact, why were the passageways kept a secret for so long?" Rowan asked.

The tree's limbs moved, as if stretching. "This is a long tale. I will try to condense it for your understanding."

Horra sat at the base of the tree while Grendel sat on the other side, both ready to listen. Rowan stood between them.

Master Knurl began. "Dwarves and elves made a well-known deal that after the war, the dwarves would receive the mountains as payment for their services provided in defeating the witches. The dwarves had already mined the lower mountains. The Fyd clan caught the elves breeching that agreement. Calcy was a fearless and honorable troll, so she challenged the elves and won. She and the elves took an oath—she spared their lives, and they would never turn against the Fyd clan or any kingdom they built. Her victory did not come without help, however. The Lady and I both assisted them. The elves then disappeared to what we now know as Endwylde—a secretive society they created in the far Northwestern Mountain Range."

Grendel gasped. "So you know about elves?"

"I once knew them. It has been many years since then. But because we helped the trolls, a bounty was placed on our heads. When Calcy built the castle, she gave us—the Lady and I—sanctuary in the passage halls until either the threat was gone or they finished the Conservatory. We hid here among the trees until now. Later troll generations came to believe the passages were holy because of their ability to keep the Creature God's anointed ones safe."

Horra frowned. "So, it isn't technically true—the passages being holy ground only royalty can access." Her head spun. Rain lashed at the glass enclosure, the storm in full swing now.

"Exactly," Master Knurl said. "When a tale is told for centuries, parts of it are bound to be left out or embellished upon. That is why, before I died, I established the druid race. I meant for it to keep the balance between good and evil and to record history and information for future generations."

Rowan tilted his head at the tree. "You formed the Magi and Archdruid clans? Why have I never heard of this before? Why did Merrow not inform me of this history?"

A bright zag of lightning crossed the dark expanse above the Conservatory's ceiling windows. A torrent of rain obscured the outline of clouds in the sky. The strike lit Master Knurl's face outlined in the Yew tree's trunk. Limbs on the tree shook as if it were shrugging. "No one has ever known. To keep us safe, we used an Im`bara spell that broke when the Grand Lady left the Conservatory to save the rest of her dryad kin from the Riven's grasp."

"You were impelled?" Horra asked, incredulous. Judging by the confused look on Rowan's face, neither Merrow nor Woodsly had informed him what the term meant. Only her love of obscure facts and her depth of reading allowed her to understand the word. "It's a powerful magical binding that has been outlawed for years."

"The Lady performed the spell. Without the elves or witches—creatures strong enough to enact such a spell—it was easy to bar."

Horra sat back on her heels. The ground rumbled again as another lightning strike cracked. The hits were rumbling farther and farther away as the night wore on, for which she was thankful. This storm was rare, coming at a bad time.

There'd be no trace of the rats if they'd escaped the castle by now, and the magical music book would be lost forevermore.

Reminded of her original mission, Horra's body tensed with determination to fetch Pidge and scramble to the passages. Only the hope that her pet could locate the vermin kept her from racing off. Yet she hesitated.

None of her history books outlined what her foremothers had done. Even if the omission was to protect other creatures' lives, it still rankled that a partial truth had withstood time. Would she have done anything different? She couldn't say. "What else do I not know about Oddar's history?" she muttered to herself.

Master Knurl's bearded lips twisted into a frown. "This kingdom has many secrets, Queen Bearer. Though you grew up believing something that wasn't completely true, it does not change the fact that your foremothers were fierce and deserved to rule Oddar. What you do with the information going forward is now up to you."

"This explains why the dwarves have always been hostile to trolls. They probably still believe the mountains should be theirs." Horra's mind raced. She'd studied Oddar history in depth, yet there were so many things she didn't know.

Master Knurl's brows puckered. "Possibly so. All who witnessed the elves breeching the contract were bound not to talk about it."

A wet wind blew in from the back of the Conservatory. The Weeping Welter tree shifted, swaying as the Lady of the Tree entered, startling everyone. She glided across the ground toward them.

Horra and Grendel rose, confused.

"My Lady." Rowan rushed to her side. Horra had never seen him move so fast.

Rain soaked her clothes, making her branchy hair droop in dark tangles. Her mantle hung in shreds, and she reeked of smoke. "It is done," she breathed out before she collapsed into Rowan's waiting arms.

CHAPTER 9

~Rowan~

Moments before the Lady entered the Conservatory

Rowan's roots tingled with the stimulating information coming from Master Knurl. The exchange brought him back to the Weald, sitting at Merrow's roots, intent on his every word. He could stay here all night listening to the old rood.

Noises in the ether inserted themselves into his mind, breaking his blissful bubble. He turned his head toward them and recognized one voice in particular—the Lady of the Willow Tree. She'd returned to the castle but was in a disordered state, judging by her frantic voice.

He turned as the Weeping Welter tree moved aside to allow the Lady entrance. Whatever magic sealed the Conservatory from outside forces broke, and wind with the essence of rain accompanied the Lady inside. The spirits outside the castle shrieked, and the trees they took shelter in groaned. His mind registered urgency and his limbs moved before he could object. "My Lady?" he inquired, unsure what to do. He rushed to the Lady's side.

"It is done," she breathed.

Rowan caught her as she collapsed. Water dampened her chilled skin, and her clothes were sodden and dirty. He glanced over at the strangler vine they'd placed on her tree, the Weeping Welter. Her power waned as the tree died. It would've required much of her strength to move the dying tree to climb inside the castle.

More incorporeal screams filled the space where silence had reigned since the fire in the Weald had destroyed all the sacred trees and their rood residents. Though the absence of voices grieved him, this sudden onslaught pierced his nerves. Were these voices a good thing or a bad thing?

The Lady didn't answer him, though he could tell by her raspy breathing she was still alive. For how long, he didn't know.

Grendel shoved him aside and grabbed the Lady's thin body. She took a minute to evaluate the dryad and frowned. "Rowan, go fetch Princess Misty. The Lady needs healing, and she's more adept at that than I am."

Rowan, still shocked by the dryad's and the voice's sudden appearance, remained immobile for a moment.

Horra growled. "Rowan, move."

He rose and rushed past Horra, who carried the Lady with Grendel to one of their wooden potting tables and placed her gently on it.

Pidge screeched, and the flutter of her wings was the last thing he heard before he opened and shut the double glass doors. The princess should be in their guest quarters.

Rowan hesitated, shaking his head and rattling his branchy crown. What was wrong with him? He prided himself on his clear thinking and methodical approach to any problem. He pushed aside the noise in his head and struggled to gain control again. When that didn't help, he stuck his fingers in his ears, a move he'd seen several of the children they'd rescued do when they refused to listen. Blocking his ears with his fingers was nonsensical to his orderly mind, but it worked. The noise died away.

Rowan's tense limbs relaxed and his mind cleared. He glided on deft roots up the stairway. A light glimmered around the frame of the last guest quarters, signaling they were still awake.

He pounded on the door right as thunder crashed outside.

No one answered.

He knocked again. "Princesses?" he called out.

"What?" Princess Glory said grumpily as she opened the door. She did not invite him in. Her hair, face, and wings were all rumpled. Behind her, the queen rested on another bed.

Rowan didn't see the other princess. "We need your sister. The Lady has returned, and she's not well. Grendel is asking for her help to aid the dryad."

The princess glanced behind her. Loud snores reverberated through a closed door. She flung an arm out. "Her *Lord*ship took a sleeping draught to get her *beauty sleep*. She won't be able to help you tonight. Maybe in the morning before she and mother leave?"

Rowan shook his head. "We don't have that kind of time. I know you don't have your full power back, but would you consider assisting somehow? It may be the difference between life and death."

Princess Glory's face swiftly changed from a scowl to a stricken expression. "Grendel is a much more experienced healer than I. Especially for dryads. I know nothing about them or their physiology. If Grendel can't help, I doubt I could make any difference."

Rowan's rushing sap chilled at her words.

She placed a light hand on his arm. "I would help you if I could, Rowan. You have my deepest sympathies. I know the Lady meant something special to you."

Surprised by the fairy's compassion but also frustrated, Rowan nodded. "Thank you. Good evening, Princess."

He didn't hear if she replied as he turned and headed blindly back down the stairs.

In the Hall, the eyes of the mounted animals on the walls gleamed in the candlelight as he passed by. He dutifully ignored them. They always unnerved him, but never so much as right at this moment.

Rowan opened the glass doors. A few feet away, the queen bearer stood over the still body of the Lady of the Willow Tree. Grendel sniffed and glanced his way. Sadness marred their faces.

"I'm sorry," the queen bearer said. She carefully moved the arm that dangled at the Lady's side and crossed it over her chest. He understood the placement—a warrior's tribute.

Grendel glanced behind him. "It was far too late for anyone to help, anyway. It's a miracle she returned at all."

Rowan's body creaked as he concentrated on not stumbling. A loud rushing sound in his ears dulled the cacophony of voices that filled the air. They grew into a sorrowful refrain. Roots passed on the news of her death. The ether was full of weeping.

Something shook his shoulder, breaking his stunned reverie.

"Rowan!" Grendel's voice joined the other sounds in his head.

A slap across his face brought him back to himself. He gasped.

"Ow, Rowan. Is your face made of stone?" Queen Bearer

Horra rubbed her claw, her eyebrows menacingly slashed over her dark eyes. "Don't make me do that again."

His face stung. He pressed his hand to the spot where she'd slapped him. The voices in his head quieted as the news passed down the lines and spirits gathered to grieve. "My apologies, Queen Bearer. I don't know what came over me."

"Shock." Grendel patted his arm.

The queen bearer studied him. "Are you all right? Do I need to pick some smelling herbs to rouse you?"

He shook his head. "No, thank you. I—need a moment." He walked around them and moved to the bench seat by the small pond on the west side of the Conservatory. He stood and stared at the blurry, silvery reflection of the moon on the water. The rain continued, but the storm had eased between the time he'd left to fetch the fairy princess and now. Heaviness filled him as if the rain soaked his fibers.

"It must be difficult when powerful emotions overtake you when you've not grown used to them." Queen Bearer Horra spoke in a low tone as if he were a scared animal. She'd used that tone often when dealing with lost children. Or Nimble. "It's hard to lose someone who means something to you."

Rowan grunted, then choked. "I have often wondered about your volatile nature. I couldn't understand it. How could I? Those pathways in my brain didn't exist." He dropped onto the bench. "I liked it better when I didn't feel so many emotions."

The queen bearer gave a bitter laugh. "I don't blame you." She sighed heavily and stood next to him. "Sympathy is not my strength, as you well know. But I'm here if you need to talk about anything." Her claw was warm against his chilled shoulder. "Now, I'll get out of your branches and leave you to sort it all out."

He nodded as gracefully as he could manage, appreciating

the space she allowed him. He ignored the soft sounds of sobbing and grief in the ether and struggled not to join them. In the end, he failed and allowed his eyes to leak, dampening the mossy lichen that covered his face.

~Glory~
Early the next morning

A FIERY GLOW etched a line across the horizon as morning bloomed. Glory, having barely slept because of the storm and exasperation with her ineffectual ability to do any significant magic to help the dryad, glanced blearily around the room. Rubbing the sleep from her eyes, she sat up in her cot, a dull ache pulsing along her temples.

High-pitched chimes echoed in her ears, distracting her from her sister's rattling snores coming from the main bedroom Misty had chosen as hers. Since Misty was the current reigning royal, she possessed the right to the biggest room, she'd told Glory when they'd settled into the suite.

Glory yawned. Though she had gifted her sister her blessing on being the next ruler, Misty's ability to hurt her with two simple words cut deep.

Beauty sleep.

Glory half-growled, half-groaned. Her sister could be so cruel. At least when Glory was mean, her hostility was on purpose. Her sister did it without thinking and thus would never become as great a queen as their mother. Better than Glory would ever be, she admitted, which was never in doubt. Glory knew herself to be too heartless for the task. Selfish to a fault. And being at the beck and call of all Fairydom would not feed her self-indulgence.

That had changed after her mother succumbed to the Erlking's curse. She loved her mother, even in the moments she'd betrayed her, acting out against the royal expectations placed on her. That her mother's ordeal traced back to Glory's actions pricked her conscience in a way nothing else could. Rebelliousness was one thing. Her mother's current affliction, something Glory could never have foreseen happening, went far beyond that, and the queen's suffering grieved Glory's heart.

The fact remained that Glory would not fit well in her mother's position, whether for a minute or a lifetime. Misty was the better choice. With a sigh, she stepped out of the bed's warmth. The stone floor was cold against her bare feet, waking her.

Rain still drummed against the castle. It crashed against the walls in sheets and pounded at the glass in the windows. Would this storm never end? Glory ignored the sounds, especially the high-pitched ringing in her ears, which intensified the ache in her head.

The queen rested, motionless, on the bed next to Glory's, her pale skin almost luminous in its pallor. Her blonde hair was the only color against the fluffy white blanket placed to keep her warm. Even the queen's wings resting beneath her head were translucent, colorless. If they couldn't wake her soon, she feared her mother may never return.

Glory placed a light kiss on her mother's forehead, dressed, and crossed the suite to pursue someone who could help her with her headache. Had she full control of her magic, she could heal herself. But she only had partial command of it, which was an improvement over what the Erlking had left her with after the first curse. Definitely after the last curses as well.

She snapped her fingers. Grendel would be the one to seek out. The giantess had done a stellar job healing her before. The beastly-looking girl was eager to help, and unless she was changing into her giant form, Grendel was the best choice for her ailment. She cast a disguisement spell that required minor magic to perform, the magic absorbing all sound of her movements as she left the suite.

Outside Grendel's room, Glory knocked on the door, hoping to wake her if she was still sleeping. Giants didn't need beauty sleep like fairies did, after all. When the giantess didn't answer after the third round of knocks, she descended the stairs, her head throbbing.

First, she checked the laboratory, but the sparse room was dark and unoccupied. Next, she checked the library. A light was on in the far corner, but Grendel was nowhere to be found. Glory's good mood soured as she exited the library and headed to the Conservatory. Though fairies had an affinity for plants, the enormous garden space held bleak memories of her and her sister destroying the plants while she was under the Erlking's mesmerization spell. The fact that she'd reveled in the destruction because she'd detested the troll princess only convicted Glory of her delinquency of character.

Glory gathered herself before she moved to enter the double glass doors. With a bolstering breath, she pushed the doors open and found Grendel bent over the still dryad. Glory's wings hung limp at her back. "Is she—?"

"Gone? Yes. We're readying her for consecration." Horra strode over from the west side of the room, a grim expression on her face. She looked more peaky than normal, though the pastiness could be due to the abysmal lantern light's glow.

Grendel's shoulders drooped. "It was too late when she showed up. She used the last of her strength to return here."

Horra nodded. "The Lady knew the risks of departing the Conservatory's safety. Leaving was her choice. She was strong until the end, returning to her home. We will honor her with a proper burial next to Hazel, her daughter."

Glory gulped. "How's Rowan?" She strode over to the table the dryad rested on as if simply asleep. The likeness of the dryad's still form to her mother's unmoving repose stole her breath for a couple heartbeats. Tears burned behind her eyes.

"He is upset. What brings you here at such an early hour?" Horra asked as she adjusted flowers around the dryad's body.

A wave of grief and heat washed over Glory. Was this her mother's fate?

Horra turned and noticed Glory's dismay. She rushed toward her. "Princess, is everything okay? Has something happened to Queen Stella?"

Unable to speak, Glory shook her head. The constriction across her chest eased, and she gasped. "I'm sorry." She waved a hand at the dryad. "She reminded me of Mother for a moment."

Horra's face softened, shifting to realization. "I can see how that would happen." Her eyes turned keen, peering too closely at Glory.

To break the mood, Glory shifted away from Horra and turned to Grendel. "I was hoping you might help me with a headache? The thunder kept me awake last night. Then there's always my sister's snoring. The pain is quite gruesome. Even my wings ache from it." She shifted her shoulders, stretching them, still nervous over the speculative way the troll princess watched her. Though she'd apologized and promised to change her ways, her ardent intensity prickled like bugs crawling across her skin.

"I have some powder that should help you," Grendel said, letting her hand linger on the dryad's arm.

"If you're too busy, I can come back," Glory said, surprising herself. She wasn't usually magnanimous. The feeling pressed against her skin like an ill-fitted gown.

"You two go on. I'm going to stay and prepare arrangements

for the Lady and help Rowan." Horra waved her claw. "If you see Sageel, send her my way."

"The powder is in the laboratory," Grendel said, moving past Glory to the stairs.

Glory followed wordlessly behind her. Outside the glass double doors, the ringing in her ears picked back up. She hadn't noticed the sound was missing in the Conservatory. "Do you have something for this constant ringing in my ears?" she asked. "I awoke to this annoying noise, and it just won't stop."

Grendel paused and glanced around. "I hear it too." She drew her furry eyebrows together to create a unibrow. "What is that?" she said. "Is it coming from the walls?"

The walls? Glory's heart jumped. "The chimes! It's the chimes."

CHAPTER 10

~Horra~

Moments after Grendel and Glory left the Conservatory, they crashed back through the doors, startling Horra. She fell against the potting table the be-flowered Lady lay upon. "Vinegar, you guys!" Her heart stuttered in her chest, adrenaline sending shocks through her tired body.

Grendel's chest heaved. "We heard the chimes, but they're inside the walls."

Horra had momentarily forgotten the Erlking's book in the wake of Master Knurl's tale about her ancestors followed by the Lady's surprise return. "Gah! I forgot. I was chasing the book down when I got sidetracked." Her weary mind fought to keep pace with the new events. "I was going to grab Pidge and—" She spun in a hurried circle searching for her pet bird. "Where'd Pidge go?"

Grendel and Glory looked at each other blankly, then swung back to her. Neither said anything.

"She's after the rats in the secret passageway," Rowan said, surprising Horra and the other two.

"Gah! Can you all stop doing that? My heart can't take it." Horra pressed her claw against her chest as the pinch of pain that came and went after the shock dissipated. She closed her eyes, took three deep breaths, and reopened them. "How do you know where Pidge is?" she asked Rowan.

"Master Knurl just informed me that the pudge wudgie is on the hunt and that we should go find her. It's important for reasons he wouldn't elaborate on." Rowan sniffed, keeping his glance from dropping to the table where the Lady rested.

Glory's wings flitted back and forth in haste. "Then let's go join her and locate the book."

Horra glared at the fairy, hesitant to trust her with the Erlking's music book. Or the passages. Leaves on the Yew tree rattled, reminding Horra of Master Knurl's declaration that the passageways were in fact not sanctified holy ground. Her heart warred against her mind. She believed Master Knurl. Roods couldn't lie, and he had no reason to do so. But it was difficult to set aside what she'd believed to be true her whole life.

Her mind won the battle. "Fine," she said with resignation. Was that a little freedom settling into her gut? "Follow me to the passages."

"Passages?" Glory's voice pitched painfully high.

Horra didn't elaborate. She second-guessed herself three times before she stood in front of the creeping briar. Unlike the other plants the fairies had destroyed, whatever magic had been placed on the vine hiding the doorway had kept the hidden space safe. The plant always looked half dead and half alive as the vines grew, then died back before new strands grew to replace them. The thorns remained—whether dead or alive— and no one pruned them. "Watch yourself. If the thorns catch you, I'll have to cut you free."

Glory's sharp intake of breath didn't stop Horra. She dropped to the ground and found the spot where a jutting stone along the castle's wall created a split in the viny curtain. "Follow me." On her hands and knees, she crawled forward and beneath the spiked barrier without looking back.

Chimes tinkled from afar and clanged from close by as she moved beyond the thorny briars, as if the plant itself were a barrier absorbing the sound in the passages. Perhaps it was. Horra realized she knew less than what she thought she did about her castle. The bouncing chimes alerted her that the book was close by. No scuttling of rats accompanied the tinkling, not that Horra could detect. She hurried through the space, which was as familiar to her as any other spot in the castle.

Her foremothers, or possibly the elves, had carved each level in different thicknesses. At a bottom level of the castle, this spot in the wall was one of the widest, with only the dungeon's being broader. Horra had always surmised the width had something to do with the walls growing thinner the higher they went, since the mountain was narrower at the top. Not too long ago, before she'd broken her mother's dying wish that inadvertently kept Horra from growing, she could walk through the hole without having to crawl. Now a regular troll size, and with the rest of her group being larger than her, they'd all have to squirm through the opening. Horra reached the end of the hole and stood, dusting herself off.

Grendel came next, just a few seconds after Horra exited. She stood as well, and she glanced around. "It's darker than I thought it would be. Do you have torches?"

"No, but wait until we move past the doorway. There's more light there." Horra pointed, but Glory, grunting and panting, crawled out from the hole, distracting her.

The fairy huffed, and dust clouded the area in front of her face before she fully emerged. Her wings sprung out. "That,"

Glory gasped, bending over, "was horrid. What in the Wilden Lands would possess your foremothers to carve wormholes in the walls?" She smacked her clothes, the dirt beaten into submission as the grime fell to the gritty floor. "It's disgusting and insane."

The chimes grew louder but then muted as if the book were moving. Perhaps Pidge had a rat on the run. Horra's claws itched to join her pet.

Scratching came next as Rowan struggled to haul his limby crown through the small space. He grunted as he shifted back and forth like a snake. The branches on his head arrived first, and Horra shoved Glory and Grendel through the larger carved doorway and into the passage to allow him room to crawl through without impaling them. They stood beside the open doorway with its unused pin.

Horra hesitated, half expecting to be struck dead by the Creature God for allowing others into the passages. Only the chimes and the other girl's breathing broke the usual silence. The chimes seemed to multiply in the open space, as if coming from more than one direction. How could that be? Horra spun in a circle but couldn't figure it out. "C'mon, Rowan," she whispered through gritted teeth.

Glory and Grendel both glanced around the dimly lit passageway, dust glittering in the air where the bleak light breached the darkness. The stained-glass window, which was built into the chapel at the top of the castle, glowed on the wall above them, the sunrise staining the reflection in different hues. The chimes continued in the background, coming from too many areas at once. Scuttling, followed by a screech of triumph, sounded from the depths. But the chimes remained.

"Why does it sound like there's more than one chime?" she asked Glory.

A rat, carrying a ragged piece of something in its mouth, pounced.

Glory and Grendel both screamed in alarm. Glory rose an inch off the floor as her wings beat the air, but it was momentary and she landed hard.

Horra kicked herself for not bringing a weapon back in with her. She caught the animal mid-leap and shook it. It snarled, froth dripping from the sides of the item in its maw.

"Horra, watch out!" Grendel yelled as another rat attacked.

Glory was nowhere to be seen. Horra had no time to consider where the fairy had gone.

She swung the first still-snarling rat at the second, catching it along the side of its head and knocking it sideways.

Rowan appeared, broken branches dangling from his body. "Oh dear," he said. "Queen Bearer?"

The first rat dropped what it had in its mouth and snapped its incisors. They were dark, sharp, and dangerous looking. "Not now, Rowan. I'm a bit busy."

A crack resounded behind her and, in the next second, something clobbered her rat. It went limp in her claws.

The pudge wudgie shrieked in the distance.

"Pidge," Horra screamed. Chimes, growing louder by the second, almost drowned out her voice.

Rowan picked up the unconscious rat. "She's fine. This critter is not." He dropped it and squared off with the open space that led to the main sections of the castle. "Do we have a plan of action?"

Horra shook her head, realizing he had broken one of his limbs off to bash the rat. "I forgot one had attacked me when we entered. Had I remembered, I'd have come prepared. Sorry."

A flash of black flew out of the depths. A half dozen of the gnarly-looking vermin ran in front of her. Each of them had pieces of something either in their tiny pink paws or in their mouths.

Glory gasped. "It's the book." It's all she could say before the rats were upon them.

Rowan stood in front of Grendel and Glory as Horra assumed an attack position—one leg back while balancing on the other, her claws at the ready. They weren't daggers, but her claws were sharp and hard as rocks.

Rowan swung his branch back and forth, catching the fleeing critters and flinging them to the side of the passage. Pidge captured the last one—the smallest.

Before Horra could watch her pet gobble the critter, another attacked her. She ducked and, instead of fighting it, captured its tail and swung it against the granite wall. It squealed and went still.

However, two more ran past Rowan as he fought off the biggest—easily twice the size of the largest hobgoblin on their staff.

A shrill note jarred her, echoing and bouncing around the stone walls.

Horra bent over, slapping her claws over her ears. Her eyes watered from the assault. When the sound died, she opened her eyes before dropping her claws.

The remaining rats lay on the ground, spasming.

Pidge's scratching claws on the rocky ground and their breathing were the only sounds. The chimes were silent.

Grendel, her face scrunched and body trembling, huddled along the wall, covering her ears with her paws. Rowan shook his head, his branches rattling.

Glancing around at the destruction, Horra's shoulders dropped. All the rats were either disabled, dead, or had been eaten by Pidge. Pieces of paper lay everywhere. She glanced over at Glory.

The fairy's lip curled upward in a half smile, and she shrugged. "Music is my gift."

Horra frowned. "If that was music, I'd rather never listen to another note again. And maybe next time start with that instead of letting the rest of us battle the little monsters."

Glory ignored her words as she looked around. "How does nobody but you know this exists?" Her eyes were wide and sparkling. "And how do I build one in our castle?" She turned back to Horra. "How often have you hidden in here?"

That was something Horra would never admit. "Often enough to escape you and the Erlking when you invaded my castle."

Grendel, no longer huddling against the wall, turned in a circle, the soles of her boots crunching against the grit on the floor. "This would be a great place for a hidden laboratory."

Horra didn't correct her on her assumption, though now that the giantess mentioned it, she could see how a hidden lab would've been a better choice of location to construct the antidote for the Erlking's mesmerization. Habits were hard to break, and she was used to working in the actual lab where they kept all their supplies.

Rowan moaned.

Horra turned to him. He was gripping a spot on his arm where one of the rats must've bitten him. The bark was stripped so that only splintered wood remained. "Are you okay?"

"I haven't felt such pain since the fire in the Weald."

Horra tore a strip off the bottom of her tunic. "Here. Wrap it with this. We'll retrieve some paste and antibiotics when we return to the lab." She didn't elaborate on what diseases the rats could be carrying.

Grendel took the cloth and helped Rowan carefully cover

the injured spot. "I have some healing ointment I can create for you."

"Thank you."

Pidge nudged a rat.

"Well, you'll never see that again. She must be full," Horra joked. She bent over and picked up a damp strip of paper with the tips of her claws. It contained musical characters. One of the Erlking's musical spells, though she wasn't sure which one it would be. Another scrap of paper had actual writing on it. A chunk of a book cover lay a few feet away.

"This isn't one thing. If it wasn't only the music book he was after, what else could it be?" Horra asked, letting the strip of paper fall.

"I guess we'll find out," Glory said as she flipped one piece over with the toe of her shoe. Both sides had writing on them, but one showed an illustration. "Looks like a children's book."

Horra widened her eyes. "My books." She ran for her nest behind the library. The wall she'd closed after she left last time stood open. Inside ... disaster.

Her heart hammered to see her special blanket torn to shreds. All the books were out of place and several were chewed. She dropped to the ground and took in the destruction.

A gentle hand fell on her shoulder. "Are you all right, Queen Bearer?" Grendel asked.

Tears pricked her eyes. "This was where Mother would read to me. It was my safest place." She sniffed. "After Mother died, I couldn't come back. Not until I hid the music book and that stupid Music Man book. I shouldn't have hidden them here."

Rowan cleared his throat. "How could you have known the rats would return to destroy it?"

Horra dropped her head, and a teardrop fell from one of

her eyes to the gritty ground. She shook her head. "He's always one step ahead of me. If the rats came here to spy on me, we'll never plan a move he doesn't know about. We'll never beat him."

"Ugh. Enough with the defeatist talk." Glory's sarcasm broke through Horra's pain-filled fog.

It was what Horra needed to drag herself back together, though. She didn't desire to fall apart in front of the fairy, whether she was friend or foe.

She swiped her sleeve across her face, remembering the last time she'd cried in the passages. What she needed was another plan. Horra lifted her head and stood. "We need to clean this up, take the pieces back to the lab or the library, and figure out what this has to do with the Erlking's plan."

CHAPTER 11

~Grendel~

Grendel and Rowan met up in the lab a short while later after splitting with the princess and queen bearer. They'd collected all the pieces from the passageway. Grendel set her sack on the tabletop, spilling the cloth bag's contents. "What exactly are we looking for?" she asked.

Rowan blinked, then set his hand-sewn bark bag on the same table. "My apologies. What did you ask?"

"Why are you so distracted?" Grendel asked, trying not to be annoyed that Rowan's attention was wandering. She was used to his hyper attentiveness toward her. She shook that thought off.

He sat heavily on one of the chairs so that it creaked beneath his weight. "Since the Lady returned, my head has been full of voices and noises from the ether." Instead of dumping his pieces of the destroyed books out, he took them out one by one. "I missed the chatter after the fire destroyed the

Weald. But I find I've grown accustomed to the solitude. It's as if she yanked a stopper from a jar, which kept the voices at bay. It's . . . overwhelming." His branchy head rattled as he shook it. Broken and jagged pieces dangled on one side of his crown where he'd rubbed it against the Conservatory's hole.

Grendel scratched her head, reminded of her fuzzy state when her palm met fur instead of skin and jewels. She'd still had her jewels the first time she changed sizes. After using her soundometer, they'd disappeared. She wasn't sure where they'd gone and was too self-conscious to talk to anyone about it. Especially since she was a classic scientist. Things like that didn't simply disappear. "What I find curious about your situation is that I had a similar experience after using my antennae soundometers. I have to wonder if there's a connection."

Rowan's hand stilled inside the bag. "I hadn't thought about that." He resumed his task of pulling out the paper remains. "The only difference is the timing, though the trek would've taken the Lady several hours from the Riven back to the castle after she freed her dryad kin."

"And what did that entail?" Grendel asked. "Did she save the other dryads and possibly the spirits residing inside the Riven's borders? Or did she dismantle the border itself?"

"I could ask the spirits," Rowan said, but his cracking voice held a note of reluctance. Morning light from the skylights bounced across the painted white surface of the walls and tables, making the moss on his bark stand out.

Grendel paused from sifting through the pieces according to color, then lettering. Rowan wasn't usually hesitant to act. "What is it that holds you back?"

Lines around his mouth deepened. "When I was in the Riven, there were spirits inside the tree I took refuge by. The elves were quite contrary, and the others were loud and obtrusive. The only thing keeping the voices tame was the rood who lived in the tree. I shudder to think of the dissonance without the rood's intervention."

All of Grendel's pieces were now sorted and spread out over her side of the laboratory table. "Would Master Knurl not help you?"

"He mentioned before that he has no links with anything outside the castle. He didn't warn us about the Lady's return, and so I have to surmise he cannot do more than he already has for our quest."

She placed several of the pieces together like a puzzle, fitting them the best she could, though she only had half of them since Rowan hadn't finished removing what was inside his bag.

Princess Glory slammed the lab door open and entered. "I thought you two would be done by now."

Grendel ignored the accusation in her tone. She knew the fairy was not irritated with them but with the fact her family had just left. "Did your sister and mother have a good send-off?"

"Ha," the fairy said, her voice derisive. She took a seat at the table parallel to Grendel's. "Yes, and good riddance. At least to my sister." The princess spun the chair around in a circle, then spun it again in the other direction. "Horra went to the Conservatory instead, to tend to the dryad." The tilt of her lips reflected the pout in her voice.

Rowan stiffened, then kept removing pieces one by one in meticulously slow movements.

Princess Glory stopped her spinning chair and studied the pieces on Grendel's table. "What exactly are you supposed to do with these?"

"Find a clue," Rowan clacked.

"To what? We know the Erlking coveted the music book.

He had his rats destroy that children's book he quoted from, some nonsense about *the little princesses all in a row*." Her voice changed to mimic the Erlking's, the cadence and menacing tone almost spot-on. She picked up one piece with the tips of her nails. "Did you notice the rats broke the magic lining the sheets when they tore them to shreds?"

Grendel blinked. She was not completely adept with magic signatures. She'd not had training in that particular field yet.

Glory picked up Rowan's bag and dumped it out before he could protest. She hovered a hand a few inches above the pile. "Nope. Not a shred of magic left to this lot. Might as well burn them for all the clues you'll gain from this disgusting mess."

Grendel's hopes dashed. What were they going to do now?

"Seems to me that your voice is the only weapon we need," the queen bearer said as she strode into the open doorway. "I don't recall the Music Man book having any magic in it, so I don't know what information it would actually provide. Unless a secret about the Erlking is hidden in the pages." She turned from the glowering fairy princess to Rowan. "When I returned to the Conservatory, Rowan, the Lady's body had returned to her limb state. I left it alone, thinking you—"

"Thank you, Queen Bearer. Yes, I would like to perform a ceremony over her remains. If you'll all excuse me." Rowan glided out of the lab.

Grendel's heart twinged at the pain her friend endured, though he worked hard to show no sign of it. She'd been around him enough to know how badly the Lady's return and death affected him. And no potion or tincture she could fashion would help him.

~Glory~

AFTER ROWAN LEFT, the Erlking's recital flew through Glory's mind as she, Horra, and Grendel gathered the shredded pieces from the lab tables to be disposed of. Was there a secret hidden within the Music Man text? She recounted it to herself. *See the little princesses all in a row? Dressed and blessed and ready for the show. One fell prey, one left betrayed, but the last little princess chose to go astray.*

Horra bent to pick up a few pieces Glory's wings knocked to the floor. "Do you mind?" Irritation edged her voice.

Glory ignored the troll, her mind only on the tale. The Shining Land's version depicted a girl sneaking off and leaving the others to take part in the Music Man's curious spells. As a child, Glory couldn't decide if the elven Music Man was a hero or a villain. Now, she knew perfectly well the spells were not *curious*, they were nefarious. Nor did she now question whether the "Music Man" was good or bad. He was no hero.

Glory glared at the troll princess. "Who said I was the one who went astray?"

Horra stopped and stared, several pieces clutched in her claws. "I didn't mention it. You did." The lab's bright sunlight highlighted her red hair like a flame atop her warty green head. "But if we're going to be honest, aren't you the one who fell prey?"

Sometimes the troll princess was too astute. Glory internally fumed. She would admit to none of it, though. "I'm not saying I was any of the characters from that stupid book."

Rowan clacked to clear his throat, and Glory cringed at the sound.

"I forgot my bag." Rowan's voice cracked in the room like a whip. "And don't you two have better things to do than debate petty matters?" Rowan lowered his voice to a deep octave, startling Glory with his anger. Though he wasn't her biggest fan, he was usually more polite than that. Well, except when he'd tied her to that dreadful half-dragon creature thing.

Rowan's mahogany eyes turned hard. "We have a diabolical individual running around the Wilden Lands, sowing plagues and seeds of discord everywhere he goes. Several creatures have died, thanks to his magic. Who cares about some silly children's book?" His voice reverberated in the small room, causing glass beakers in the cabinets to clink together.

Glory's eyes widened, but she noticed hers weren't the only ones. Both Grendel and Horra stared at the wood boy with their eyebrows raised and mouths open.

"Rowan?" Horra asked carefully, in a neutral tone. "Are you all right?"

Rowan pounded a fist on the table, knocking some of the paper onto the floor. "No, I am decidedly not all right." He turned and strode from the room, leaving behind his bark bag that he'd returned for.

Glory glanced at the other two. "What was *that* all about?"

Grendel frowned, showing her fangs. Not as pronounced as the troll princess's tusks, they were still quite monsterish. "He said the sounds from the ether have increased since the Lady returned to the castle. They've been disturbing him."

"Is that a reason to bite our heads off?" Glory crossed an arm over her stomach and flicked her other hand out to emphasize her distaste.

"Yeah, I liked him better when he wasn't as emotional, too. These feelings have to be so unsettling for him. He sees himself as very in control, and he certainly likes it that way." Horra frowned at the doorway but turned back. "His reaction to the Lady the first time she showed herself was weird. And he keeps acting stranger each time she's involved."

"So you think it's only the Lady he's reacting to, not the noise?" Grendel asked.

Horra shrugged. "It could be anything." She turned to glance at Glory. "Be kind to him while he—and we—figure this out."

Glory tensed at the unspoken accusation. "When was I not kind?"

The troll planted her claws on her hips and leaned toward Glory. "When you argued about the Music Man book. You know he hates when people argue around him. He's sensitive."

Glory sputtered. "He wasn't in the room."

Grendel stepped between Glory and Horra. "That's enough." She pushed her hands through her fuzzy hair. "I understand why you two drive Rowan crazy. You're both impossible when you're together." She turned on her heel and stomped out.

Glory straightened and waved a dismissive hand. "Who is she to call me impossible? All I was doing was defending myself. That's called a free exchange of opinions in my kingdom. If anything, she-who-changes-to-a-scary-giantess-beasty-thing is equally unbearable. I mean, did you see her when she shifted into that monster?" Glory shuddered.

Horra turned a frowning glance her way. Her face smoothed before she let out a giggle. "That was pretty horror-ific. I mean, one minute she was a small woolly giant, then she was this enormous ball of orange fluff running off and shrieking with those antenna thing-a-ma-jiggies dangling from her ears." Her giggles turned into outright laughter.

Glory clenched her jaw, but the laugh sputtered its way through her lips in a spit-inducing chuckle. The action was very un-princess-like, which only fueled her laughter.

Horra pointed at the fairy, then chortled harder.

Unable to stop herself, Glory let out a whooping cackle. They were both in tears within mere seconds. Neither could seem to stop the impulse, especially when Sageel poked her head into the room to see what the commotion was all about and her apron's neck strap caught on the metal handle on the broken door, catching her so that she dangled for a moment.

With a snap of her gnarled fingers, Sageel's uniform unhooked. She then accused them both of drinking giggle juice, a bubbly piskie brew that induced uncontrollable giggles or burps, before she whirled and left in a huff.

Glory snorted. She'd only had the drink once and had burped for two hours straight. The disapproving maid didn't realize she'd never touch the stuff again unless tortured.

Another glance at the troll, and both of them fell into more uncontrollable laughter.

CHAPTER 12

Rowan didn't go directly to the Conservatory. He couldn't. He marched from the castle into the courtyard, between the kitchen and the stables. The rain had stopped and puddles filled the low spots along the rocky land between the buildings. Though the damp breeze held a chill, the cold didn't bother him as much as it once had.

His splashing footfalls dropped heavily upon the hard ground, damaging the smaller feeler roots that remained on the edges of his feet. He didn't care. Between the fact they were supposed to have dried up and fallen off by now, the Lady's death, the internal onslaught of noise only he could hear, and the bickering royals, his ability to remain calm and collected had vanished.

He entered Nimble's stable at the end of the row of barns, hoping for some peace and quiet to settle his frazzled nerves before he tended to the Lady. It was warmer inside the barn, and the air weighed less on his limbs. This small comfort offered no escape from the voices permeating the air, though. Three steps into the barn, he nearly walked into the wyvern leaning against Nimble's fencing. It was the same creature that the Lady requested and rode to the Riven.

This wasn't the escape he'd hoped for.

Rain, and possibly sweat, gleamed across the wyvern's scaly hide, and dried froth flaked along the edges of its mouth. The dragon snorted at Rowan, then turned its head back to Nimble, who had his head flung over the fence. Had the gulgoyle wished to escape, the wooden structure wouldn't keep him in. Possibly only habit kept the fire creature a prisoner of the weaker barrier.

"Well," Rowan said and stopped. What did one say to a dangerous dragon? Merrow's instructions floated through his mind. *"Brush the creatures down. Feed and water them so they're made comfortable. Don't be afraid of them. Animals react to fear."*

But that training was for Torren's horse and Horra's half-dragon, Nimble, not the wyvern. He hesitated.

Boards in the barn creaked, and a face formed from a rough-hewn pole. "Hello, dearest boy!" The distinct voice landed a punch to Rowan's gut.

Neither of the animals took any interest in the sudden appearance.

"Merrow?" he asked. He struggled to make sense of his presence. "I thought—"

"That the fire had destroyed all traces of the roods? It had until our Lady of the Willow Tree untangled the spells the Erlking placed on tree roots. I'm delighted to see you." The wood around the rood's eyes puckered. "Your growth rings must be extensive to have grown so big in such a short time."

"What—how?" he cracked out, unable to gather his thoughts into coherent order.

The face nodded. "All will be revealed in good time, young druid. We are still adjusting, adapting. I can't stay long. I have not found a tree yet, which restricts my abilities. And the Weald is unhabitable at the moment." His face faded, then returned. "I must go. I cannot maintain this form. Take heart, my boy. And don't forget what I taught you." Merrow's voice hushed, then the pole returned to its original worn form. His mentor was gone.

"I have missed you." Rowan touched the pole, knowing Merrow was no longer there. He hoped the old seedkeeper heard him, though.

The barn door opened and Torren strode in, a bucket of oats and another of water in his claws. "Rowan," he said, startled. "I was told by the stable hand that the wyvern had returned before the rain stopped. They were too scared to tend to it, so I came instead. I didn't know you'd be out here too."

Rowan dropped his hand from the pole. "I needed a break from the queen bearer and the fairy princess."

"Ah. Say no more." Torren chuckled. "They're still at it, huh? I've been so busy with my knight duties that I haven't had time to miss them."

Grendel entered the open doorway behind Torren and stopped when she noticed the wyvern. Her eyes widened. "What is that?" she asked.

"It is the wyvern Rowan freed from the Riven," Torren said. He took a strange-looking utensil from the wall and swiped it across the wyvern's hide, drawing the water from its slick surface. Water shed in a line from the flexible surface of the tool onto the dusty floor. "I never thought I'd see one in my lifetime, but they're not as dangerous as you'd think. As long as you don't act scared of them. They're pretty amazing, actually."

Torren smiled as he worked on the dragon, whose tail wagged like an excited pet.

Grendel eased closer to Rowan, then jumped back when the tail swung in her direction. "O-kay. Rowan, can I talk with you?"

The wyvern grunted and leaned toward Torren, who chuckled and scratched a spot on its neck. The tail lifted and fell in a banging motion.

"Yes. I think we would be safer somewhere else." Rowan led the way back outside. He waited until they moved to the center of the courtyard by the water pump before turning to the giantess. "What can I help you with?"

A corner of Grendel's lips dipped in a frown. "I'm worried about you. You seem ... I don't know"—she shifted, tossing one of her hands out—"upset or tense?"

Rowan wasn't sure if that was a question. He'd thought she was going to ask him something pertinent. "Why would I not be?" he said. "The Lady returned, died in my arms, and now is nothing more than a pile of wood in the place she called home for generations. There are voices and noises in my head that won't go away no matter what I try to do. And we've gained no progress in unraveling how to stop the Erlking's influence over the Wilden Lands." When he finished, his voice echoed off the stone walls of the castle.

Torren stuck his head out of the stables, his green face wide in surprise. "All okay out here?" he asked.

Rowan inhaled, though he didn't need to breathe. The action helped center him. He blew the air out. "My apologies."

"You're overwhelmed. I'm familiar with that emotion." Grendel glanced at the ground before looking back his way. "I try to focus on something—big or small—that I *can* do, instead of all the things I can't do." She shrugged. "It's comforting to take command over something when everything seems so out of control."

He ran a finger over the pump's handle, wiping some condensation away. The air was still heavy with rain, though the storm had moved on. Clouds reflected in the mud puddles littering the courtyard. "I welcome any suggestions."

"Let's try to reconfigure the soundometers. Maybe we can figure out what all the noise is. Maybe it's linked with how the Erlking manipulates music."

The tightness in Rowan's chest eased with her suggestion. Doing something productive was always helpful. "I would like that. After I've seen to the Lady's remains, of course. And only if it's just us."

"We could lock the other two out?" she said, a lilt in her deep voice.

"Indeed," Rowan agreed. He glanced at the sky once more. The gray gloom mirrored his mood. "I'll be there shortly."

~Rowan~
A short while later

ROWAN ENTERED the lab after burying the Lady's limbs beneath her Weeping Welter tree. The vine had spread to cover the entire tree now, and the limbs were withering. Though her loss still stung, performing the rites Merrow had taught him over the Lady and her tree had instilled a sense of resolution.

Grendel stood above a large beaker, which sat over a flame.

"What are you doing?" he asked.

"I'm brewing a distress tea. Mother used to prepare them

for me right before tests. Tests always made me nervous." A mortar and pestle lay askew on the table next to the giantess, the vestiges spilling from the bowl. Dried remains of other ingredients were scattered around her. He didn't know her to be so disorderly.

Rowan's hands itched to clean everything up. "Are you nervous now?" Rowan asked, unable to decipher her actions and emotional state.

"No, but you are. And since you can drink, this will help ease your nerves and settle your emotions." She added in a small batch of dried flowers, pinching them as she dropped them in, and stirred the brown liquid with a long-handled spoon.

"What's in it?"

Grendel glanced at him, then looked away. "Nothing to worry about. It's all natural and safe."

He frowned. "But you won't tell me what it is? Why would I drink a potion I don't know the ingredients of? Is this another of the giant's secrets?"

"No. Just a trade secret, if you must know. Eventually, I aspire to have an apothecary of my own. If I gave away all my potions, there'd be no reason for anyone to buy them from me. Buyers would just mix everything themselves." She stirred in a dark sap. The mixture popped and sizzled against the heated sides. Grendel smiled. "That's to add some fizz."

Grendel took the beaker off the flames and set it on a wooden trivet.

Rowan's bark tickled as the particles from the potion floated into the air and rested against his trunk.

"Don't look so dubious. It's perfectly safe, and I'm drinking some myself. And you said yourself that you can't taste anything, anyway." She walked over to where Rowan stood right inside the door. "Now, about the soundometers." Pieces of her first experiment already sat on the table where she—or someone else—had cleared the useless book and paper debris from the passageway. The bags were nowhere to be found.

"Maybe we're trying to solve the wrong puzzle with them." Grendel took the wires and examined them. "I mean, it was detrimental for me to hear all the noise they amplified. After listening to Glory in the passageway, what if we merely need to change the frequency of the sounds? Sort of mix it up so the Erlking's music doesn't have his desired effect?"

Rowan moved around Grendel and sat in the next seat. Heat from the cooling burner warmed the air to his right. He grasped the broken devices, assessing them. "You could be on to something. But how do we do that?"

"Magnets hum when you create metallic resonance around them. If Princess Glory—or anyone, actually—used either a low-key or high-pitched resonance near it, it might interrupt the Erlking's spells. So, maybe we configure some sort of low-key or high-pitched noises creatures can't normally hear."

"Like a whistle only animals can hear?" Rowan said. "I've heard of them. Didn't the witches once apply them to call the war dogs to battle?"

"Their slathering hounds, which the elves slayed in their Witching Wars, yes. It's not perfect science. What I heard with the soundometers on was illogical." She motioned to them. "There wasn't a single note but a cacophony of noises and voices. The racket was potent. I'm not sure how to counteract that, but maybe Princess Glory, with her wide musical knowledge, could help."

"You think by adding more noise into the ether, the creatures will—what? Be freed from the spell?"

"Well, isn't that similar to what you did with the wyverns? Broke them out of their musical pattern?"

Rowan gazed into the giantess's hopeful face. "That's the

best solution we've come up with so far. But we'd need to test it out first."

Grendel's face split into a wide grin.

CHAPTER 13

~Horra~

After leaving the laboratory earlier

Horra joined her father in the throne room, where he had created a makeshift desk. He sat on a wooden dining room chair since his stone throne was currently rubble.

"You finally did it," she said, nodding at the table lined with parchments, letters, and maps.

He rubbed his tired-looking face, the dark-green stubble creating a scratching sound. He must not have shaved this morning. Tufts of hair on his head stuck out in a couple places, and one spot lay flat from where he'd slept. "Against my better judgment, yes. You missed the send-off for Queen Toppenbottom and Princess Misty."

Though spoken easily, his tone held a note of admonition. "I was taking care of the arrangements for the Lady's remains."

He nodded, accepting her excuse. "Did you find the book

you were looking for? I forgot to ask when you filled me in on the Lady's return." His sigh was heavy. The lines around his eyes and mouth had deepened to grooves.

She noticed a few silver threads intermixed in his green hair and fought against the fear it ignited in her gut. Illness had robbed the ruby from her mother's lovely hair before she'd died. Those strands had been white, not gray, though, which gave her the strength to answer her father. "We found remnants of the book. The rats chewed them to bits and destroyed any magic they held."

"Rats?" he asked, the bluster gone from his demeanor.

Horra neatened a pile of parchment decrees. Though she knew the passages were not the holy spaces she'd grown up believing they were, she didn't relish admitting to their existence when her father looked so tired. That was a confession for the future. She cleared her throat. "Pidge took care of the rats."

"Then what is your next step?" His eyes were steady, unmoving.

Horra was still not used to being in charge. She'd rarely seen her father indecisive. Being uncertain was all she was now. Nothing she'd done forged even a dent in the Erlking's terror. Unable to find anything else to straighten on the table, Horra locked gazes with her father and admitted the truth. "I don't know."

King Fyd's bushy eyebrows rose into his disheveled bangs.

"We—the others and I—are devising a plan," she rushed to explain. Her comment was mainly true, though they hadn't formed definite plans. She had to provide an acceptable answer, however, or he might lecture her again.

"See that you do. And if you need any other motivation"—he sat up, his chest protruding—"a group of concerned parents *visited* us this morning after the rain stopped." He drummed his claws on the wooden table. "I'm surprised you didn't hear them protesting outside the castle entrance. Loudly."

Horra blanched. They'd been inside the passageway and, between the chimes and the battle with the rats, heard nothing.

Her father continued. "More children have gone missing. They are demanding we send search parties out for them. Or this." He held out a larger sheet. "The giants are joining the smaller creatures. Too many of their children are missing now to ignore. Oddar is no match for the giants."

Horra's mouth dropped open. "But it's not our fault. We returned every child we found as soon as we could. We fed them, cleaned them up, and kept them safe within these walls." Horra took the portrait-sized sheet, a signed affirmation from the Giant Ministry. "The giants have a ministry?"

The king let out a breath. "Apparently. And since we are the only formal leaders in the central Wilden Lands, they are counting on us to solve the problem. There's no mention of your giant friend, Grendel. I'm unsure how they will react when they find we have been harboring her when they believe she's missing."

Heat drained from Horra's face. It hadn't been her choice to keep the Largeness family in the dark about Grendel's presence.

"Are you up for the challenge, Queen Bearer?" His voice was deep and full of emotion.

Her courage dropped, smashing into pieces inside her like a broken vase. "I don't have a choice, do I?"

Her father's gaze grew watery. "No. I'm afraid you—we— don't."

~Glory~

AFTER LEAVING THE LABORATORY, Glory moved her belongings from the suite of rooms she and her family had shared back into the golden room. She would never admit to anyone she preferred the small dank room at the end of the hallway now. Especially after having thrown such a fit about it in the not-so-distant past before she'd snuck out to meet the Erlking.

The guest bedroom now signified freedom from her royal duties. The accidental gold vein she'd unleashed illuminated the space better than any light globe she could conjure. And though her magic reserves were growing, fear of depleting her magic kept her from using it on trivial things.

"Ugh," she groaned at herself, at how she was changing. "I'm becoming such a troll."

She took her time while also mulling over the Erlking's musical spells and how she'd stopped the rats in the passageway with only a single sharp note. Singing it off-key on purpose, she'd done it to gain their attention. She hadn't realized it would incapacitate the little grubbers.

But would it do any good when faced with a host of critters and the Erlking himself? Somehow, Glory doubted that.

It didn't take long to tuck her things away, so she lay down to rest, folding her wings carefully behind her. They and her head still throbbed, but the pain was manageable now. In all the excitement, she had forgotten to ask the giant girl about a cure.

She closed her eyes, and Maestro Lyrie's music lessons came to her as she considered the evil elf's musical spells. Maestro had been a zealous director. He'd drilled her on song composition, music theory and its history, advance note management, and all the elements of musical arrangement. None of his lessons had addressed how to insert magic into music. Magic merely happened when fairies played.

Besides the glee of stealing something from beneath the Erlking's nose, her curiosity of the strange spells drew her like a glimmerfly to a flame. Fairy magic created bright, hasty tones—pleasant melodies in a repeated structure. Their songs were cohesive and logical. Besides the dark magic element, the Erlking's song structure was not orderly in the way music should be.

Glory struggled to make sense of the dissonant notes with the relentless rhythms used in his spells. There was no repetition, and the notes would turn flat or sharp. She had scoffed at such spells, thinking them nothing more than an infantile attempt at playing an instrument. Awkward and unruly.

Maestro once forced Glory to sit in a storm to catch the rhythm of nature. She then had to compose a song from what she'd heard. The crescendos, the rise and fall of the currents, and the silent moments of reflection had lent themselves to an inspired piece she'd titled "Wind's Song." Maestro's tears when she'd played her outro had guaranteed her place as a Composer of the Highest Order.

With all that knowledge at her fingertips, she still couldn't figure out the Erlking's spells. Glory twisted in her bed, working herself into the crooks of the lumpy mattress. She grunted in disgust. Nothing in the troll's kingdom was geared toward any other creature's comfort. Sitting up, she transformed the mattress into a smooth cushioned surface, free from lumps. Unlike the lighting, this wasn't a trivial issue but one of necessity. "Should've done this long ago," she said, before reminding herself she hadn't the ability before now. Smiling, she magicked the scratchy blanket into a cloud-soft spread.

Satisfied, she lay back down and fell into a deep sleep.

Music invaded her dreams. She stood on a musical measure

like one would a ladder. Flat half notes chased her up and down the lines, then across the grid until she fell into a whole rest symbol and disappeared inside it. She reappeared on the board of a harpsichord, where an invisible hand played a prestissimo tempo, a frantic symphony of movement. She dodged and dove across the keys, but she couldn't evade the fury. The unseen force tripped her over and over again until she lay tossed among the chords. Notes tugged at her tender wings, ripping, tearing in their assault. She cried out in anger and agony.

Pounding on her door jostled her awake. Heart racing, Glory threw an arm over her damp eyes to block the sunlight streaming through the tall window, which reflected boldly off the golden walls. She needed to add curtains to her list of things to magic into place.

Thunk, thunk, thunk.

Her dream dissipated like smoke as the knocks grew louder, reigniting her headache. She wiped away her tears and cleared the sleep from her eyes. "Okay, okay. I'm coming." Glory threw back the fluffy comforter and, in five strides, reached the door. She yanked it open to find a frazzled-looking Horra on her threshold. "What is it?" she asked, her head throbbing.

"Meeting in fifteen minutes in the laboratory." The troll spoke in a clipped tone.

Her heart skipped a beat. "Has something happened? What's wrong?"

"Find out at the meeting," Horra said over her shoulder as she left Glory standing in the doorway.

"Why did I stay at this stupid castle?" she grumbled.

~Horra~

HORRA WALKED AWAY from the fairy princess, her lips pinched together over her tusks. The fluffy white bedspread over a pristine mattress gave her a flashback to when the fairies, under the Erlking's influence, took over her castle. When she'd finally returned home after getting lost crossing the Wilden Lands, they had fairy-tized the rooms with gauzy fabrics and pastel colors. Their takeover disturbed her on all levels then and now.

It was too much to hope that the moment they shared laughing in the lab might've brought them closer together. Horra fought the temptation to be insulted by Glory's magicked items. She should rejoice that Glory's magic had reappeared after what the girl had suffered. Part of Horra's reluctance was that she'd warned the fairy about the Erlking yet the girl had gone off and placed herself in danger anyway. She half deserved what she got. Guilt niggled her conscience at that thought. No one deserved the Erlking's spells. She puffed out a breath, trying but failing to let some of her stress go.

Between the speech Master Knurl gave on her kingdom's history, allowing the others into the passageway, fighting the rats, and then her father informing her about more missing children, her taut nerves threatened her sanity. Everything rolled together in a raw and jagged ball inside her gut.

Horra plodded to the laboratory without thinking. She arrived at the broken door and shook her head to clear the cobwebs from her mind. "Gah! Don't lose it now," she muttered as she swung the unsteady hanging door open.

Grendel and Rowan stood inside the room with pieces of wire, chunks of Pidge's feather stems, and other debris around them. They bent over a tiny item. "What're you guys doing?" she asked.

Rowan jumped as if he hadn't realized she was there. Grendel scuttled away to avoid being poked by his branches.

Horra snickered. Usually, she was the one on the poked end of Rowan's branchy crown. "I made noise when I walked in. What are you guys so focused on that you didn't hear me?"

"Following Princess Glory's example, we're creating a specialized whistle," Rowan explained as he ran a hand across his lichen-covered trunk.

Horra stopped walking and stared. "A whistle?"

Grendel removed a metal rod from a burner and used the melted end to weld something onto a rock. "What the princess did was fortuitous. With a whistle, we can create high-frequency sounds in the ether sphere. We're hoping it will scatter the spell, breaking its command on the critters doing the Erlking's dirty work." She described the rest in technical terms Horra didn't understand.

Horra stopped Grendel with a raised claw. "I'm sorry to interrupt, but I'm calling a mandatory meeting. Glory will be here in a couple minutes."

Rowan shifted, alert now. "What's happened?"

She glanced momentarily at Grendel, then inhaled deeply. "The Erlking is accelerating his mission of stealing children. The giants are now involved and are on their way to Oddar."

Grendel's head jerked at the mention of the giants. "What? Why? Have more giant children gone missing?"

"It seems so. Your ministry has joined with our local creatures, demanding we find the children. Our relationship with your kingdom is tentative at best. We are not strong enough, especially with our diminished resources, to stand against them should they find out we've been hiding one of their children without telling them." She glanced at Grendel then. The girl stood wth her head and shoulders hunched. "I don't anticipate trouble, but I also don't expect them to be happy with our deception."

Grendel dropped her metal rod, her hand shaking. "This is not good news."

"Do you wish to hide in the passages when they come?" Horra asked, half hoping she would.

Grendel didn't seem to hear her. "Do you know if Galumph is still missing? Did they say?"

"I'm afraid not."

Tears glittered in her flecked eyes. "I should've kept looking for her after you found me." Grendel turned to Rowan. "We need to finish these and test them." She sniffed wetly.

Horra patted the girl's arm. "Grendel, what do I tell them if the giants ask or find out about you? I don't enjoy pressuring you, but this could veer into an inter-kingdom disaster."

Her eyes grew wide. "You can't tell them I've been here. They won't understand. Loyalty is important to giants." She wrung her paws. "I can't believe Galumph slipped my mind. My parents will never forgive me." Tufts of her red hair waved frantically as she shook her head. "Never."

Horra inwardly cringed. The giant girl would obviously be of no help when it came to her kind or their visit. It was moments like these that Horra wished she weren't responsible for such a vast kingdom.

CHAPTER 14

~Glory~

Minutes after the grumpy troll royal woke her, Glory barged into the lab, interrupting a tense discussion. "Can someone provide me with some headache powder?" Glory's request came out as more of a demand. But she didn't apologize.

Horra, Rowan, and Grendel all turned to glance her way, every pair of eyes aglow and cheeks flushed. After no one said anything for a couple of beats, she added, "Please?" The word usually worked with her mother. But that thought stirred unwelcome emotions inside her, which she quickly buried.

Horra was the first to break her statue-still posture. "In the last cupboard, in the jar with the blue label. Use the water from the sink in the back."

After realizing no one was going to retrieve it for her, Glory spun and headed toward the other end of the laboratory. "Thanks a lot." She couldn't help the note of irritation as she strode across the narrow space at the front of the tables, since the three other creatures blocked the wider center aisle. The last cupboard contained several powders and ingredients. She sifted through the glass jars, which weren't in order. "Trolls are allergic to organization," she muttered beneath her breath.

After searching two cupboards, Glory found the labeled blue jar in the back of a third. A glance at the others across the room informed her they were still holding a heated discussion. "Are these glasses clean?" she asked, examining the beakers sitting on a towel drying next to the sink.

Silence.

Glory glanced over to find them all staring at her with open mouths. "What? This is a lab. There's no telling what concoctions these beakers have held. And there are things called germs, you know."

"They're as clean as you're going to get them." Horra's clipped tone carried across the room.

"Fine." Glory swished water inside the cleanest-looking beaker, rinsing it before filling it with more water. She measured as per the label, two ounces per dreg of powder. After adding the white granules, she swirled the water once again, then gulped it in small sips. Her wings constricted against her shoulders. "Blech. That's awful. What do you put in this?"

Horra's green cheeks puffed out like a frog's vocal sac. "Do you mind? We're trying to establish a plan to save the Wilden Lands, and you're worried about a little headache?"

"I asked once before, if you remember, then we all got sidetracked. And though I have some of my magic back and healing myself should be easy, I can't force the pain away. So it's not simply a little headache. Something is going on." Glory laid the beaker down hard on the table, and the glass clinked loudly in the room.

Rowan let out a clacking cough, making Glory cringe. "The

voices in my head have not relented, either, since the Lady reappeared. The clamor does not pain me, but it is quite distracting and difficult to think beyond it, especially when the noise ebbs louder. Could the two be related?" he asked, his fingers steepled together in front of him.

No one spoke.

An idea formed in Glory's mind the instant the ache in her temples eased. Her wings slackened, the muscles loosening. The ache faded faster, she realized, than the fizzing tonic her healers used. She walked closer to the others and sat on a tall chair, resting her arm on the table. "The Erlking's musical spellbook confused me when I first stole it from him. The notes didn't make any sense. It's not actual music that gets played, not by traditional wisdom. The Erlking is far from conventional. But what if—" She hesitated, trying to break it down so they could understand, since music and all its elements were complicated.

"Go on." Horra's voice tightened with impatience.

Glory held her hand up to stall the troll's ire. "What if he's not actually creating music with the instruments he plays, then adding magic to it? What if he's purely creating chaos and then siphoning magic spells into the cacophony? That would explain why all the dissonant chords and frenzied measures fill his spells." Her confidence in the thought solidified as she spoke.

"Except he used magic when he invaded the castle," Horra pointed out, waving her claw wildly in the air. "I mean, I thought the music was noise from the beginning, but it wasn't like what you're describing."

"Yes, but his attempt at taking over your castle immediately didn't succeed, did it? His target"—Glory pointed at Horra—"wasn't affected by his music, so he changed up the spells. Or he already had a Plan B in play, since the rats became his spies after he introduced himself to me as a dark elf. Musical instruments first, then he spelled the critters into becoming spies, and finally, his musical spells. It could be why when I let out that high-pitched note—"

"Screech," Horra amended.

Glory ignored her. "It affected the rats. Perhaps we should've kept one alive to see if it broke the spell the Erlking put on them."

Grendel snapped her fingers. "I should've thought to do that. About the noise—a creature would go mad listening to what I did. But the rats didn't appear crazed. We already knew the music fueled his spells somehow. How does what you're implying help us defeat him?"

"The only way I know to stop the Erlking's influence is to mute or deflect the noise he employs. That's why cloth in the ears kept us from becoming mesmerized. Is there a way to mute or deflect the noise he's filtering into the ether to stop his influence on the critters and the children?"

"Without destroying the instruments?" Rowan asked, though it sounded more like a demand to Glory's ears. "Don't forget—the wood is part of the dryad's trees. If we destroy them, we kill the dryads."

"Has anyone seen any dryads since the Lady returned?" Glory glanced at each of them. "Could they already be dead?"

Horra moved to sit across from Glory at the back table. "She said 'it is done' when she collapsed. I thought she meant her mission to free her kind. Could her words have meant something else?"

"Her mission wasn't only to free the lost souls, but to undo the ties that bound the Riven together. Also, she unraveled the spells on the roots across the Wilden Lands, freeing the roods." Rowan turned his gaze toward the Conservatory. "There had to be spirits there we didn't know about. What if they are part of the recent uproar?"

Horra slid back off her chair. "We need to talk with Master Knurl."

~Rowan~

The Conservatory was quiet when they entered, the midmorning light shining brightly around the garden space. Rowan sensed Pidge asleep in her nest—a rare occurrence. She'd eaten her fill and more of the rats in the passageway and was sleeping it off. Rowan led everyone over to the Great Yew Tree. "Master Knurl. We need your help."

The trunk popped, and the wizened face of the rood appeared. "How may I assist you, young druid?"

"Now that the Lady has broken the Im'bara spell, are you able to find out if she did indeed rescue the other dryads from the Riven?" Rowan wouldn't admit how deep his fear of returning to the tumultuous place ran in his soul.

"I couldn't connect with the Lady when she arrived. The air has been static since the storm, so I continue to have difficulty communicating with anything outside the castle. I am afraid I cannot help you."

Pidge's screech filled the silence the rood's words left behind. She circled the glass ceiling before darting over and landing next to Rowan on unsteady legs. Her stomach protruded more than normal. She preened and rubbed her beak on the Yew's bark.

"Master Knurl, can you tell us what kind of static you're referring to? Could it be the Erlking's magic, or something else?" Grendel inquired from behind Rowan.

The tree creaked. "Magic, yes. But also, many voices are joining the disorder. I have recognized my brethren, but as soon as I sense one, they disappear. As for the dryads, I sense a shifting resonance coming from the direction of Endwylde."

"What's that supposed to mean?" Glory asked, her voice sharp.

"The elves." The queen bearer grabbed her pet and dragged her away from the tree. Pidge cackled unhappily before fluttering off. "Do you think the change in the Riven has drawn their attention? And what of the others who were stuck inside that shifting maze?" Horra's voice rose as she spoke, matching the fairy's tone.

Rowan planted his roots into the soil. "Let's not jump ahead of ourselves or create problems that might not be there." He raised a finger when the queen bearer opened her mouth to reply. "We need to consider all the possibilities and not get caught up in threats we cannot fully identify. If we wander too far out in the thistles, we'll miss the real dangers coming our way. Now, let's sit down, decide what we need to address first, and forge a plan."

Silence.

"That was very succinct," the queen bearer said.

Rowan relaxed. "Thank you, Master Knurl, for your input, though it was not helpful."

"Rowan," Horra shrieked. "That is not nice to tell someone."

The rood frowned. "Nevertheless, he is correct to say that. I can only tell you what I know to be true. Everything else is speculation." A rumble rose from the ground, shaking the tree's limbs.

Rowan and the others took hasty steps back. "Master Knurl?" Rowan asked as sap rush through his core from fear.

A wide limb whipped out and clutched the top of Rowan's crown. "Rowan, my boy." It was Merrow's voice this time, his essence seeping through the old Yew's fibers, making Rowan's heart race. He'd missed his former mentor, but two visits in such a short period was alarming. "There isn't time to explain, but I've received a vision. Take this gift and don't hesitate, my young druid. I know you will do what you have to when the time comes." Merrow's voice faded.

Tingles, akin to ants marching beneath his bark, traveled from the tips of his crown to his roots in the soil. Then, as fast as they came, they were gone.

The branch cracked and broke, dropping to the Conservatory's ground, scraping across the lichen on Rowan's bark. Pidge screeched and darted for the pond.

"What is that?" Horra asked, her brown eyes wide. She pointed a claw.

Rowan shook his crown. Besides the raw scratches across his outer layer, which wasn't a big deal, he wasn't sure what the queen bearer meant. "What is what?"

"You're sprouting," she said, her mouth open wide enough that he could fully see her tusks.

A clacking voice interrupted them. "I apologize," Master Knurl said. "I drifted off. What was it you asked me?"

Rowan frowned. "You did not drift off. Merrow invaded your tree to present a message." He rubbed at his itchy trunk.

Grendel stepped up to him and narrowed her eyes. "Your leaves are turning gold and you appear to be budding."

Glory snickered behind them.

Horra elbowed the fairy in the gut. "Stop that. It's not funny. Whatever Merrow did must be important."

Rowan was unsure what the fuss was about. He switched topics. "Master Knurl, you mentioned a shift coming from Endwylde. Would that be the elves?"

The tree scrunched his face, then smoothed it. "I do not know. The power I sensed could be a shift in the Riven. Both are too far for me to gauge, and the disharmony in the ether is affecting my ability."

"What if it *is* the elves? They are more powerful than all of us combined." Glory marched away, then paced back.

Rowan ignored her erratic movements and recalled Master Knurl's discussion about troll history. "That's not true." He turned to face the queen bearer. "A small group of your non-magical foremothers—a dryad and an oread—overthrew several elves before they built this great castle and formed Oddar."

Horra's brown eyes widened. "But they only faced a handful of elves, who were probably more intent on pillaging than fighting."

"Someone needs to check on the Riven," Grendel said. "That way, we'll know for sure what the situation there is."

Silence.

"We also need to find the children," Horra said. "That's what I brought everyone together to discuss. More have gone missing. Glory, if what you said about the Erlking using the children as his army is right, and more children have gone missing, it could signal the Erlking is nearing completion of his plans for them. They are as much a priority as the Erlking is." Horra flung her arms out. "We have to leave now, and we need to split up."

CHAPTER 15

Before her companions could question Horra's declaration to split up, Sageel, followed by Torren and Murda, rushed into the Conservatory. "Queen Bearer," the old hobgoblin maid gasped. "Your father is requesting your presence in the throne room." She wheezed, then whispered, "It's the giants. They've arrived."

Grendel let out a startled "eep" sound. "They can't find me here." Her body trembled, and she grimaced.

Horra recognized the signs that the giant girl was losing control. The last time she'd done that, she'd broken through the front doors, where the giants were now, and bolted.

Glory groaned. "Oh no. Not this again."

Rowan held up a finger. "Surely your kind will understand—"

Horra bumped into him as she grabbed the orange giantess

and directed her past the Yew tree to the back of the Conservatory. "This way. And hurry."

Grendel hesitated for a blink of an eye before she allowed Horra to push her toward the hole in the back wall. Her fur puffed as she morphed.

"Run!" Horra pushed Grendel past the Weeping Welter tree, which no longer moved to allow them to pass.

Grendel, growing and sprouting more fur, skimmed through the ropy branches, then fell to the ground with a shriek. On arms and knees, she crawled through before one growing foot got stuck. With a jerk, the boot came loose and the fur-covered foot was gone. Stones from around the outer wall crumbled and fell, sealing the entry. A roar pierced the air before Grendel's footsteps rumbled away.

"What's this?" Sageel asked, her eyes narrowed at the no-longer-hidden spot. "Is that how you got out of the castle the first time 'round?"

Horra frowned. News of the secret entry was bound to spread with everyone using the hole as a doorway. Pebbles scattered as the rocks stopped falling, fully sealing the space. She'd either have to dig it out or never utilize it again. With a sigh, she rose from her stooped position. "Yes. I used to be the only one who knew about it."

Sageel straightened, a grin on her face. "That's my clever girl."

Rowan bent next to Horra, taking up the rest of the space between the trees. His blooming crown snagged her hair. She brushed at the branches, but it only tangled her curls more. "Space, Rowan."

"Forgive me, Queen Bearer," he said, though he didn't move. With one long arm, he reached in and collected the boot. It had been part of a door-troll uniform, the only size they had big enough to support the giantess's enormous feet. "Did you see which way she went?"

Horra detached her curls from his branches and moved away. "No. The rocks blocked my view, and she didn't run in a straight line."

He jerked upright. The bark on his face appeared smoother. "We have to find her. She is the only one who can help me test the whistles." He rushed back toward the Yew tree, where Murda and Torren both stood waiting for them.

Glory smirked. "So you're saying there's something you can't do?"

Horra's temples throbbed. "Enough! We have to come up with a plan without Grendel. She's a big girl, literally, and she can join us when she cools off again."

"After you greet your guests, Queen Bearer," Sageel stated as she hustled past them all. Though she'd been out of breath when she'd arrived, the old hobgoblin was quite spry.

"Is that why you're here?" Horra asked the other two trolls.

Torren snickered. "Your father wasn't sure you'd come willingly. We're your official escorts."

Murda's sheepish expression confirmed Torren's words.

"Pickled pig's feet. Let's go, then. Rowan, you and Glory start planning the experiment. I'm sure with Glory's extensive musical knowledge, she will be an excellent stand-in for Grendel in this experiment. I'll be back as soon as I can."

Torren waved for her to go ahead of them. Did they honestly think she'd slip out instead of meet the giants? Horra had to admit it was tempting. Nevertheless, she strutted out of the Conservatory like the royal she was.

Raised voices drifted through the open doorway in the Hall of Monstrosity. Her mother's portrait watched her as she strode past. Though Oddar's history differed from what she grew up believing, her mother and grandmothers had been brave and fierce. She took comfort in that knowledge and bolstered herself to face the giants.

"There's only so much Oddar can provide," her father was saying to a gathering of five giants. Mr. and Mrs. Largeness were not among the group, thankfully. Horra did not relish explaining why they'd harbored their missing eldest child or describing why their daughter was not currently available should her presence become known.

Horra reassured herself that Grendel could take care of herself. She'd proven that more than once. Setting the issue aside, she stepped next to her father's chair.

She bowed her head at the five giants, then faced her father. "How may I be of service, my king?" she said as formally as she could, wishing she had worn something more appropriate for their guests.

Torren and Murda displayed a formal knight stance against the walls on opposite sides of the room. They joined three other knights, including Captain Erast, who looked away from her. She was glad to see the contrary knight, though her interaction with him had not been enjoyable previously. Ignoring those memories, Horra fixed her face with an unemotional expression and turned toward the giants.

"Queen Bearer, please meet the Giant Ministry. Your Honors, this is my daughter, Queen Bearer Horra Fyd."

With the introductions finished, the king tapped a claw on the arm of his chair. "Thank you for coming so quickly, Queen Bearer. The giants have arrived to petition us to lead a search party for the missing children. I was just explaining how Oddar has already taken up the torch in this area. However, because you have spearheaded this subject, I'd like you to share your missions, the challenges you've faced, and your plans going forward."

Horra inwardly groaned and worked to keep her expression

professional while gathering her thoughts. The last thing she needed to do was natter on for hours, explaining everything from the beginning. She called upon every ounce of Woodsly's dignitary training to form a response and a plan that would satisfy creatures that, should they become unhappy with her for any reason, could crush her at will.

~Rowan~

MOMENTS AFTER HORRA left the Conservatory, Rowan stood beside the Yew tree, Grendel's boot still in his hands. Emotions bloomed and took residence in his core, flowing out to his extremities. His mind sputtered, slowing. The air around him stilled. Sounds in both the physical world and the ether dissolved into silence. He stood, boulder still, unable to move or think.

"Wood boy?" Glory snapped her fingers in front of his face. "Hello. Are you with me?"

Her sharp tone sifted through the lichen lining his ears. "Yes." His voice quivered. He shook his head, unsure what had just happened. "My apologies, Princess Glory. Did you ask me a question?"

She clicked her tongue. "Uh, yeah." Her gaze was intuitive. "What's going on with you? First, you sprout golden leaves and buds. Now, you're spacing out. Are you ill?"

Rowan contemplated her words. He lifted his arms, but they looked the same. "I cannot see this sprouting you refer to."

Glory pursed her lips and grabbed his arm. "This way." She dragged him, her wings fluttering wildly enough to create a breeze, over to the pond area. "Look at yourself in the water."

Light from the windows above shone upon them, mirrored

cheerily on the placid surface. Rowan bent over the edge. Where there had formerly been green leaves budding on his crown, it was now full of clusters of catkins and yellow leaves. Seedling buds hung from his stems. "I'm blooming."

Glory huffed. "That's what we've been trying to tell you."

He considered this. It had to be Merrow's handiwork. But why? He was too young to mature this way. The seedkeeper had mentioned a vision and told him to do what he had to do when the time came. "Merrow speeded up my growth pattern."

Glory examined a catkin cluster, running her fingers through the pieces. "Granted, these adornments are much more appealing than bare limbs. But ... why?"

Rowan straightened and stepped away from the fairy's prodding hand. "That's what I'd like to know." Pricks of energy came from every part of Rowan's body, signaling a biological change on a molecular level. He recalled a vague memory of something similar happening to him before he unrooted. His memories were not intact from that time, since his brain stem had still been developing. It was more of a feeling than a memory. Rowan shook his blooming head. "We need to test the whistles. I'd like you to look them over for viability."

Glory's face drained of color. "Me? Why can't we wait for Grendel to return?"

He narrowed his gaze. "Were you not trained in emergency response and advanced critical planning in your Shining Land?"

"Well, yes, but—"

Rowan moved back toward the table where they'd placed the whistles, most still unassembled. "It's good you possess an expert-level knowledge in music. You are uniquely qualified to tune the whistles to the right frequency using your trained ear."

Glory's groan followed his footsteps across the Conservatory.

Pidge scree'd from above, but the bird did not join them.

Rowan handed her the first one, the crudest-built one. It matched the woodwind mouthpieces from the book he'd found in the troll's library.

She puckered her face in disbelief. "My specialty is music, not building instruments."

When he said nothing but stubbornly held the article out to her, she sighed and took it.

"Fine. But it won't be my fault when these experiments fail." She studied the carved wooden whistle. When she blew into the end, it ushered a hollow sound that didn't carry far.

Rowan frowned. The note was supposed to be too high or low for the ear to hear. "That isn't right. Try this one. It's a unique take on a tootler used to call dragons."

"Unique is right." Glory reluctantly took it, and the next, until they assembled and then tested their way through each of his creations.

"I do not understand. I followed the diagrams in the book."

Glory turned a whistle over in her hand. "What wood did you use?"

"Stringy pine."

She blinked. "Well, there's where you first went wrong. Stringy pine is too soft. And what's inside?"

Rowan glanced off into the distance, his gaze unseeing. "A piece of Pidge's feather stock. It was the only flexible material we had."

"Music is a precise science," she said.

Rowan swung his head to look her way.

"Yes. I said science. Like in a potion, you need to apply the best-quality ingredients, and you can't sub anything."

Rowan stuck his chin out. "I thought you said you weren't an expert on building instruments."

Her wings beat furiously, and her cheeks darkened. "I

might not know how to build them, but I am a Composer of the Highest Order. I'm classically trained on musical instruments and the instrument of my voice—which I believe you've already witnessed. It's easy to know when something will or won't work after you've played enough musical contrivances, as I have."

"So what would you suggest, then?"

She flicked a hand out. "If we're fighting music with music, I need *my* instruments, not something crudely carved in haste. We have a wide array of instruments back in the Shining Kingdom. I have enough magic to form a fairy path now to go back and fetch them. I'll return quickly, and we can test them when I'm back."

He wasn't sure if he should trust her. "How do I know you'll do as you say?"

"Do you require a magical oath?"

Rowan clasped his hands in front of him, sensing a small amount of anger in the fairy's words. "That may be best."

She tsked. "Fine. I promise to return home with all haste, gather any instruments I think would be beneficial to our mission, and return with them quickly." Sparkling magic glittered when she uttered her last word, sealing her magical pledge.

He bowed his head. "Thank you."

Without looking back, she flung the doors wide open and strode through them.

Pidge screeched and took off flying toward the doors.

Rowan beat the bird to the doors, closing them and ending her attempt at escape.

Pidge fluffed her feathers and chittered unhappily.

Rowan ignored the bird. He picked up the whistles and tossed them in the scrap pile the hobgoblins used to start fires.

CHAPTER 16

~Horra~

Four hours later, Horra rejoined Rowan in the Conservatory. Her throat was raw from talking, and her neck ached from tilting up to speak with the giants. "Where's Princess Glory?" She eyed the wood scraps and oddly carved instruments in the bin.

"She returned to her Shining Kingdom," Rowan said while carving holes in a flute.

Anger was the first emotion to sink in. Disappointment quickly followed, ending in relief. Horra sat on a wooden ladder chair she'd formerly used to stand tall enough to work at the table. "It's probably for the best. She wasn't much of a team player."

Rowan lifted his budding head and frowned. She hadn't noticed when he was bent over that the moss had cleared from his face, leaving it a beautiful silvery hue. "The princess vowed to return with some solidly constructed instruments we can operate to combat the Erlking's music magic."

Horra relaxed. "Oh. So then, what are those?"

Rowan filled her in on their discussion and subsequent plans. He turned his head when he finished and held up the flute. "I am determined to create a workable instrument." He eyed her. "I thought you'd be happy that the fairy is stepping up to help us instead of sitting around complaining about everything. Yet your expression does not reflect that."

She shrugged. "Oath or not, I still don't trust her. What if she has a way of breaking the oath? She could be lying about being this big master of music. Maybe she—"

Rowan blew into the flute. A sharp note filled the air.

Horra snapped her mouth shut. She glared at the satisfied woodgoblin druid.

"That was much better than the others I've carved." Rowan sent her a calm gaze. "She'll be back. Even if she doesn't return, I've almost formed a breakthrough with my instruments. We may not need her help if I can perfect them."

Horra groaned. Not one of his creations had functioned correctly or worked when they needed them to. Even the bells he'd constructed before they entered the Riven ended up not being needed in the end.

"First Grendel running, then the giant's meeting, and now Glory leaving. It's too much, Rowan. This task is impossible." A weight Horra wished to avoid settled on her shoulders. Though she knew from the first moment Woodsly had offered her charge of Rowan's seed that she was in over her head. Back then, she'd had hope. Now, with all the children missing and the parents from all over her kingdom worried, her hope was wavering.

Rowan rested a hand over her trembling claws. "We're as close to the answer as we've ever been. Don't give up now. Merrow once told me it's darkest right before the dawn."

Her stomach gurgled. It was late, and she had eaten little in the past day. She grimaced. "I'm going to find something to eat. Things will make more sense after that."

Rowan said nothing as she left the Conservatory in search of Sageel. Her favorite maid would take care of her. That thought brought her more comfort than anything else at the moment.

Horra meandered through the Hall of Monstrosity, taking in all the awards, trophies, and portraits. She stopped at Queen Calcy's portrait to contemplate her ancestor's actions in securing the mountains and creating Oddar. Her history books told of Calcy's determination—a troll seeking a better life away from the muck and mud of the swamps. Labeled a champion of change, Calcy, like Horra, would've faced tough choices for her band's survival. She couldn't fault her multi-great grandmother for that.

Horra ran her claw over the canvas's flawless surface. She had to give it to the fairies. They could dole out destruction, but they could also reverse it just as easily. "Which is probably why Glory thought it would be a simple thing to have the Erlking return her beauty," she said, the revelation coming from somewhere in the depths of her mind. "When did I start siding with that fairy?" She shook her head.

Stomach still grumbling, Horra moved away from the peaceful hall and entered the throne room. One of the massive doors opened, the grit on the ground loud as the heavy stone moved against it.

Someone wearing a furry coat entered, but the darkness beyond the doorway didn't illuminate the creature. They were shaggy and bedraggled.

Her father's warnings of the recent uprisings made Horra jerk to attention. "Who is it?" she yelled.

The person let out a little "eep" and jumped at the same time. "Oh, Horra. You scared me." The creature with Grendel's voice turned away from the outside and stepped into the castle. The way the sunlight glowed from behind blocked her features. She wasn't wearing a coat. Her fur had thickened into a lustrous covering. She wore a boot on one foot, while the other was bare and furry.

Horra gaped at the girl's appearance. The giantess resembled a woodland firefox, except she was larger and rounder. Tufts of orange-red fur stuck out in several areas, some matted with dirt and weeds.

She looked more wild animal than giant.

"Grendel? What happened to you?" Horra stared at the furry giantess.

Grendel wrung her pawed hands. As soon as she realized what she was doing, she dropped her arms, hiding them behind her back. "I—I was scared that if the giants saw me, they'd realize who I was. And—and look at me," she wailed.

Horra strode over to her, grabbed the girl's arm, and led her past the threshold. She pushed the heavy stone door shut, sweating with the effort. When she returned to Grendel, the giantess had quit crying and stood sniffling, the fur on her face damp. "Come with me. Everything will be better with a full belly."

"Okay." Grendel's meek answer sounded especially pathetic since she looked like a massive fluffy cat.

They entered an empty dining room. Horra directed Grendel to a chair. "Lunchtime has passed. I'll be right back. Don't go anywhere."

Grendel nodded, more despondent than Horra had ever witnessed her.

Horra signaled for Sageel, telling her briefly what she

needed. The maid raced off to gather what she'd requested and send for Rowan.

Back in the dining room, Horra rejoined Grendel. She hesitated. The giantess was never this stoic. "Are you injured? Do you require something more than nourishment?" Her eyes flew over the girl's body but saw nothing more than dirt, weeds, and fur. No weeping cuts or injuries that needed immediate attention.

"What? Oh, no. I'm—well, not fine, but not physically injured." Grendel's flecked eyes had darkened, but they were clear. A good sign, Horra hoped.

Before Horra could ask anything further, Sageel burst through the servant's doorway with a tray of two large mugs and food.

After the maid left, Horra took the carrot juice and handed it to Grendel. She sipped on her spruce juice while the giantess stared at her bowl of vegetable stew.

"It wasn't your parents," Horra said to fill the uncomfortable silence.

Grendel shook her head. "Doesn't matter."

"I'm not the most empathetic creature in the Wilden Lands, but I understand how scared and frustrated you must be." Horra tried her best at diplomacy. It was grueling watching Grendel, who she considered a friend now, appear so despondent.

Grendel sniffled, her furry brows furrowed adorably across her forehead. "Do you? Because I don't think anyone can understand what it's like when the curse overtakes me. I'm practically blind to everything except trying to escape it." She swiped a paw across her damp cheeks. "It's unbearable. I have absolutely no control over myself."

Horra thought about that. "I think you have more control than you believe." She raised her claw when Grendel opened her mouth to argue. "You were gone a shorter time with this change. And you reverted to your normal size without brewing the contracting potion. Unless you had the potion on you?"

She shook her head.

Horra gestured with a claw. "See? I believe the Erlking failed in his mission to curse you. It hasn't worked properly. Yes, you change when things overwhelm you, but you don't remain under the curse's influence." She leaned in closer to the giant girl. "I have to wonder if the spells are flawed somehow. Maybe that could help us when we search for the children. And Rowan has made some progress with a whistle," she added brightly, hoping to lift her friend's spirits.

Grendel's dark eyes shone. "Flawed spell or not, this"—she waved at her body—"will scare the children. I'm terrified of it."

Horra bit the inside of her lip, unsure. "The children are already frightened. Seeing a floofity beast girl will probably make them laugh."

The giantess said nothing, probably not believing Horra. They sat in silence as they both ate with gusto.

Horra wished she could say or do something to ease her friend's burden. But, sunk in her own gloom, the words didn't come to her.

~Rowan~

ROWAN BOWED his head to keep it from scraping across the castle's doorframe as he entered the dining room. A young housemaid informed him that Horra had requested to see him immediately, but didn't tell him why. "Queen Bearer, you requested for me to come?" When he lifted his head, he saw a furry Grendel sitting next to Horra at the wooden table. Her head rested next to an empty bowl and she snored softly.

He stilled for a moment as memories of the Lady being placed on the Conservatory table raced through his mind.

"With those seeds all over your head, you're almost as fuzzy as she is," Horra quipped as she clanked her silverware on her dirty plate.

Rowan glanced at a bundle that dangled at the side of his face. "These are catkins. They are not the actual seeds." He darted his glance to Grendel.

Horra scooted her chair back and rose, facing him, leaving the dishes for the maids to clean up. "She's fine. Tired and grubby, but okay. Changing twice in such a short time makes you hungry and exhausted. Can you help me carry her to her room so she can rest up?"

Relief rushed through his fibers. "Certainly."

Queen Bearer Horra sat Grendel back in her chair. "You grab her shoulders and I'll take her feet. She might have bruises, so try to be gentle."

"How did she get so—" He waved his hand toward her.

"Furry? We don't know. I discussed with her how I don't think the Erlking's spell worked correctly on her."

"Why do you think that?" Rowan swung an arm, shifting the queen bearer sideways, and lifted Grendel from the chair easily.

She planted her claws on her hips. "I could've helped."

"I am capable of carrying her," he said as he allowed the queen bearer to lead the way to the guest hallway.

Along the way, she explained what she and Grendel had discussed before he arrived.

Rowan nodded as he fitted himself through the guest-bedroom door to Grendel's bed, where he placed her gently on top of a plain blanket. Recalling Merrow's instruction on hospitality, he asked, "Does she need to be covered?"

"She'll be fine. She has her fur to keep her warm." Horra glanced around the room at the numerous beakers and jars partially full of various ingredients.

Rowan followed her example, wondering what she searched for. He noted that the disorder was unlike Grendel, who was normally neat and organized.

Horra picked up a jar labeled "boiled oil of aged wattle." "Was she working on something?"

"Besides the failed soundometers? Not that I am aware of." He considered it, though. Wattle, taken from mucus of noxious slugs, was used by leathersmiths to tan swamp-swine hides. The ammonia in the milky mucus worked to fashion softer hides, and it also removed the bristly swine hair.

That thought forced Rowan to hesitate.

Horra yawned, her jaw opening wide. Rowan glanced away from the spectacle. "Ugh. I'm exhausted," she said. Her eyes had the same glazed look they'd had after escaping the Riven.

Rowan frowned. He'd hoped to forge a plan. With Glory gone and Grendel out of commission, and now the queen bearer needing rest, he acknowledged that wouldn't happen. "Let's reconvene after you've rejuvenated. I will head back to the Conservatory and do the same, whittle more flutes, and feed Pidge."

"She doesn't need to eat for days," the queen bearer said groggily. "But I could sleep for a week."

Rowan followed mutely behind the queen bearer as she trudged off to her bedroom and he down the stairs to the Conservatory. He realized halfway down that he, too, was experiencing a lapse in energy. All the fresh growth sapped him quicker than normal. Merrow had warned him that adolescent woodgoblins underwent changes that depleted them. Their body's energy would focus on growth and nct activity.

But it should've taken him years to reach that point in his development. He had to wonder why it was happening so soon. He scratched an itchy spot on his crown and bumped a cluster of catkins. Possibly it was the rich soil in the Conservatory causing this odd maturation spurt. If not, what reason would there be for such rapid progression? The only hypothesis he came up with was that his mission as a druid was fated to be short-lived. And that thought gave him no peace.

CHAPTER 17

~Rowan~

After Rowan's brief respite in the Conservatory, he headed to the armory, where he retrieved a stash of tonewood he'd used to create his extermigrubber weapons. Modeling them after the first flute he'd constructed, he carved three more and polished them with snake oil. Though his other trials were unsuccessful, he needed to keep his hands and mind busy.

The sun no longer shone upon the Conservatory, which explained why it had become so difficult to see. Though he had taken in the needed nutrients from the rich soil, he was still exhausted. He retracted his roots, moved to the center of the garden space, and leaned against the Yew tree. Pidge screeched from above, then fell silent. Even the frogs that called the little pond their home remained mute. With a sigh, Rowan closed his eyes to enjoy the quiet. He fell into a deep trance.

Voices of roods and other spirits broke through his somber

bubble. He opened his eyes and realized he was no longer in the Conservatory but in the Weald from before the fire.

Rowan stood, transfixed. His heartwood expanded inside his body. How he longed to return to his home. Glimmerbugs darted around his head in an enthusiastic dance, as if celebrating his return. He detected the breeze from their furiously beating wings against his bark, and his sap rushed through him. "Merrow?"

"*Yes, my boy.*" The seedkeeper's voice rang out through the yew trees.

Rowan swung his head around, intent on finding his mentor. "Where are you?"

"*I am here, and I am not.*" A breeze whispered through the trees and swirled around his trunk, lifting the last remnants of moss like a caress. "*And I am not the only one here with you in this space of your memory.*"

Before Rowan could ask, another voice chimed in.

"*Good day, young druid.*" Woodsly's voice chilled Rowan's sap instantly. "*I see you're doing well. That is good. I apologize for breaking through your mental barriers, but we needed to reach you before your next journey began.*"

"For what purpose?"

Woodsly continued. "*Encouragement and gifts. You are about to face a daunting task. I believe Merrow warned you of it in the moments he broke through the Erlking's interference. You are the instrument, not the instrument maker, so take heart and do not allow frustration to blind you to your purpose. There is a great crowd of witnesses here in the ether walking beside you, though you cannot sense us. You are not alone.*"

Rowan glanced at the stone path that was as familiar to him as the grooves in his bark. "I do not understand," he said to the roods.

"No, I'm sure you don't. This isn't like the tests I gave you. Real life is more confusing. And fragile." Merrow's voice was warm but evasive. *"All will be revealed at the right moment, dear boy. I'm sending you two critical things that will help in your mission. Until then, trust in your knowledge and don't be afraid. We will always be near."*

The wind, which was a breeze before, picked up and became a storm, blowing debris from the stone pathway into the air. The Erlking's voice shrieked and broke into a thousand chitterbug calls. Rowan clutched his ears to shut out the noise, but it remained and grew. The glimmerbugs whipped around as if terrified. He bent over, shutting his eyes tight and bracing against the onslaught.

The noise ceased.

Rowan opened his eyes, and he was back in the Conservatory, leaning against the Yew tree, his heartwood pounding inside his chest. Pidge pecked at his crown, clearly agitated. He waved her away and strove to regain his bearings.

"What just happened?" he whispered.

No one answered. Not even Master Knurl, whose presence he could not sense in the tree behind him.

In his hands were two things: a paper and a set of magicuffs. The sheet crinkled as he stood. He opened it and gasped. The roods had gifted him the formula for the Weald's foundation stones. It included the unknown sigils he'd seen in the Riven, plus a few more he'd never seen before.

A dark sadness pierced his fibers. His experiments were not what would defeat the Erlking. The test Woodsly and Merrow had referred to in his vision would call upon him to be the instrument—a sacrifice, perhaps? His already unsettled heartwood grew even more distressed.

Several hours later, the night sky turned into an overcast

gray morning. Rowan had taken from the soil what sustenance he could, then extracted as much extra as his fibers would contain. But it wasn't only the extra he'd taken in that settled heavily inside him.

Smoke curled into the air from the ironwood as he carved the sigil seals onto his bark. The marks on the bottoms of his feet were sensitive, so he plunged them into the ground. The burns tightened as the magic in the soil forced the wounds to crust and close over. Without the lichen and moss to hide them, Rowan worked to embed the sigils into the intersecting ridges of his bark.

The door to the Conservatory rattled, then opened. Grendel poked her head in. "Rowan?"

"Over here," he called and set the ironwood aside.

Grendel sniffed as she walked his way. "What's that smell?"

"I'm adding protection symbols to my bark. Did you sleep well?"

She rubbed her head, then grimaced at a snagged section. "I remember nothing after eating last night."

"I carried you to your room with the queen bearer's aid." He considered asking her about the oil of wattle but dismissed the notion. If the giantess favored ridding herself of her orange fur, that was her business. He had bigger things to focus on. "Were you injured?"

Grendel frowned. "I'm sore, but nothing serious, no." She sat next to where Rowan had placed his flutes. "What are these?"

He took a few minutes to explain what he'd done and why. "I whittled them small enough to fit in a pocket. I tested them on Pidge last night and she came to me when I used them. We still need to test them in the field, but I wished to wait for you and the queen bearer to waken."

The glass door opened at the same time Rowan spoke, and in walked Queen Bearer Horra. "Were you talking about me?"

Pidge screeched and fluttered out of the tree and toward the stone entryway to greet her owner.

The queen bearer tossed something in the air to her pet, then tossed other pieces around for her to hunt.

It was no surprise that the bird was finally hungry. He'd sought to feed her the previous night, but she hadn't come out of her nest. "I mentioned you, yes. Now that you're here, I'd like to engineer a plan of action for our next steps."

The doors flew open once more, and in walked Princess Glory, her filmy dress flowing and her wings fluttering. "Planning? Without me? How rude." She plunked a bag on the table and an odd-looking wind instrument fell out. It resembled the Erlking's pan flute in that there were several pipes, but each of the pipes on this one had holes like a flute or whistle.

"What is this instrument?" Rowan asked.

Princess Glory smiled wide. "This is a musical arsenal." She handed the gleaming item to Rowan. "Let me introduce you to the aethrial."

The queen bearer scoffed. "Are you joking? That one small thing is an arsenal?"

He didn't hear the fairy princess's reply as he studied the instrument. Inconsistently spaced holes were crafted along the device. In fact, there were several holes in the center pipes running its length. The wood was not the same on each of the pipes. One was a lighter-color, and another had a red hue. "Interesting," he said. "Does each one create a different sound?"

"Exactly! And few people know how to operate it." She grabbed it back from him. "And I am one of those few."

Grendel looked inside the bag the fairy had emptied. "Is that it? I mean, don't get me wrong. I'm glad for anything that will help us. But how will this one instrument, diverse as it sounds, help?"

The princess beamed. "That's a brilliant question. This might answer it." She reached inside the ornate cloak she wore and tugged out a children's book: *The Music Man.* "I found this in our Shining Library."

Queen Bearer Horra gasped. "You had a copy?"

In a rare show of magnanimity, the princess gave the book to the queen bearer.

Queen Bearer Horra ran a claw across the glossy cardboard. "The cover is different. This looks like a dark-haired fairy. My copy had a more elven-looking man dressed as a dandy with a droopy hat."

Princess Glory's enthusiasm lessened. "Yes. Fairies prefer to design every book they publish with fairy resemblances. It's much more aesthetically pleasing that way."

Flipping pages, the queen bearer found the section the Erlking had quoted, then moved on. Her claws stilled on the book. A page was missing, the manuscript falling open to reveal an uneven tear along the binding.

"A spell I might exercise against him."

The princess's and queen bearer's gazes met, and an understanding seemed to pass between them. Then the queen bearer held the book for Grendel and Rowan to see.

On the page before the ripped-out sheet was a photo of a lovely child bearing the aethrial. On the last page was an image of the Music Man in chains, weeping.

"I could hug you," the queen bearer said.

Princess Glory stepped away from her quickly. "No—"

But it was too late. Queen Bearer Fyd grabbed the sparkling fairy and squeezed her tight. Princess Glory's wings hung limp as she endured the embrace.

Grendel squealed with glee. "Group hug!"

She rushed over to the other two girls, her furry arms swallowing them.

Rowan stepped a safe distance away from the trio. However, he had to admit that, for the first time that morning, hope blossomed inside him.

CHAPTER 18

~Horra~

After several seconds of a heartwarming hug, Horra and Grendel let Glory go. "I take back half the bad things I've said about you," Horra said to Glory.

Glory, smoothing her crinkled fabric, sent her a humored glance. "Only half?"

"Well, you were pretty awful." Horra gleefully hugged the book. "I didn't think we would ever find another copy."

"Yes, well, rodents don't run wild in the Shining Kingdom." She straightened her lilac-colored dress and the silver cape she wore over it. Finally unrumpled, Glory turned to Rowan. "You're looking pretty dapper today, wood boy. Got any beauty secrets you'd like to share with me?"

Rowan cleared his throat. "No. Now, Queen Bearer, you mentioned yesterday that we needed to split up. Now that we're all reunited, what did you have in mind?"

Horra studied the woodgoblin. His bark was clearing up

nicely. Lichen, which had plagued him since before his unrooting, only grew along the lower portions of his legs. She narrowed her eyes. Knowing him as well as she did, Horra sensed he didn't wish to focus on his changes. "Yes. As I see it, we have two missions. The first is to save the children before it's too late. The second is to face the Erlking and do everything in our power to derail his spells and release any creatures under his thrall. And thanks to Glory, we may actually have a chance now."

She turned from Rowan toward the other two, noting the shimmer of a halo that surrounded the fairy. "What is your plan for the aethrial?"

Glory beamed, light following her movements as she picked up the instrument, which she'd dropped when Horra hugged her. "Before I found the book, Rowan and I were discussing the puzzle of the Erlking's music, which isn't music at all but noisy chaos. We wondered if there was a way to counteract the spells. I don't need to add magic to my music. It merely happens when I play. But what if I boost it with my simple spells as I'm playing? The children's minds are freed, the critters all stop doing his bidding, and we defeat the Erlking like in the book."

Horra frowned. "You think it would be that easy to counteract it and capture the elusive Erlking?"

"That has not been substantiated yet," Rowan answered. "I, too, have been hard at work creating flutes that emit a sound only critters can hear. It worked on Pidge, so I have confidence it will also work on the other critters."

"I see," Horra said, hearing her father in her words. She worked hard not to show her skepticism about her companion's invention. So far, none of Rowan's devices had done them any real good. "I'd like to test them before we head out, just to be sure they won't backfire. Grendel, since your sister is among those the Erlking has taken, I'd like you to head up the search for the missing children. We may be able to lure Murda away from her duties and have her go with you. She's wonderful with lost children. I'll check with Father after this meeting."

"What about me?" Glory asked, her shoulders and wings drooping.

Though Horra had slept like a swamp log the night before, the weight of being responsible again for others settled heavily on her shoulders. Instead of answering the princess, she did what Woodsly had been so good at—she challenged her to come up with her own answer. "You have proven yourself invaluable to the group today. Where do you think you can serve our kingdoms the most? Fighting the Erlking, or finding and freeing the children?"

Glory hesitated, her smile dropping, as if she had forgotten she'd have to actually do the hard work. "Those are the only choices? Can't we lure the Erlking here and then attack?"

Horra shook her head, a bit of disappointment souring her stomach at the other girl's reaction. "You know as well as I do you can't dictate anything to that fiend. We have to search for him."

Grendel sent her a gentle smile. "If you join me in finding the children, you'll secure a chance to save them. You'll be a hero."

Glory waved a dismissive hand.

"I'll take that as a yes." Horra fought to keep the goodwill she'd felt toward the fairy in mind. "Rowan, that leaves you and me to return to the Riven. We need to find out how the Lady left it and rescue anyone who may have remained behind. It's possible we'll run into the Erlking along the way."

Rowan bent his head. "And how do you propose the two of us fight him?"

The stone that had been dangling in Horra's gut shifted and dropped. "With your flutes?" When he didn't respond, she continued. "I don't know, Rowan. If you have a better idea, I'd love to hear it."

Sunlight filtered through the cloudy skies, illuminating the silver bark of Rowan's body. The tips of his crown were now a pristine white. Horra finally understood why the Ghost Tree attracted Rowan's attention. The unblemished surface was a stark change to the mahogany hue blotched with moss that it had been.

Rowan steepled his fingers. "I'd like to test my instruments before we leave."

"And just how will we do that?" Horra asked.

THEY ALL GATHERED in the front courtyard. Horra held Pidge's leash. She wasn't sure yet what Rowan had in mind, but after her meeting with the giants, she was eager to solve this test and move on to their next step.

Rowan glided forward and handed the whistles to Horra and Grendel. They dangled from leather straps the woodgoblin druid had added before they'd headed outside. He stopped in front of the fairy. "Do you wish to join the test?"

"Can I play first to show you what the aethrial can do?" She held the instrument ready, anticipating the answer.

"I am eager to hear it." Rowan waved an arm, directing her to start.

Glory took a moment to place her fingers. After a deep breath, she began to play. Her fingers moved elegantly across the holes, but no sound came.

Horra scrunched her brow as she glanced at the other two.

Then the air came to life. A tickling breeze traveled over

Horra's hide. Clouds above them danced and then dissipated, revealing the sun. The chilled morning air warmed, and light rays glimmered as if with fairy magic. Horra imagined this was what the Shining Kingdom always looked like—a prettified, picturesque vision of a duller reality beneath.

Glory moved in time to her music, her eyes closed and wings open, as she gracefully danced in a circle around them. The fairy princess swayed and twirled as if enjoying the music that Horra could not hear.

A glimmerbug buzzed in front of Horra's face, startling her. Horra frowned. It was only the beginning of Springtide, and the thaws were not complete. Winter hibernations still held, so the bugs shouldn't be out and about yet.

In a last motion, Glory held firm to one hole, her other fingers straight up in the air. When she finished, Glory was breathless and displayed an expectant expression.

Though the air had been full of petrichor—the scent of rain-washed soil—it thickened, washing over Horra's hide like comfortable clothes. "What was that?" she asked.

Rowan said nothing. He stood transfixed and unmoving.

Tears trailed Grendel's furry cheeks. "I miss my family and my home." Her words ended on a whine.

A satisfied expression crossed the fairy princess's face. "I call it 'Introspection in D Minor.' I added a recollection charm for emphasis. Did it work?"

"Was I supposed to hear something?" Horra asked, scratching her head. Though she had witnessed the atmospheric changes and noticed the smell of washed soil, she had remained unaffected.

Glory's sweet expression fell. "You—? I should've expected that, since the Erlking couldn't attract you, either. Are you tone-deaf or something? Anyway, what about everyone else?"

"I am not tone-deaf. I hear perfectly well, thank you."

Horra couldn't help but snap at Glory. She glanced at Grendel, who silently sobbed next to Rowan. "It's probably a good thing I didn't hear you since you made poor Grendel cry. Was that what was supposed to happen?"

Glory blinked and turned to Rowan. "What about you? You have an opinion about everything."

Rowan cleared his throat. "It was ... interesting."

Horra snickered.

Glory glared. "What's that supposed to mean?"

Rowan scratched his chin, seemed surprised when he didn't find the moss that had covered it for so long, then dropped his hand to his side. "I heard some of it. The song went in and out of hearing range for me. It was evocative, however, which I believe was your intent. The question remains: Will this help us in our quest to dismantle the Erlking's effect on others?"

Glory opened her mouth but quickly shut it.

Grendel blubbered and sniffed, running one of her arms across her snotty nose.

Ew. Horra turned away from the giantess. "Your music obviously works on some level, Princess. You cleared the clouds and called the glimmerbugs out of hiding. Maybe it will help the children to recall their lives before the Erlking snatched their minds and wills from them. We won't know if anything works against the Erlking until we come across him." She sent Rowan a meaningful look.

Rowan's expression didn't change.

Horra inwardly sighed. The woodgoblin had come so far in understanding creature interactions, but he still lapsed in moments.

"Thank you for your presentation, Princess. Perhaps we are not the best test subjects." Horra's words seemed to codify the fairy. "Now, we need to test Rowan's flutes next and see if we can call Pidge before we leave."

"Wait. I'd like to try once more, if you'll allow me?" Glory said, an eager expression on her face. "I'll play a different arrangement. I was working on it before the Erlking, and I was hoping to see what you guys would think?"

Horra glanced at the sky. They had lost enough time already, but she knew better than to turn the fairy down. Nothing ended well when she did that. "If you can do it quickly."

Glory nodded. She drew the aethrial up, closed her eyes, and started again.

Tinkling sparked in Horra's ears. Much like the fairy's laughter, it fizzed and popped in her ear canal. Then silence dropped over them like a blanket.

It reminded her of the suspended moment on Nimble when they'd run into the Erlking's magical trap, and when Kryk had presented her with the woodencloak.

And just like those events, the stillness broke and life exploded around them.

Glory dropped the instrument and opened her eyes.

"What did you do right there?" Horra asked her. She hadn't meant to be so demanding, but she didn't apologize.

Glory blinked once, then grinned. "I added a suspension spell. You must've heard about them. Our army used similar spells in the War of the Warts. It freezes the target for a moment or two, allowing our fighters to scuttle away from danger." She rubbed a dainty finger across the instrument's holes. "Why?"

"Are you able to do that for longer, or is it only a momentary spell?" Horra asked, her mind spinning. If the roods could suspend time long enough to hold a conversation with her, could the fairy's magic do the same?

Glory crinkled her face in thought. "Mother can secure someone longer, which is how she survived that dreadful war. That's why I was so sure the Erlking would never catch her, or keep her if he captured her. I am not yet strong enough to play for more than a few seconds."

Horra glanced at Rowan. "Did you feel it?"

Rowan twisted his neck as if trying to ease a kink. "I felt many things. To what do you refer?"

Horra flung an arm out. "The suspension. Like when you, Torren, and I jumped over the log while riding Nimble." When he didn't react, she continued. "When grubby worms infested you and you couldn't talk correctly."

Rowan's face fell slack. "I did not sense that, no."

Frustrated, Horra paced. "If you could perform that same spell with the Erlking, we might sneak past his magic before he finds a way to escape again."

"O—kay." Glory hesitated. However, a glint had entered the girl's eyes that hadn't been there a moment before. "I could try. But I thought you and Rowan were going to the Riven and Grendel and I were going to the mountain keep to find the children. Are we not going to split up, then?"

Horra growled, planted her claws on her hips, and glared at the ground as if it had caused her frustration. "I—"

The thunder of a horse's hooves rattled the ground, interrupting the cheery birds that had been flying in happy circles above them. Horra turned.

Torren, dressed in his military uniform, raced the Stempner steed up the smooth stone path. When he spotted the four of them in the front courtyard, he turned the horse their way. "I have news!" he yelled before jerking to a stop and jumping off. "Balk found a child wandering around the forest near the outside of the Riven. It's a bocan child—not his—but he's forming a search party and they're going to scour the area."

"A separate search party? With whom?" Horra asked, surprised. He'd always been an independent mercenary.

"With anyone who's willing to go with him." Torren panted as if he were the one running, not the animal. "He said this girl went missing before his daughter did."

CHAPTER 19

~Grendel~

Hope surged in Grendel's heart at Torren's words, shaking away the lingering sadness she'd experienced while the fairy princess played her music. If they'd found a child who the Erlking kidnapped earlier than Galumph, perhaps it wasn't too late to rescue her sister. "Was the bocan child all right?" she asked Torren.

Torren ran his claws through his windblown green hair, something she'd seen him do before when he was uncomfortable. "Half-starved and dirty, but otherwise she seemed okay."

"Was she able to talk about what happened to her?" Queen Bearer Horra asked.

He shook his head. "Her memories weren't completely clear. But from what I gathered from her broken descriptions, she and four others entered a strange forest. She only shared glimpses of odd things after that." Torren glanced at the queen bearer. "I can't be a hundred percent sure, but it sounded similar to what you and Rowan told me about the Riven."

Rowan, who stood next to Grendel, stiffened.

The queen bearer's jaw worked, clenching then loosening. "I didn't see anyone besides Rowan and Glory in the Riven. Well, and Pidge. Wouldn't we have seen others?" She turned to Rowan.

"We knew there were others there. If you recall, several spirits were clinging to the Ghost Tree." His voice was low. "It was a miracle we found each other in that forsaken place."

Grendel sensed a reticence in Rowan's demeanor. Like she did in her experiments, she examined what caused her woodgoblin friend's sudden shift. She realized he'd been aloof since she'd found him that morning.

The other's conversation had continued while she'd been inwardly deliberating.

"... but you didn't intend to have anything to do with the Riven." The queen bearer's tone edged on accusatory.

"The Lady broke the spells, didn't she? That has to be why they found the bocan girl," Torren argued back. He ran his claw through his long hair again. "Look, I know it terrified me before. But you guys came back alive. I'll be fine."

"Did you ever consider that there may not be two places to go?" Princess Glory stuffed the aethrial into her bag, the canvas swallowing the instrument like Pidge gulping a small critter whole.

Grendel frowned. "What do you mean?"

"*He* may have changed his plans. Maybe that girl was there from before. Maybe between the time we escaped and that dryad Lady returned to free her kind." Her voice emphasized the last part of the sentence. "Do you really desire to waste time searching through a dark and dank mountain with no light?" Her wings twitched as she shivered.

"Which is faster to travel to?" Grendel asked. All of them turned toward her, and she was suddenly self-conscious. "Sometimes the best plan is the one of least resistance. Is the closest the Riven, or the Erlking's mountain keep?"

Rowan held out a finger. "That depends. We entered the Riven in one place and exited from another. We were farther away upon exiting than when entering."

That sparked an argument between him and the queen bearer.

Grendel's skin itch-tingled, a sign she was growing perturbed. "Stop." She waited while they all quieted. "Let's take it from where you entered, since you'll probably know that spot better than where you left. You said yourselves it was unclear how you ended up where you were. Now which one is closer?"

"The Riven," the queen bearer said before Rowan could reply.

Grendel nodded, satisfied they'd determined the best choice. "Then let's start there. If we need to, we can change the plan."

Torren bowed to her in a rare show of deference. "Thank you. I'll go round up our rides. We'll leave after breakfast." He spun around and, with the reins in his hands, marched his horse to the stables.

Princess Glory snorted. "Who's running this show? You, or your cadet in training?"

Queen Bearer Horra sent the fairy a noxious look. "Gather your supplies and snag some grub. We're out of here in an hour."

Grendel nodded. "Send my breakfast to my room, please?" Thankfully, they didn't ask, and she didn't tell them she had something important to do first.

GRENDEL EXITED the kitchen to find everyone packing items onto a regal carriage in the back courtyard beside the stables. She slumped and wished she could fade away into the shadows. Pidge perched on the edge of the back seat, her reflective eyes darting about. When the bird turned toward her, she stopped, then screeched.

The queen bearer, the fairy princess, Rowan, and the knights glanced her way and did a double take.

Grendel knew they would notice her change of appearance. However, their stunned expressions were more than a little disconcerting. Grendel rubbed the back of her bare neck with her paw-ish hand. The potion using the aged oil of wattle had done a remarkable job of removing her fur and moisturizing her skin, but nothing would reverse the other physical traits of the Erlking's hex. And the potion she'd concocted with the oil only worsened things.

Grendel had donned the hooded smoky-hued cape over a set of clothes the hobgoblins had sewn to fit her. Somehow, the last transformation had shifted her height. She'd tucked her too-short pant legs inside a pair of troll knight's black military boots. None of that was what caught their attention, however. She fought off a sigh. It was the fact that the potion she'd used to remove her fur left the skin beneath with a gray pallor. Even the whites of her eyes had suffered the unintended side effect. She was sure her appearance was much like that of a caped shadow.

Rowan clearing his clackity throat broke the awkward silence. His gaze was much too intuitive. "Did you pack what you needed?"

Everyone moved at once, each attending to their own task.

"I believe so, though one doesn't always know what to pack

for this kind of event." Grendel handed him her bag, which jangled with the wrapped beakers of ingredients. To prepare for certain needs that might arise, she'd attempted to gather enough of certain elements that might heal or restore. "What's this?" She pointed to the carriage.

The stunning conveyance took up much of the courtyard space. The exterior was clear with wavy glass, the wheels were thin and tall, and the seats a plush golden velvet. Two facing bench seats swooped upward in an arch in the center, like a throne. Footrests on each side were made of thin strips of white painted wood, along with handrails for guards. It was glorious for a fairy vehicle but left much to be desired for a giant girl who was terrified of fast speeds and open-sided carriages.

Princess Glory clapped her hands. She wore a gauzy white dress with gold accents, probably to match the wagon she stood in. Her iridescent wings stood out against the stark white. "This is the newest version of our flight carriages. I borrowed it when I returned to the Shining Kingdom. It seats six comfortably." She waved her arms elegantly over the plush interior. "And it's built using sea crystal from the Deep Shore, making it lighter weight than our other transports, so it will travel faster."

Grendel held back a groan.

"I wonder if her sister knows she *borrowed* it," the queen bearer muttered against the saddlebag straps she was tightening. Beneath the straps, Nimble huffed, and smoke curled from his nostrils. The Stempner beside him stamped a front leg and quivered.

Grendel wondered the same thing. She considered whether to retrieve her supply bag from Rowan, or let him add it to the other packs. However, considering the two animals were unevenly matched, the only choice was to keep it safely on her person. "Is this going to work?" She nodded at the animal team.

"The princess is going to operate fairy paths, so it will be fine," Rowan said as he tucked something into a saddlebag on the other side. Again, Grendel sensed a reserve in the woodgoblin druid's demeanor. He placed her bag next to it and tethered it tight.

Torren and another female troll, Murda, joined them. Grendel recognized her name from earlier when the troll queen bearer had mentioned her. Less brusque than Horra, Murda's long, braided hair was green, the sign of a common troll.

Several minutes later, the group was finally ready to leave.

The king exited the castle via the kitchen entry. "May you be swift in your travels and return safely." He bowed, performed a quick about-face, and disappeared inside the castle.

~Horra~

"EVERYONE HAVE THEIR EARPLUGS?" Horra asked as she stuffed her ears with sponges. She'd just finished tying her supplies up and, with Torren's help, ascended the narrow stairs into the carriage.

Torren, Murda, and Grendel mumbled yeses as they settled in. Grendel sat on the opposite side from Horra and her knights, taking the space next to Glory.

"Yes. Thank you, Queen Bearer." Rowan sat upon Nimble, since the space inside the carriage was limited and the seats suited for fairies, not a woodgoblin druid who resembled a fully grown oak tree in stature.

"Ready?" Glory stuffed her sponges inside her ears. She raised her arms.

Horra nodded, and a blueish-green light surged from the fairy's hands, blanketing them in cold, tingly magic.

In response, the Stempner and gulgoyle moved as if to run but were instead lifted off the ground. Air rushed over them as the carriage rose with the spell. Pidge screeched and hurried to follow them.

From the corner of her eye, Horra caught a flickering image of a wyvern keeping pace with them. There was nothing she could do to stop the creature. Possibly, it would come in handy if Glory's path magic failed.

Horra's hair flew wildly around her head. She would've braided it, but the coarse thicket of curls never cooperated for long, and she hadn't desired to waste time on it. "Argh!" she grumbled.

With a snap of Glory's fingers, a bubble sprang into place around them.

Without the noise of the wind, Pidge's screeching echoed from somewhere in the distance. She didn't sound happy.

Horra's hair fell into her eyes. "Couldn't have done that first?" she asked Glory as she rearranged it back into order. A flash of the wyvern assured her it was closer to them and not attacking her pet. Birds, which darted about at their disturbance, were nothing but spots as they rushed by. Pidge was fast, but not nearly this fast. Horra would've insisted the bird ride with them, but she was much too big to fit into the small seating area.

The fairy smirked. "You should follow your knight's example and braid your hair. By the way, you're welcome. I included you all in this spell as a courtesy. If you don't like it, I could—" Her words drifted off as she lifted her hand.

Horra glowered and bit back the insult on the tip of her tongue. It would serve no purpose other than to prompt the fairy to return her anger with an insult. "Okay, stop. Thank you, oh regal one, for your beneficial employment of magic for us lesser creatures. We don't deserve you."

Glory's teeth shone white. "That's better. You're welcome."

Torren covered a laugh with a claw as he pretended to scratch his cheek.

Horra huffed and glanced into the distance. A wave of dizziness came over her as she sought to spot her pet. They were moving faster than she could have ever imagined. Closing her eyes, she breathed deeply to rid herself of the sickening feeling.

She didn't dare glance behind her at Rowan to be sure the druid still sat upon the gulgoyle. All she could do was pray he and Pidge were safe and that they would land quickly.

CHAPTER 20

~Horra~

The landscape blurred beneath the fairy's carriage as they rode. Horra stopped trying to locate Pidge. She had to trust that the pudge wudgie would find them, great huntress that she was. Bile burned the back of her throat. She'd been so lucky that her first trip via fairy paths had been at night. It was impossible to see anything in the darkness. Beside her, Murda shifted, her body tense, belying the fact that Horra was not the only one disturbed by their swift flight.

"Ah, Bough Valley is beneath us now." Glory's wings fluttered excitedly—almost as if she were flying. Fairies could fly, Horra knew, but she'd never witnessed it. "We're almost there."

Horra's head spun at how fast they moved. Is this how the Erlking had traveled from place to place? They knew he could wield the fairy paths after he'd taken Queen Toppenbottom, her guards, and their carriage. But was it the queen's or his magic he used for the spell? "Did the Erlking know how to create fairy paths himself?" she asked Glory.

Glory frowned at the mention of his name. "If you're asking if he had enough power to perform the spell, yes. If you're asking if I told him how to create the path, no. It's innate, like you snapping your claws and creating a spark."

"But not all fairies can do it," Grendel pointed out. Horra tried not to stare at the girl, but her ashen appearance was still too new and jarring. She preferred the bright-orange skin and tufts of red hair to this.

Glory gave her a cursory side glance. "They can, but not this high up. Like our limited ability to fly, other fairies can create a path to lift off the ground a few feet, but they would have to navigate around objects instead of flying over them."

This was new information to Horra. A thought came to her. "I remember you said once the Erlking is of mixed heritage. Do you think he could be part fairy?"

A frown creased Glory's otherwise unblemished face. "Not possible without the wings. It's a dominant fairy gene. Even quarter fairies have them. Ah, we're here." She perked up. "Hold on. My landings aren't as smooth as Mother's."

They sailed over the large valley Horra had screamed into before they'd all entered the Riven. Her heart squeezed and her stomach followed suit. She'd thought it was intimidating then, but riding over it at breakneck speed in an open carriage was nightmarish.

Nimble struck the ground first. His legs had been "galloping" the whole air ride. The Stempner stumbled once and righted himself when the startled gulgoyle tilted sideways, away from him.

Murda slid into Horra, and Horra slipped sideways into Torren. Torren struggled to stay inside the open-top carriage. Horra reached out to grasp his uniform, but she didn't act fast enough. His top-heavy body structure worked against him, and he toppled over the side and plunged to the ground.

The very rocky ground—right next to the valley's perilous drop-off.

"Stop!" Horra screamed.

They slowed, then stopped, leaving Torren a few feet behind.

The bubble protecting them from the airflow popped, and Glory rose with a satisfied grin. "Actually, that wasn't so bad."

Murda climbed off Horra and straightened her uniform. Though her hair had been in a neat braid, strands now stuck out in several places.

Horra grimaced at Glory. "You lost a passenger, but that wasn't so bad? Couldn't your protection spell have a fail-safe to keep your passengers inside?"

Murda jumped out of the carriage and hurried to help her fellow knight back to his feet.

Glory's demeanor shifted into haughtiness. "He didn't die, nor did I wreck the carriage. I call that a win." She fluttered to the ground.

Horra glanced at Grendel, who shrugged as if to say the fairy got them there. What else could she want?

Horra huffed and used the narrow stairs to climb out of the tall carriage. It was much easier going up than down the narrow steps, which was probably why Murda had bypassed them altogether when exiting.

She joined Murda and Torren, who rubbed his head. "Are you all right?" She recalled the time she'd had to club her friend with a rock inside the Erlking's mountain keep. Too many strikes to a troll's head—thick though their skulls were—was dangerous. "How many fingers am I holding up?"

"Four," he said, a grin tugging at his green lips. He chuckled at her frown. "Just kidding. Six."

Horra cuffed him on his arm while Murda rolled her eyes. "Not funny." She wiggled the two fingers closer to his eyes, then lowered her claw. "But you're obviously fine if you're making jokes."

"Queen Bearer," Rowan called from the front of the carriage. "Come. Look at this."

The area was much as she remembered it. The strange groves of trees with their bent trunks still stood. Grass and flowers were sparse. The eerie prickle on her neck that she'd experienced the last time she was here was gone, though.

Horra moved around the garish crystal transport and joined Rowan. She determined to ride Pidge home. Even if she had to travel several days, it was better than Glory's fairy path. Next to Nimble, Rowan hunched over something on the ground.

"What's wrong?"

He pointed to a large indentation—no—several in a pattern. *Giant's footprints.* Horra reached out and touched one. Thanks to all the recent rain, the soil was soft enough to maintain their shape.

Rowan cleared his throat. "We're not the only ones who have been here lately."

Horra scanned the area. Several different-sized footprints trailed in lines beside the larger ones. It was as if a crowd had passed through not long ago—probably in the past day, since it had been dry before and the marks wouldn't have shown then. "Maybe the giants have already searched here?"

Grendel moved to stand beside Horra and studied the prints. "Child-sized." Her words came out choked, and her ashen face paled further.

"The trees say groups of children are on the move in the area." Rowan's gaze was dark and serious. "And they're all headed to the same place."

~Grendel~

Panic gripped Grendel's heart at the thought of her sister being among the children who might've passed by here. There was no way to tell if these footprints were her sister's or not. They could be from any of the missing children.

But what if it was Galumph? They could save her. The constriction around her chest eased. "We need to find them." She yearned to search *now.*

Queen Bearer Horra's claw on her arm drew her attention. "Let's let Rowan figure out what he can from the roots first before we head willy-nilly into the unknown. The Riven, even if it isn't intact, is a dangerous place. We need to be careful."

Thoughts of Galumph circled in Grendel's mind. Images of the chubby baby she'd been after she was born to the terrible-tantrum toddler stage. And finally, her sister's intense fascination with bugs. Grendel had been sure her sister would become a bio-insectologist. There wasn't a critter she didn't know something about. The girl was a menace when it came to her experiments, but she had no doubt Galumph was incredibly smart concerning insects.

"But Galumph, the children—"

Princess Glory stepped beside the queen bearer. "I hate to say it, but she's right. You could get lost too easily if even remnants of the magic lingers."

Fear and rage built inside Grendel. She clenched her fists, then closed her eyes to stifle the emotion, but her blood rushed through her body, signaling the change.

Murda's calm voice broke through her concentration. "Take a deep breath. Hold it. Now let it out again. Slower. And another."

A snarl broke from Grendel's throat, and she sputtered.

"Again," Murda said, her voice unwavering.

After several attempts, Grendel let out a last breath and opened her eyes. She'd regained control of her emotions but was still shaky. "Thank you."

Murda smiled. "Anytime. I used to endure panic attacks before a test. My mumsy showed me how to work through my anxiety."

"I didn't know that," the queen bearer said. "You were always top of the class."

The other troll shrugged and walked over to pet the wide-eyed Nimble. Grendel hadn't meant to scare the poor animal. Her heartbeat slowed. She shook her hands out as if she could shake off the effects of the change.

Rowan, his hand and roots sunk into the ground, stood and stretched, his bark creaking as he did. "They're headed that way." He pointed to their right. "Past the Riven."

Beside her, Queen Bearer Horra stiffened, and Torren frowned. Even Rowan stilled.

Frustration flickered to life inside Grendel. "We need to follow them. Show up before they rejoin that evil fiend."

Her outburst incited the others to jump, breaking them from their reverie.

Nimble rumbled, his flesh hardening, before he settled back into his gulgoyle form.

Queen Bearer Horra sighed. "Torren, tie up the animals and leave them with the bag of feed Murly packed. Rowan and Murda, you two unpack the supplies and ready them. Glory, take charge of Grendel. C'mon, everyone. Let's move."

Glory slammed her fists on her hips. "Me? Why do I have to be in charge of the little beastess?"

Grendel inwardly grimaced. She probably deserved that.

The queen bearer whirled around to face the indignant fairy. "First of all, that's incredibly rude to say. Second—"

Rowan straightened to his full height. "Ladies, let's not start this again. Glory, that remark was uncalled for. It was gracious of you to allow us use of your carriage, but that doesn't award you the right to insult anyone. Especially given that you, too, have been a recipient of the Erlking's spells. If we cannot band together, we will fail this mission. Do I make myself clear?" His voice boomed.

Grendel had never been afraid of the woodgoblin druid until this moment.

The queen bearer and her knights' eyes were all wide with shock.

Princess Glory blanched. "Sorry."

Rowan leaned his face closer to the princess's.

She dipped away, her wings grazing the ground, but finally gave in. "Fine. My apologies, *Grendel*."

Rowan turned to look at Grendel. She swallowed before answering. "Apology accepted. Thank you."

"Respectfully, I'm not sure what got into your bark, Rowan, but I accept your point. Let's move," Queen Bearer Horra said.

The knights and Princess Glory scattered, leaving Grendel with the queen bearer and Rowan.

"Rowan," the queen bearer muttered quietly, "what's wrong? I'm worried about you. You've become so volatile lately. Is it because we're going back into the Riven?"

He closed his eyes for a heartbeat. "No. I don't like it, but we survived last time and we're actually prepared this time."

Grendel watched her friend closely. "I'm worried too. You've been off lately. Is it something we can help you with?"

He lowered his head. The seeds dangled heavily from the branches. "Nothing can help." Without another word, he walked away to gather his equipment.

CHAPTER 21

~Rowan~

Rowan used his time digging through the saddlebags to settle his fibers. He'd surprised himself as much as the others with his verbal explosion. Yes, the fairy princess and the queen bearer were maddening to deal with, especially when they argued. But he couldn't divulge to the queen bearer or Grendel what bothered him more.

And his task shouldn't surprise him. He'd been sown as a sacrifice. But knowing something and living it out were two different things.

Nimble, sensing his distress, grunted and sidled away from him. Rowan patted the gulgoyle, soothing him. If only it were so easy for him to find comfort.

He grabbed the bark bag he'd packed. The symbols he'd etched into the lining were the same ones he'd placed on his bark for protection and strength. He'd need everything the sigils could provide. Beneath it, he drew out the woodencloak.

He strode around Nimble toward the queen bearer and held it out to her. "This is yours."

Horra's eyes turned watery. "You fixed it?"

He shrugged. "I added more symbols—ones I noticed in the Riven. It's more than a patch, and hopefully with the new seals, the Erlking won't be able to sense you anymore."

Her lip quivered. "Thank you." He moved to leave, but Horra placed a claw on his arm. "I'm sorry about earlier. She knows how to needle my hide."

Rowan nodded.

"But I'm responsible for my reactions. I promise to do better."

"Thank you, Queen Bearer. You will be a wonderful queen when this is all over." He gave her a slight smile.

Her eyes leaked. "Thank you, Rowan. That means a lot."

"Is everyone ready?" Princess Glory's shrill voice rose above the din as they all suited up with their supplies.

The queen bearer closed her eyes, took a breath, then reached beyond Rowan to grasp her golden sword. Untying the tethers, she lifted it. "If anything happens to me, wield this." She shoved it against his trunk. "Carry it. And don't be afraid to utilize it."

Rowan clasped the sheath the king had crafted specifically to transport the royal sword. Though he wasn't overly fond of weapons, it was an honor to carry the blade. He slipped an arm through the shoulder strap. "I will make you proud."

She spun, unlatched the jeweled dagger in its leather sheath she always carried with her, and secured it to her belt.

Rowan sensed Pidge shortly before her screech filled the air. The pudge wudgie had pushed herself to follow behind them.

He also sensed another, bigger presence. The wyvern. A search of the sky only revealed the black pudge wudgie. He wasn't sure what the dragon's presence meant, and he had no way of blocking it from their mission. His only consolation so far was that the creature had shown no malice toward any of them. The wyvern had even seemed helpful in relation to the Lady, so he hoped that attitude would continue with them as well.

Pidge fluttered to the ground next to Rowan and the queen bearer. Feathers ruffled as if emerging from a windstorm, the bird dropped to the ground heavily and sat rather than stood.

"Torren, some water, please?" Horra called out as she scratched her pet, watching as the bird's beak remained open like she was panting. She glanced at Rowan.

Rowan studied the bird. "She will be fine. Her vitals are okay. I believe the flight wore her out."

After Torren gave her some water, Rowan tossed her chunks of jerky he'd created with a denser concentration of protein than what the trolls usually fed her. Within minutes, Pidge was back to her usual perky self.

He took her over to the trail they'd found. "We need to track the children. Can you help us find them?"

She cluck-chirruped in response and took off at a run.

The group hustled to follow.

~Horra~

HORRA RUSHED AFTER HER PET, the landscape changing not too far from where they'd landed. If she recalled correctly, she'd fallen into the Riven only a small distance from a copse of bendy trees. However, several small thickets were spread out in the uneven area, and she couldn't be sure which one she'd previously been near. Everything looked the same, until they crested a small hill and the change was obvious.

Pidge stopped, twisting her head sideways. Though the recent torrent washed most of the odor away, a smoky haze hung over a blackened forest of tree corpses that had once been part of the Riven's maze. Her mind spun back to the moment the Lady had returned to the Conservatory. The scent of smoke had been thick on her soaked mantle. Had she performed the same spell on the Riven that her daughter, Hazel, had on the Weald?

Like the Weald, little remained. Whatever the dryad had done here had clearly been with the intention of devastation. Horra whirled her head toward Rowan to gauge his reaction to the fire-ravaged forest.

Rowan stood statue-still, his face impassive.

The others followed shortly behind Rowan, their gazes shifting across the blackened landscape, shock and surprise clear in their expressions.

A pained bellow echoed in the distance.

Pidge darted her head to their left.

Horra followed her gaze and found an area where something churned the ash. "Grendel?" she called over her shoulder as she picked her way across the charred land. She placed an arm against her face to keep the detritus floating in the air out of her nose and lungs.

"Coming."

Pidge fluttered, dropped, fluttered on, then landed as Horra trod warily to where the sound originated. Luckily, the fire had been out long enough that no hot spots remained. The stench of magic was gone. At least, she hoped nothing remained.

Behind a large bundle of burned tree kindling, Horra found the source of the bellowing calls. "Oh, no."

The Erlking's midnight-colored kelpie lay bleeding behind

the broken and blackened tree trunks. Fire had singed its wing feathers, mane, and tail.

It glanced up at Horra, the whites of its eyes a contrast to the dark terrain. It breathed out a feeble call. Swollen and red, a wound festered on its back haunch. It struggled to move, but it was too weak to fly away.

"It's okay. I'm not here to hurt you." Horra used her gentlest voice.

Grendel rushed to its side, and the animal's bulging eyes widened. "Oh dear," she said. "Is this the—"

Behind them, Glory crashed out of the haze. "Calliope!" Her shrill shriek caused the kelpie to scramble and fail again.

"Whoa, whoa, girl." Glory, her gold-and-white dress smudged beyond repair, reached out a hand to the animal.

"Stop. The poor thing is terrified," Horra whisper-hissed at the fairy. "Grendel, do you have something we can apply to the wound on her back quarter?"

"I think so." She dug through her pack. The bottles inside clinked and clattered until she located the one she sought. She held up a jar of off-white paste. "Princess Glory, do you know of any healing spells—particularly, purging ones you could employ while I apply this?"

The kelpie's breaths came quick, the residue in the air swirling with each puff.

Grendel moved to step closer, and the kelpie jerked. Calliope's body didn't comply with her desire to flee.

"Wait. Let me calm her first," Glory said, drawing out her aethrial. She took a careful breath, and her fingers danced across the holes.

As before, Horra heard no sound. In seconds, though, Calliope lowered her eyes. They flicked back open as the animal forced herself to stay alert to what she saw as danger. But it wasn't long before the kelpie's head followed her drooping eyes. Another few moments and her body relaxed, breaths coming at a more natural pace.

Horra motioned for Grendel, who crept around her to the animal's side. Her gentle hands applied the paste in an even layer from the outside in. The giantess cut a chunk of fabric and placed it over the wound, sealing it with some medicinal sap to keep it in place.

"There," Grendel said, satisfied. "I don't see any other wounds besides burns. Do you guys?"

Glory drew closer to the kelpie, her hand outstretched and a glowing pearlescent ball of magic hovering above her palm. "This should ease her scalded flesh." With a flick, she sent the magic toward the kelpie.

Calliope's ears twitched, but otherwise she didn't move. Her feathers stitched themselves back together, and the wicked burns scabbed over.

"What do we do with her now?" Horra asked. Guilt over injuring the creature while the Erlking escaped ate at her gut. "We can't leave her without knowing if she's okay."

"Allow me," Rowan said.

Horra hadn't even realized the woodgoblin druid had followed them.

He dug his hands into the earth beneath the kelpie, the ashy dirt falling as he lifted her carefully from the ground. "I'll take her to the other animals so she doesn't frighten when she awakens."

Her heart burst with pride at Rowan's compassion. Usually, she'd have to instruct him on what to do and how. "Thank you."

He nodded and slid his way back through the desolation, his bark surprisingly unmarred by the dark residue.

"Is it me, or is our wood boy growing into a man?" Glory

asked, dispatching the warm fuzzies Horra had experienced while watching Rowan.

"Yes," Horra said, a tremble in her voice.

"I agree," Grendel said. "Maybe that's why he's been so forlorn lately?"

A shriek rent the sky above them as the wyvern circled in a serpentine motion, chased by another and then another.

"Is that a good shriek or a bad shriek?" Glory asked.

"That isn't only one wyvern." Horra's heart pounded in her chest. "So I'd guess it isn't a good thing."

The trio rushed back the way they'd come, Horra letting the other two go before her. She dug the dagger out of her sheath and clutched it in her claw. Her head swung around as more wyverns joined the first in the air above them. She couldn't tell if it was in response to them being territorial after being held prisoner in the Riven for so long. She'd thought the creatures happy to be freed.

Whatever it was, she guessed it wouldn't be pleasant.

The three of them crashed through the damaged forest to the safety of the cliffside. Murda and Torren stood at attention at the sooty forest's edge beside Pidge. Torren opened his mouth and pointed behind her.

Horra spun and saw what he saw. Orbs of light floated several feet above the ground. Wind rustled, blowing through the Riven's remains and swirling the ash-laden air. Fallen limbs parted as a group of twelve tall figures strode deliberately along the unobstructed path. The air in front of the group was clear, but the ash and dust billowed outside the space as if an invisible wall or a magic bubble protected them.

The tallest man, who stood in the middle of the group, held up his arm, and the others stopped. He wore a silver robe and a pointed dark-gray hat. A white beard spilled from his face down to his waist, and long white hair spread across his back.

His pointed earlobes brushed past his shoulders, proving him ancient in elf years.

Horra moved to stand in front of Grendel, clutching her dagger tight in her claw. She took a defensive posture that Woodsly had taught her once upon a time.

Wyverns landed on either side of them. Horra wasn't sure which side they were on until the animals all faced the elves and hunkered toward them in a forbidding formation.

Torren and Murda moved in front of Glory as any good troll knight would do in these circumstances. Though they also fell into their defensive positions, their eyes grew wide with trepidation.

This was far worse than running into a group of worqs. At least with them, non-magical creatures stood a chance. Horra's gut turned watery, and she fought not to let her fear show.

With another wave of the elf's hand, the wind died. Still, the fog swirled around the clear corridor where they stood, regal and tall. "Who dares to trespass on elven land?" His voice boomed across the expanse between the two groups.

CHAPTER 22

~Rowan~

R owan settled the kelpie with the other animals and the carriage. Concerned voices flew through the ether. They were there then gone before he could catch what was said.

Pidge screeched in the distance—a warning call.

Rowan's roots tingled, revealing a deep magic source in the area. He rushed back to rejoin his band, who were awaiting his return.

Orbs of light floated in the air above a dozen long, caped individuals.

"*Elves,*" a female dryad whispered to him.

"*Wyverns,*" another voice quavered.

"*Dangerous,*" a rood he didn't recognize proclaimed.

"*Stand your ground, my boy,*" Merrow's voice warned him.

Sap raced through his body as he rushed back to his friends.

The elves were already there, standing like soldiers over the decimated forest. They were as tall as he was, and each wore a long silver or gray robe. Rowan knew without being told this was the Sylvan Council.

Rowan swung his gaze to the wyverns. They were like watchmen, their focus on the elves, not on his band, for which he was thankful. Fighting both wyverns and elves was not a battle he'd delight to engage in. The queen bearer and her knights stood in defensive, ready positions he'd seen Horra exercise often on their missions.

"Who dares to trespass on elven land?"

Voices erupted in the ether, disagreeing with the elf's words.

Rowan cleared his throat, startling his companions enough to pivot from the elves and toward him. "Where is your deed for that claim?" he said.

Rowan spread his roots across the rocky terrain, grounding himself. Though not as effectual as sinking them into soil, it allowed him to broaden his base imperceptibly. His woody soles nicked against the rocks, leaving a trail of sap behind. His magic joined the land's.

One wyvern swiveled its head to gaze at him. It blinked golden eyes, then twisted back to stare at the invaders. Their white teeth flashed in the murky haze. The dragons were on their side. Resentment and anger tingled along the ground from the animals.

The elf who spoke and seemed to be in charge raised his face in defiance. "We do not have to prove anything to the likes of you or any of your kind."

"I could say the same," Queen Bearer Horra yelled back. "I am the only anointed leader here. You are no longer relevant. Go back to your isolation."

Crackling magic formed around the two elves who stood

next to the first. Snapping white flashes flickered in a showy, threatening manner. "Your inferior presence is unnecessary here. Leave before you force us to do something you will regret."

A wyvern hissed, and a blast of misty magic sprung from its mouth. The elf's snapping flashes ceased.

Anger unfurled like a smoke plume inside Rowan. "Do not threaten us. Queen Bearer Fyd is correct We stand upon sanctified Oddar ground. It is you who invaded the Wilden Lands, against the sacredness of nature, creating the Riven as a barrier to hide yourselves and your rogue kingdom of Endwylde. You were the ones responsible for sealing off the forest and sending your poisoned spells into the ground, twisting everything to your will. It is you whose presence is unwarranted now that the Great Lady destroyed your foundation, releasing your enchantments and freeing the lost souls trapped here."

Nobody moved.

The first elf raised a hand, and the other two stepped back. One motioned with his arm.

A female elf pushed through the center. Unlike the others, she wore a long, flowing gold gown with a green velvet hooded cloak. Long dark hair flowed in straight lines down her back, contrasting with her pale skin. Her pierced ears were half the length of the others, and golden hoops ran across the length of each outer lobe. She tilted her head sideways and held them with a steady gaze.

"We did not intend to poison the ... Riven." Her voice was honeyed and smooth.

A need to understand tugged at Rowan's mind. His anger dimmed and his heart rate slowed. Maybe he'd been too harsh—

"Stop that," Horra snapped, jerking Rowan back to

attention. "Have you forgotten that trolls are immune to your *persuasion?*"

At once, the influence placed upon Rowan's thoughts cleared. He shook his head, and anger rekindled in his core.

The dozen male elves took a step toward their female counterpart.

Dragons rose from their resting positions, their tails still but the dangerous poisoned ends swishing.

The woman scowled at the wyvern and motioned for the others to stand down. "Very well. We are looking for a renegade half-elf." Her voice changed from polished to demanding.

"You'll have to be more specific." The queen bearer narrowed her eyes in contempt, her dagger held ready in a clenched claw. "A couple of those have caused our kingdom much grief."

The golden-clad woman pursed her lips. "We are aware of the first who escaped. He called himself the Erlking. Am I not mistaken to believe he has been dispatched?"

Queen Bearer Horra grinned. "My grandmother Queen Petra Fyd *dispatched* him."

The woman's smile was toothy. "I see. It is not he who we seek. We hunt the cursed elf who refers to himself as the Conductor."

The dragons bellowed at the name. Several crashed their tails into the ground before settling again.

Rowan recalled one of the tree spirits referring to the second Erlking by that title. Beside him, Princess Glory stiffened. "I am not aware of anyone who goes by that title. There is, however, a different Erlking who has been a thorn in my side for quite some time now. He uses music magic in detestable ways. Tell me, why did your Sylvan Council curse him?"

The elves shrieked and objected, as the elf spirits had in the Ghost Tree.

Color spread across the female elf's pale face. "We do not speak of such things."

The queen bearer groaned. "This is getting us nowhere, and we have too much to do to argue with a bunch of out-of-touch ancient elves." She tucked her dagger back into its sheath.

Rowan plunged ahead, hungering to gather as much information as possible. "I've been told his offense had to be terrible for you to remove his ears. Is this correct?" By now, his roots stretched several feet beyond his group and behind him. "What was it he did to warrant such a harsh punishment?"

The elf woman's hand curled out, and before anyone could react, a miasma of magic flew toward him.

Wyverns moved, but not fast enough. They took to the air, their shrieking cries echoing.

Rowan braced for her strike. Like a lightning rod, the magic impacted him before burning a path down his body and into the ground.

His companions screamed, their faces filled with terror.

The spell was more than uncomfortable. None of his fibers were spared as the magic washed through him, burning and cleansing. He stood his ground, letting it do what he hoped it would—remove any trace of the Erlking's poisonous spells his seed had suffered. It was a gamble, baiting the female council member. In the end, he prayed it would be worth it. When the spell had done its worst, the ground around him appeared as charred as the forest he faced.

Grendel rushed toward him, but Murda held her back. Queen Bearer Horra surveyed the damage before glancing his way, her eyes keen and calculating. Princess Glory's wings reverberated like a deadly rattler snake's tail. Wyverns writhed in the air above them, their cries ringing out.

Rowan glanced into the disbelieving faces of the elves. He drew out the golden sword that gleamed in the dull light. "You have just sealed your council and probably Endwylde's fate."

~Horra~

A few seconds prior

DISBELIEF ROCKED through Horra when the female elf sent a shockwave of a spell at Rowan. The light from the magic was blinding. "No!" she screamed but was held back by Torren's powerful grip.

"Don't touch him," Torren said. "We can't lose you too." His body shielded her from the spell's brilliance as it lit the woodgoblin druid up like a torch. It traveled from the tip of his crown to his roots, which spread across the area for a dozen feet on both sides.

Though Horra appreciated her longtime friend and knight's concern, she wasn't the one who could defeat the Erlking. Rowan was. She punched and yanked, but she was no match for her classmate's muscle. And now the elves had gone and murdered ... She stopped struggling against Torren's hold.

Rowan lifted his head, his dark eyes aglow with the dying sparks of magic. His bark lightened, and the seeds hanging from his limbs trembled and transformed. In front of her, where Rowan had stood, was not a Yew-born woodgoblin but a living Ghost Tree. "Wha—?" She barely heard Rowan's threat about the elf's fate.

The golden sword Rowan held glimmered at the edge of her vision.

Master Knurl's words came back to her: *Calcy and the elves took an oath—she spared their lives, and they would never turn against the Fyd clan or any kingdom they built.*

Understanding dawned on Horra. Rowan's determined expression and stance verified it. "I'm all right." She shrugged Torren off and faced the elves again. "You attacked a ward of Oddar. Rowan is an honorable druid of the Weald, which is a forest protected by Oddar. You have broken the pact your ancestors and mine agreed to. Your lives are forfeit."

Silence greeted her. The elves were still as statues, not even blinking.

Horra let the tense moment stretch as she'd seen her father do when someone had committed a contemptible act. It allowed the offender to snap first.

Wind from the wyverns flying overhead blew past the group, whipping the ashy dust outside the magical bubble the elves had created around themselves. Bleary rays of sunlight highlighted the destruction before them. Though the female had mentioned hunting the Conductor, Horra wondered if that was truly what stirred the group to emerge from their seclusion. She didn't think so. It had to be the destruction of the Riven's barrier to their kingdom that had spurred them to action.

Her thoughts flew through her mind in the blink of an eye before the elves finally moved. The males were the first to do so, stepping back and away from the female. Her chin jutted farther upward at their obvious disassociation. "Cowards!" she shrieked.

Glory appeared beside Horra and, using her aethrial, sent a streak of glittering magic through the air, creating a sparkling boundary around the elves. "That should suspend them for a moment or two," she murmured low to Horra.

Horra stepped forward. In two strides, she crossed the Riven's charred boundary. "That's why the Riven couldn't harm me or Rowan. Even though the Erlking placed more hexes upon the land, it wouldn't supersede your initial spells, which couldn't harm one of Oddar's citizens. We'd be lost forever to the maze or possibly died of starvation, but you couldn't outright attack us." She turned to look at Glory. "And that's why the spiders went for you instead of me."

The fairy frowned, her concentration on her magic keeping the elves from running away. "Eh, I'd still rather be from the Shining Kingdom."

Without acknowledging her sarcasm, Horra continued. "Is that why your mangy outcasts, who both call themselves the Erlking, came after us? Because you couldn't touch us and they could since they were no longer considered members?" The pieces came together in her mind. "If he could overtake Oddar, become its ruler, or even take us as his prisoners, your council couldn't act against him. It was the ultimate revenge against you."

The men shuffled, unable to step beyond the fairy's magical border.

The woman hung her head. Anger and contempt twisted her face when she finally looked back up. "Trolls are despicable, disgusting creatures. You wallow in swamps and eat slop that we wouldn't even feed our foulest beasts. You're warty, green, and hideous beings that aren't worthy to spit on my shoes, let alone rule a kingdom that possesses power to bind us in any form. We are mightier in every way."

Beside her, Glory snickered. "She's got you there, Horra."

"Oh, horrors." Horra feigned shock. "She called me hideous." She glanced at Glory, who struggled to keep her magic in order as she sputtered with giggles. Horra nodded at her. "She's insulted me worse than that."

Horra sent the woman a fierce smile, one that showed the full length of her tusks. "And now, Sylvan Council, here you are at my mercy. I would think having your life in my claws might inspire you to act a bit more civilized."

Her Critical Hostile Engagement classes finally came in handy. She turned to Rowan. "The sword, please."

Light gathered around the golden blade. It blazed as she lifted it into the air. Horra clasped it in both claws and plunged the blade into the burned remains of the Riven. "Judgment time."

CHAPTER 23

G lory's eyes widened as Horra drove the sword into the ground of the Riven. "Are you crazy?" she whispered to Horra. "You said ycurself this ground is dangerous." She was glad the elves paid mcre attention to the troll than to her, because the spell holding them faltered for a moment.

The wyverns shrieked louder, the awful pudge wudgie scree'd from afar, and Nimble's bellowing calls distracted her from her task of holding the elves.

Horra's blade, plunged halfway into the blackened toxic ground, vibrated and hummed as the animals quieted.

Did the elves know what she was doing with the illustrious weapon? Glory didn't wait to find out. She sidestepped to avoid the sword's possible blowback, not an effortless task while holding the magical barrier in place.

The wyverns landed again, falling in a circle around the elves this time. Their bodies pounded against the ground, and

Glory let her spell go. The dragons were more capable of guarding the elves than she was.

"This land was Oddar's before you annexed it, saturating the forest with your repulsive spells. As the elven leaders, the blood of the Riven's victims is on your heads. I demand by the magic of the land and by the sword that the Riven be redeemed, restored back to the hands of the Creature God and to Oddar. I also require recompense from the elves for their trespass of violence today," Horra said, her eyes alight with anger.

The elves stepped closer together, away from the dragons. If Glory wasn't mistaken, the wyverns were all grinning. She almost felt sorry for the elves until she remembered they were the ones who created the Erlking.

Grendel, who stood on the outside their group, backed up. She looked like a trembling dark apparition among the scorched forest. "Oh no," Glory breathed and grasped for the giant girl's arm before she shifted to her monster form.

Murda joined Glory at Grendel's side. "It's okay. Horra knows what she's doing." The troll knight spoke to Grendel, but Glory disagreed. Trolls didn't have magic. How would Horra know how to direct an invaluable magical object?

The air shifted as the enchantments in the sword and the earthen magic linked forces. Light exploded out of the sword, blowing like the wind.

Glory ducked her head. She'd only seen such a display once, and her mother had warned her that if she gazed into the epicenter of brightness, it would blind her. "Look away!" she screamed, hoping the others would listen.

A mewling roar sounded as Grendel tore away from them, changing into her giant form, terror clear on her ashen face.

"Wait. Stop!" Murda called after her, but the girl's giant

strides were too long. She was gone, a shadow amongst the rubble within mere seconds.

The radiance died away. Glory blinked to allow her eyes to adjust to the once-again murky atmosphere. The forest remained singed and smoking, and the elves stood where they'd been before Horra unleashed the power of Oddar's sword.

Horra looked around. "Where's Grendel?"

Glory snorted. "You scared her silly. Who knows?"

The troll frowned. "Oh, vinegar."

~Grendel~

GRENDEL'S PULSE raced as she darted across the dead and terrifying forest. The hum from the sword had unleashed the voices in her head once more, spurring her change. A small part of her brain told her to stop panicking. The other, larger percentage disagreed. She heeded the latter and kept running.

~Rowan~

ROWAN CLOSED his eyes against the dazzling magical light display the queen bearer set into motion. The rush of the power blew across his body, rattling the seeds on his branches. Since he had entrenched his roots in the solid stone ground, the blowback did not topple him.

In some moments, he doubted the troll queen bearer, but in this situation with the elves, she'd risen to meet the crisis. Pride in his friend's intuitive actions surprised him. He hadn't experienced the sensation before.

A mewling growl drew his attention. He opened his eyes to see Grendel bolt, her body morphing as she dashed into the dark recesses of what once was the Riven. Disappointment crashed into him. He wouldn't be able to heave his roots fast enough to trail her. He took a mental note of the dust that plumed from her heavy footfalls in the direction she ran. When he was mobile again, they would need to add finding Grendel to their list of missions.

"Well done, Queen Bearer," he said instead of ruminating on Grendel's disappearance. He realized he could sense through the forest's roots where Grendel sprinted. In fact, he could sense many bodies in the forest. Finding them would no longer be a challenge. Whatever the elf had thrown at him—burning his hexes away—had returned to him the clarity he'd possessed while living in the Weald before the fire.

"Thank you, Rowan. Are you all right, though?" The queen bearer spared him a glance while keeping her focus on the elves. "That was a pretty hefty spell you endured."

"I'm better than ever." He smiled without elaborating.

"Queen Bearer, what would you have us do?" Torren broke into their conversation.

Rowan raised a finger. "Might I propose a suggestion?"

"I'm all ears," she said.

"Instead of taking their lives, which, by ancient Wilden Law decree, not to mention Oddar's authority, would be your right as sovereign leader, we force them to pledge an oath to never encroach on land that is not lawfully theirs from this moment forward. And demand they restore the damage they and both Erlkings have done to the Riven and across the Wilden Lands—cleansing the land back to its original state before they took control of it. Requiring this, you will restore the balance of the Sylvan and therefore their kingdom. If they do these things, they'll spare their lives. If they do not, their lives are forfeit."

The elves stood mute, though their clenched fists conveyed their indignation. Rowan watched each of them closely since they'd already proven their violent tendencies.

Whispers in the ether informed him about a group of giants approaching from behind the elves moments before the rumble of their massive footsteps revealed them to everyone else.

Two of the elves bolted, darting sideways, but the wyverns bared their teeth and flung their tails around, stopping them. The bubble the elves had placed around themselves flickered and died. Without their magical barrier, the ashy air swirled around them.

Five giants, six goblins, a dozen gnomes, and four bocans—one of whom was Balk, the mercenary who helped them in the past—rounded a small hill. Behind the first group stood a group of woodgoblins and hobgoblins.

"Well, if it isn't Queen Bearer Fyd." Balk stepped in front of the giants to greet them with a smile. "And is that Rowan with you? You've changed much since the last time we met, young druid. I see you found the fairy princess and a few other creatures?"

"Balk," Horra said. "It's good to see you. Yes, to all of your questions. Much has happened." She didn't stop to explain the wyverns or the elves. "Are you searching for the children?"

"We are. Sprites informed us that a group of children moved this way a week ago." He narrowed his eyes at the elves. "Is that why you are here, or is there something else going on we should know about?"

Dryad spirits, whom Rowan had sensed in the forest around the Riven, drew closer to their group. Their excitement tingled along his roots.

"Justice." Their chant was a single voice echoing on the wind, which picked up and dashed around the elves.

"You all have arrived in time to witness a magical covenant between us and the elven Sylvan Council." Queen Bearer Horra waved her claw toward them.

The elves no longer appeared haughty. Their fear seeped into the ground like spilled water, brushing along Rowan's roots with an acidic zing.

Horra hastened to explain what happened after the Sylvan Council showed up. "So, now we see if the elves will cooperate, or choose a death sentence."

Balk's group murmured amongst themselves.

"Rowan, can you help me seal this deal?

"Of course, Queen Bearer," he said aloud. In a whisper close to her ear, he added, "Perhaps we should hurry this along? Our friend who ran away is on her way back."

The queen bearer's eyes widened. She gave him an almost imperceptible nod.

He spoke to the others, allowing his voice to deepen and carry. "Witnesses, raise one hand in the air as witness to us and to the Creature God." He nodded to the queen bearer, placing his hand over hers on the sword's hilt.

The queen bearer took a deep breath and let it out quickly. "So, what say you of the Sylvan Council? Do you choose the deal I laid out before you, or death by your own transgression?"

The female opened her mouth, but the male who spoke first nudged her aside. "I am afraid, Melian, you have worn out your usefulness as a mediator." A snap of energy shot straight toward the woman's throat. She shrieked, but no sound came out.

Rowan wondered if he could learn that trick for when the queen bearer and fairy princess argued.

The man opened his arms in a gesture of surrender. "I am

Belamir, leader of the Sylvan and great-grandson of Delacor, who accepted the pledge with your ancestors generations ago. I apologize that some of us have forgotten the things that have passed." He glared at the woman. "We accept the terms of your gracious offer." He bowed his head in deference. "Thank you, kind Queen Bearer Fyd for your *mercy*."

Rowan caught a note of ingratitude in the way the elf said "mercy."

A cheer rose from all the dryads still hiding among the rubble. The wyverns blasted into the air, whipping detritus and magic around as the sacred oath was sealed into place.

Sensing the elves held back on their oath, Rowand didn't cheer even though the queen bearer had performed the arbitration splendidly.

Melian crumpled to the ground.

Rowan flinched.

"Wha—" the queen bearer stuttered. "Why?"

Rowan shook his head. "The oath. She chose not to submit."

"I didn't think—" The queen bearer's throat worked as she swallowed hard.

Balk walked up, interrupting them. "Congratulations, Your Majesty. Your father will be very proud of you." He glanced at Rowan. "Remind me not to make deals with you. You're worse than she is."

"Excuse me." The queen bearer, looking ill, stumbled away.

"Did I say something wrong?" Balk asked

Rowan stared at the queen bearer's back. "No. Though she acts fierce, she doesn't have an appetite for death."

CHAPTER 24

~Horra~

Horra's stomach lurched as she rushed away from Rowan and Balk. Though the arrangement with the elves was completed, she didn't fancy showing weakness in front of them.

Murda and Torren rushed to join her without asking. Murda stepped ahead of her and Torren covered her back.

She swallowed the bile rising in her throat but lost the battle as they reached the carriage. Horra dashed, bent over the edge of the ravine, and heaved, emptying her stomach. It burned her throat and nose. Dry heaves followed. Finally, her sickness eased.

"Here. Take sips." Murda handed her a handkerchief and a water pouch. She and Torren stood like a wall, shielding her from any passers-by.

"Thank you." Her voice was rough. She wiped the tears off her eyes and cheeks, then blew her nose before taking a small drink. Her breathing leveled, and she lowered to the ground, sitting on her shins. The cliff stretched below her in a dizzying view. She shifted to the side and moved again when rocks bit into her hide through her trousers.

Horra lifted her head to the sky, but Torren blocked her view.

He gave her a knowing look. Compassion creased his face.

She recalled the same thing had happened to him when they'd found his father's remains. Blinking back new tears, she let out a breath. "I'm okay."

"Of course you are." Torren's strong voice buoyed her.

Nimble rumbled, and smoke curled into the air. Her pet sensed her distress.

She moved to stand but stumbled. Torren caught her arm and righted her. As soon as she regained her footing (one leg had fallen asleep already), he let her go. Horra walked over and leaned against her fiery pet, soaking in the warmth for an extended moment. Feeling steadier, she poured a small amount of water into her claw and scrubbed it across her face, hoping to erase all signs of sickness. She cleared her throat. "The children."

"We'll find them," Murda assured her.

Rowan returned to the group before they could make their way back to him.

"Queen Bearer, the giants left with their group to search for the children. The elves have spread out to cleanse the Riven." Rowan glanced into the distance. "I sense the Erlking is not far away, though he cloaks himself in darkness. I cannot penetrate it to know exactly where he is, but I know the approximate area." He pointed north and away from the Riven.

"You're sensing his presence?" she asked, surprised.

His lip lifted in one corner, not quite a grin but also showing the woodgoblin's satisfaction. "The spell the elf used untangled the hexes the Erlking placed on my seed. She may have meant it for my demise, but it worked the opposite. It allowed me to open back up to the ether, like I did in the Weald."

Horra tried not to gape. "That's wonderful, Rowan. Though you scared the vinegar out of me. I thought you were a goner when she sent that spell." She rubbed her chest to ease her stress. "Don't let that happen again without warning me."

Rowan's lip dropped. "I didn't mean to scare you, Queen Bearer. I was not sure how our discussion with the elves would play out. But I noticed a divide between the male elves and Melian. Their politics played into our hands."

"Hmm." Horra didn't agree or disagree with him. "Do you think you could lead us to where the Erlking is hiding now?"

Rowan glanced into the distance again. "I sense his position has not moved."

"Can you sense the children?" she asked.

He frowned. "No. They are hidden from me as well."

Horra turned toward a large stringy pine tree. "Grendel? Do you choose to join your parent's group to search for your sister? I'll understand if you do."

The hooded girl stepped out from behind the tree. "How did you know I was there?"

Horra glanced at the sky. "You were a shadow on the wrong side of the tree."

Grendel dropped her head and shrugged. Her clothes looked new—browns in place of the black fatigues she previously wore. Dark wispy fur covered her, and her facial features now fully resembled a woodland firefox. "You saw my parents?"

"They appeared after you disappeared. They didn't see you, so they don't know you're here. You could show up and surprise them. You don't have to tell them where you were or anything that happened. I'm sure they'd understand. I think they believe they're searching for both you and Galumph."

A shudder washed over her thinner, animalistic body. "Look at me. This is so much worse than it was before." She shook her head. "No. I can't let them see me. Not yet."

Rowan tipped his head toward her. "You may never return to your natural state. Recall what he did to Princess Glory before we found you. He won't bargain with anyone. You can't hide from them forever."

Though Horra hadn't sought to pressure the giantess, she was proud of her companion for breaching the subject with Grendel. He was turning into a great druid.

Grendel swiped a paw across her cheeks. "I know. I just can't with my parents." She sniffed. "I have to face them someday. I'll let them find Galumph first, then maybe it won't be so hard."

Glory's skeptical expression mirrored Horra's opinion.

Horra sighed.

"If you don't mind, Queen Bearer?" Murda snagged her arm, drawing her aside.

"What is it?" Horra asked.

"Would it be all right if I stayed here and joined the other group to search for the children? I have experience helping them."

She nodded. Though she enjoyed having her friend and knight with her, it would take one responsibility off her shoulders. "That's an excellent suggestion." She placed a claw on her knight's arm. "Please be safe."

Murda pounded a fist to her chest, lowering her head in a show of honor.

Horra watched the girl walk away, hoping they would see each other again.

Glory walked over, her eyebrows arrowing down. "What

are you doing? Are we splitting up? I don't have any desire to tag along with her or that other group." She waved her dainty hand at Murda and shuddered.

Horra sighed. "Gah! I can't believe I'm going to say this, but can you drive us to wherever Rowan directs?" She instantly regretted asking as a sly smile crossed the fairy's face.

~Grendel~

GRENDEL CHECKED the bandages she'd placed on the kelpie. Calliope's flesh trembled beneath her hands, a fear reaction to her presence. It took more effort than Grendel liked to not graze the kelpie's skin with her sharp claws. "Good girl," she told the creature when it stayed still long enough for her to undo the strips.

The bleeding had stopped, and the swelling had lessened. The infection from the wound was barely noticeable.

"Well?" Glory asked, eager for her assessment.

"She's going to be okay." Grendel unwrapped another strip, added more of her healing lotion, and gently sealed the bandage. "And she's more perky, since she's eaten."

The oats they'd left for the other animals were now gone. She assumed since they'd fed the half-dragon and Stempner before they came, the sick kelpie must have eaten them.

"Do you think she'll be well enough for us to bring her along? I don't trust leaving her here for the elves to nab." Princess Glory dogged Grendel's steps as she checked the other burns and small wounds.

"The creature means something to you?" Rowan asked.

The princess's hard glare softened. "Well, yeah. It's not her fault the Erlking has the real golden bridle and controls her with it. She's as much a victim of him as we are." She patted the black horse's neck. It sniffed the fairy's wings in return. "I am capable of compassion."

"No one said you weren't," the queen bearer said, diffusing the situation.

Nimble bellowed and glanced behind them. His tail slithered along the rocky ground, sending rocks rolling. Some clattered close to the ravine's edge.

"Oh no." Horra ran a claw down her face. "I forgot about the wyvern." She glanced at the sky, but the group had disappeared.

In the blink of an eye, the two-legged dragon landed next to the gulgoyle.

Grendel jumped and screeched, startling Torren, who searched their packs for a rope to hook the kelpie to the fairy's carriage.

Clicks emanated from the wyvern's chest as it greeted the other animals. It peered over their heads at the queen bearer as if it knew she was the one in charge.

The queen bearer's shoulders slumped. "You've got to be kidding me."

The animal trumpeted a call. It was the first time Grendel had heard it create any noise.

Grendel surveyed the carriage with a critical eye. "There's not enough room to hook both the kelpie and the wyvern at the back of the carriage. The gulgoyle and Stempner only work because Nimble is tall enough that his wings don't interfere when they're moving."

"Who's brave enough to ride him?" the queen bearer asked.

"Not me." The fairy princess was quick to respond. "Besides, I have to drive the carriage." With a flourish, she magicked her gown into a white pantsuit with gold embellishments.

For a moment, Grendel ached to ask the princess if she could help return her skin to its normal orange hue. Her thoughts drifted back to her experiment and how it might've gone wrong, and she missed the rest of the conversation, startling when everyone jumped into action.

Rowan and Torren strode to the front by the animals. Glory flicked glittering magic at her feet and lifted herself into the carriage.

The queen bearer, sensing Grendel's confusion, guided her toward the conveyance. "You're with me and Princess Fancy Pants. Nobody offered to ride the wyvern, and it's already followed us this far. I doubt we could lose it if we tried. And it seems as if its brethren deserted it." She pivoted. "Rowan, don't forget the sword."

Rowan retrieved the weapon, strapped it onto his back, and approached the kelpie. He laid a gentle hand on her muzzle. The winged horse jerked her head up and down in protest. Rowan dug into a hidden pocket and produced an apple, which Calliope chomped greedily. When finished, she nickered at the woodgoblin.

"She'd be purring if she were a cat." Grendel repacked her bag on the gulgoyle.

"It is a benefit of being a druid. Animals respond to me easier than to others, though the food did not hurt."

Pidge screeched when Torren approached her. "Sorry, girl. There's no way I'm riding in that death trap again." He scratched her neck and produced a dried chunk of meat from behind his back. With a gulp, the piece was gone, and her attitude was less hostile toward the troll knight.

When everyone finally settled and Grendel sat beside the sparkling fairy, Glory snapped her fingers and they were airborne once again.

Grendel's heart hammered in her chest from fear and

exhilaration. She didn't mind the carriage, but considering Torren fell out, she braced herself against the narrow side of the wall. The afternoon's warm air rushed around them, the atmosphere full of the familiar scent of stringy pine trees. In the blink of an eye, the fairy secured another protective bubble around them, shutting out both the air and the scent.

"Hold on tight," Princess Glory said, her wings tucked tightly together. "I've used a lot of magic today, and this ride will be slower and bumpier than before, especially if I have to focus on flying and maintaining the bubble."

As proof of her claim, the glowing green magic flickered beneath the Stempner's and gulgoyle's feet. Luckily, Nimble's wings hauled them back into place before the magic sputtered to life.

Frowning, Horra said, "I should've ridden the wyvern."

CHAPTER 25

Calliope wasn't much different from Nimble, Rowan decided, except in size. Calliope was not as large as the Stempner, and only half the size of the gulgoyle. However, the kelpie was strong enough to bear him without issue. Rowan's feet didn't dangle far from the animal's body, which would help when they landed.

The carriage, traveling several feet to the side of him, swayed in the air, the gulgoyle's powerful wings keeping it afloat while the fairy's depleted magic faltered.

Their lives were in danger, and he needed to land quickly even if they didn't make it as far as he'd hoped.

He nudged the kelpie faster so he could take the lead. Now that he was in the air, sensing the Erlking's location proved more difficult, so he directed them toward where he'd last discerned the evil elf to be.

Warm afternoon air rushed about, streaming through his limbs like a song. He savored the exhilaration of flying free again. The landscape below him dashed by. With the ravine to their east, he traveled along the forests lining its edge until it leveled and the Sterling River unfurled below them. The Iron Mountain Range transitioned into meadows and curving timber lands, which he knew from their missions led to the swamplands.

This land was alive with Springtide in a way the mountainous regions could never aspire to. Green sprigs of new grasses and wildflowers poked through the ground, giving the area a satisfying and beautiful green cover.

Ahead, he spotted an open meadow. It lay in the shadow of the forests around it—a drastic contrast to its barrenness. This was the area he targeted. Even if he hadn't sensed the Erlking, it would've caught his attention, at least from the air.

They drew closer.

The kelpie quivered at the same moment Rowan witnessed a brief flicker in the air.

Believing it to be the wyvern, Rowan didn't pay it any mind, focusing instead on a place large enough for the carriage to land. Not far away was an open space before the clearing. He leaned forward, spurring the kelpie toward it.

They lowered, dodging the branches of larger trees. Here, the forest thinned out some, allowing him to view their destination more clearly.

Another flicker flashed along his right side. Rowan glanced at it, hoping to avoid the wyvern's tail, and realized it wasn't the dragon at all.

"Whoa," he yelled, but it was too late.

A tree limb whipped out before he could direct Calliope away, catching the animal along her right forelimb. The horse squealed, balking, her eyes wide with fright.

He noted shadows in the tree, possibly the Erlking's minions, but he had no time to consider it.

He didn't have time to warn the others, either. The golden sword caught as Calliope thrashed against the tree limb, catching the strap and tearing it off him. Rowan grabbed for it but missed. It glinted in the sunlight, dropping end over end until it disappeared.

Thankfully, he'd tucked the magicuffs inside a bark pocket where he could still feel the weight of the magic-nullifying object.

Rowan blinked, the need to sink his roots into the ground urgent. Whatever was below him used spells similar to the Weald to disguise itself, and he hadn't sensed it until it was too late. Not only that, but the tree grappled with them as if a rood had control of it. This was a puzzle he was intent to figure out. He let go of the kelpie's mane and shifted sideways, his aim to fall off the kelpie and allow it to fly free, away from danger.

He plunged to the ground, extending his roots. Shimmering magic surrounded the forest floor, much like the woodencloak's outline. The air was ripe with noxious spells. The Erlking had to have used all the magic of the Wilden Lands to pull this stunt off. And Rowan was in the thick of it.

There was no way to avoid the Erlking's miasma of spells, so he saved himself from the worst damage. He drew back his vulnerable roots and used a spare amount of magic to seal them up. He aimed his trunk, which could survive the impact, for the ground instead.

The branches along Rowan's crown crunched first, then his body cracked and pain spiraled through him. The voices of his friends screaming his name echoed above the forest. He yelled back, but a combatis rigoralia, the same kind of death bringer spider that trussed Princess Glory up in the Riven, shot a web at his mouth, gagging him.

Two worqs grabbed him. Excruciating pain from his right arm—broken, he was sure—exploded inside him, inhibiting his ability to retaliate. They tied ropes around his arms, tugging them behind his back.

He refused to walk, so they dragged him over to a group of bedraggled-looking, gaunt children. Several stacked wood in a pile. One fed a fire where a third turned a massive swine carcass over the open flames. Smoke swirled upward. There was no wind here to whip it around, and the heaviness of the magic clung to the air like a thick fog.

A worq clicked and grunted out some words. If Torren were here, he might be able to translate. However, the meaning became clear when they shoved Rowan into a hole in the ground filled with chitterbugs. Rowan screamed into the webbing covering his mouth as they crawled over his body, engulfing him.

~Horra~

MOMENTS AFTER ROWAN fell off the kelpie, Horra rushed to the side of the carriage, searching for his body. The last time she'd seen him fall—his tumble from the wyvern in the Riven— he'd turned into sticks on the ground.

Like Woodsly.

Horra shook that thought away. Rowan had survived his fall. He would be okay. He had to be.

She spied no bundle of sticks or intact woodgoblin body. Where had he gone? She screamed his name, but he didn't answer. "Land this thing," she shrieked at Glory.

"I'm trying. Your stupid half dragon is freaking out, and I can't land it while he thrashes around." Glory's face was red. Her wings thrashed, whipping her hair in their current. The cold green magic bearing them safely in the air sputtered again. The vehicle dropped.

Horra's stomach followed suit. She gulped back panic. "Torren, take Pidge next to Nimble," she yelled over her shoulder. Luckily, they'd traveled slow enough for her pet bird to keep up with them.

Pidge scree'd, and a flutter of wings let Horra know her knight was doing as requested as she hung, once again, over the side of the wobbly conveyance. Only a moment later, their path steadied. The fairy path held them once more. She sat away from the edge, her stomach churning.

Red cheeks contrasted with Glory's pasty face. Sweat dotted the fairy's forehead as she held her hands out, her fingers curled like claws. Her chest rose and fell rapidly.

Grendel was bent over the other side, searching for Rowan as well. She called out his name with no answer.

"Hold on. We're landing." Glory clenched her jaw as she spoke.

Grendel didn't move, so Horra dove for the girl, tackling her so that she fell inside rather than outside, like Torren had.

They landed awkwardly, jerking when the Stempner's and gulgoyle's feet caught the ground. Trees flashed by, too close for comfort. They tipped one way, then the other, before all the wheels settled. Nimble navigated through the forest, but his dodging of obstacles sent them swaying at dangerous angles.

"Whoa! I said whoa!" Glory's shrill voice pelted Horra's ears like an ice pick.

The animals ran on for another few feet before slowing, and the carriage shimmied sideways with the abrupt change of speed.

Horra closed her eyes and ducked, Grendel huddled beside her on the bottom of the carriage.

Crack!

The impact jarred them, tossing Horra into Grendel. Still, Horra kept her claws over her head. Another second passed before she realized they had stopped. Dropping her claws, Horra glanced up. Tree trunks, limbs, and leaves greeted her. They sat at an angle, the carriage's backside up in the air after having collided with a sturdy oak tree.

Behind her, Glory panted as if she'd just ran up a hill. "That," she wheezed, then swallowed, "was too close. I think I might faint."

"Drop your head between your knees." Horra climbed over the cowering giantess to reach the fairy. When the girl didn't listen to her, Horra shoved her into a sitting position, the carriage groaning and rocking as she did. That accomplished, she eased Glory's torso down so she bent over her lap. "Focus on something else, like sparkling flowers, then take a deep breath in. That's right. Then let it out. Remember how I did it when we were hiding in Nimble's shell?"

Wings limp, Glory whimpered but didn't fight her, a sign of how shaken the fairy was.

Horra empathized.

Nimble bellowed, and Pidge chittered at the gulgoyle.

"Is everyone all right?" Torren's voice drifted through the air.

"Peachy," she called back. "Grendel?" She nudged the girl's foot.

"I'm okay," came her muffled reply.

"You two stay here. I'm going to search for Rowan."

Neither Glory nor Grendel moved.

"All righty then." Horra climbed her way carefully to the door. Since it sat tipped at a precarious downward angle, at least she'd be able to jump out without too much fear of breaking a bone. The door didn't immediately open, however, so she kicked at it. "Glad I wore boots," she muttered. The see-through material splintered on her third kick.

Torren searched around the tree the carriage hung from. He whistled. "The animals are okay, but Princess Misty is not going to be happy about this."

"Ugh," Glory groaned into her knees, sounding slightly sick. Luckily, the fairy's breathing was coming in even beats. She would be okay after a few minutes.

The steps, however, hung sideways. They would be useless for Horra to climb down. The jump was farther than she expected. "Help me, will you?"

Pidge fluttered by, but Horra wasn't brave enough to jump onto her bird's back. "Not you, Pidge. I need Torren."

"You're too big for me to catch." Torren turned around and braced himself. "Step on my back and jump from there."

Horra did and landed hard on her right foot, twinging her ankle. "Ow. Gah!"

After checking to be sure she was fine, Torren chuckled. "You were never good at tumbling."

"Like you were, you big lummox. You always landed sideways or on your stomach." She brushed her shaking claws down her shirt. "You're right about one thing. That contraption is a death trap. Next time, I'm riding with you."

His laughter helped Horra regain her composure.

Minutes later, Horra had her pack on before donning the woodencloak. She was grateful Rowan had updated the wards and sigils. She just hoped they would work.

Torren glanced at her. "You think you're going to need that?"

"Something caught Rowan unaware, and we're near the Erlking—what do you think?" She puckered her lips in thought. "We'll need to be stealthy." The pudge wudgie nudged her side. "I'm fine, Pidge."

"Should I tie her up?" Torren asked.

"No. She has a keen eye." An idea occurred to her. "Why don't you and Pidge scout out the clearing? I'll follow you on foot. It'll be good to have both perspectives. One of us might see something the other doesn't. Meet back here before sunset if you find nothing, and we'll regroup, construct a new plan."

He saluted her and, within seconds, he and Pidge were in flight.

Horra followed the horse's tracks and skid marks back to where they'd landed. She studied the opening in the trees. The sunlight formed a ring around the area like a target.

Horra flipped her hood up and tucked her thick hair inside. Though the sun shone from its midday position in the sky, the air here was curiously cool. She strode a few steps forward, and a warm breeze washed over her. She froze, frowning. The area around the Riven had been like this too. Had the Erlking created another maze-like space?

Horra's heart pounded as she trailed back the way she thought they'd come and stopped. Nothing looked familiar. She couldn't see Torren or Pidge anywhere. Possibly, they'd already landed in the forest clearing.

A rustling sounded from her right, and she pivoted to glance that way, tripping over something she hadn't seen at her feet. She tumbled, landing on her hands and knees.

Shadows dropped out of nowhere, chilling her. Her thoughts turned muddled. What had she been doing? Why was she on the ground? Stringy pine trees and immense oaks loomed over her. She tried to stand, but her legs wobbled and she didn't make it. Crawling, she crept her way over to a hawthorn tree and used it to help her stand. Her hood slipped.

Buzzing erupted.

Horra instinctually yanked the hood into place and tightened it around her head. Her heart raced in her chest, her hide crawling with warning. She closed her eyes and took a deep breath, then another, pressing her head back inside the hood as far as her thick curls allowed. Her confusion cleared.

Just like it had in the Riven.

Her hammering heart, though, sunk. Opening her eyes, she saw the forest for what it truly was. Like in the Riven's maze, she was no longer in the same forest as she had been a few seconds ago. And only time would tell if the land would shift and spit her out somewhere different.

"Vinegar and beans!" she groaned.

Dried moss hanging from low tree limbs swayed, though there was no breeze. The air was thick and held a tang of magic. She drew the hood over her nose and mouth. Shiny, iridescent green-black bug carcasses lined the tree trunks. She stood rock still and stared.

Pidge and Torren.

Her heart thudded heavily in her chest. Would they also fall into this enchanted forest? She itched to stamp her foot and scream.

Was this why she hadn't seen Rowan after he fell? Carefully, she turned in a circle, gathering the lay of the space. The bug's wings fluttered with her movements. The trees continued on forever in every direction.

Now what was she supposed to do? If she moved, would the bugs attack? If they attacked, what would happen? She shuddered to think of the possibilities. Her memories of the Riven's horrors kept her motionless.

But Rowan needed her.

Her kingdom needed her.

And Horra needed to rally her courage.

"Please help me," Horra prayed silently, her soul begging for the Creature God's favor.

Her mother's face, and each of her fierce ancestor's faces,

flashed through her mind. The memories ended with her father's expression when he'd told her he believed in her. They'd all overcome every situation they'd come against. She could too.

A small seed of hope sparked in her gut. It was enough. She pursed her lips and took a step forward, ready to face whatever the Erlking had set into place.

Colorful wings flared.

Another step.

The bugs took flight, dashing about in a frenzy. They buzzed by her head and caught on her clothes.

"So much for this woodencloak," she muttered. Horra took off running, dodging trunks and bushes, bugs and boulders, and—

Children?

Hobgoblins, gnomes, goblins, and four shrunken giants lined the area in front of her. With ripped clothes, matted hair, and dirty skin, they created a feral-looking barrier.

She slid to a stop, the ground here as damp as everywhere else, assuring her this wasn't like the Riven whose landscape and weather were separate entities. Their last rainstorm had affected this area. Bracing herself against the rough bark of an oak tree, she stared at the menacing faces of the children who waited for her.

They stood with their hands raised and mouths twisted into grimaces.

Horra did an about-face and darted in the other direction, only to run into more children. Another extensive line of savage children strung out to greet her.

There was nowhere to turn. Horra was surrounded.

CHAPTER 26

~Glory~

M inutes after the pushy troll left, the panic inside Glory dissipated. She wouldn't admit it to anyone, but focusing on sugared flower petals helped her overcome the anxiety attack. It had never happened to her before, but she'd also never crashed a carriage coming off a fairy path, either.

She was shaky, and her magic was all but completely spent until she could rest again. It would probably take her a few days to recover the power she'd possessed at the beginning of their trip. Magic was like a muscle. If you didn't exercise it often enough, it atrophied. Which was why she had been so desperate to regain what the Erlking had stolen from her.

"Princess?"

She felt Grendel move from the floor to the seat. Placing her palms on her thighs, Glory sat up and faced the ghastly girl. After experiencing so many creatures shrinking away from her after the hex, she steeled herself against the initial spark of aversion the shadowy caped girl elicited. "Yes?"

"Should we go after the others?" Grendel asked, her voice more timid than normal. She glanced around while wringing her paw-like hands.

Guilt over teasing Grendel about her beastly presence bloomed inside her. Grendel had been nothing but kind to her. She'd helped Glory when she hadn't requested to be healed. The giantess had even restored some of her magic. Glory shoved her contrition down. The girl didn't need her to wimp out. They both needed to be strong.

Glory donned a brightness she didn't feel and smiled. "It would be better than waiting for the fiend to find us. Don't you agree?"

Grendel sighed, a feat since the girl's mouth was now a wolfish-looking snout. "Right. Yes. Let me unstrap my bag. I might need it if Rowan's injured."

Glory kept her smile in place until Grendel jumped out and disappeared around the front, where they'd tied their supplies on the half-dragon. She clenched her outfit's silky fabric in shaking hands. She now regretted creating the white cloth, knowing she was more than likely going to destroy it by traipsing through a forest full of who knew what. With a shrug, she surveyed the distance to the ground. It was too far to jump, and in her weakened, shaken state, she didn't trust her wings.

Though the carriage dangled, it rested with its end up on a sturdy tree. Not wishing to waste her magic in case she'd need it for more important things, she crawled over the side and hung on to the carriage's base before dropping several feet to the ground …

And onto her backside, spraining her right wing. Sharp jabs of pain thrummed through her. "Ugh!" Glory rolled over and, as expected, stained her satin legs with grass and mud.

Grendel handed the bag containing the aethrial to her. She snatched it from her hand before stopping herself. "Sorry. I tweaked my wing, and they're super sensitive. And I ruined our newest carriage. I'm not mad at you. All this has made me crabby." She waved her hands in the air.

"Yeah, I get it," Grendel said kindly.

More guilt nibbled Glory's insides. She puffed out a breath. "Yes, you do."

"Which way should we go?" The giant girl squinted into the distance.

Glory removed the aethrial from the bag. She'd play while they walked and maybe the music would cheer them up. She pointed the instrument to their left. "That way."

As they walked, Glory played an upbeat song. It was hard not to flutter her wings while playing music, but she refrained since it sent shards of pain across her wing. Sunlight glowed around them. Bird's songs filled the air. The air warmed enough to remove the chill.

A screech pierced the air.

Grendel's head snapped up. "Is that Pidge?"

Glory lowered the instrument to her side. "I don't know. All birds sound the same to me."

A dark figure dashed above the treetops. The male troll rode Pidge, and it looked like they were fleeing.

She laid her hand on Grendel's arm. "This doesn't look good—"

Tree limbs cracked.

"Worqs!" Torren shouted. "Get back to the carriage."

Glory glanced at Grendel, who shook with fright. She tugged on the giant girl's arm. "Let's go!"

Together they ran. Small saplings snapped and snagged their clothes as they fled. The air was heavy with moisture and the scent of damp ground.

Between one moment and the next, the forest darkened and trees appeared out of nowhere.

Glory skidded to a halt, and Grendel rushed past her a few feet before she, too, stopped.

"Where are we?" Grendel puffed.

"I don't know." A feeling of déjà vu shivered over Glory's skin. She rubbed her shoulder, trying to ease the ache in her injured wing.

Susurration filled the air.

Glory gulped. "Oh no. This is so not good."

~Grendel~

THE TERROR in Princess Glory's voice threatened to shatter the thin margin of control Grendel held over her beastly curse. "Wha—what's wrong?" Her voice edged higher, ending in a whine. She hated herself for this weakness. She'd never been afraid before the Erlking hexed her, except when she stressed about how she'd perform on a test. Now, except for a few solid moments she'd spent at the troll's castle, that's all she was—a scared, shivering coward.

"Shh. Don't let them hear you," the fairy princess whispered, her luminous eyes wide and her wings rigid.

Grendel swallowed the spit in her mouth. "Who?" she breathed.

"I don't know. Just them." She bobbed her brunette head toward the tree to her left.

Besides bugs on the bark, Grendel didn't see anyone or anything. "I don't—"

The princess slammed a finger to her lips so that Grendel couldn't finish what she was going to say.

They stood that way for several heartbeats.

Grendel shifted into a more comfortable position.

Glory let out a half groan and shook her head vehemently. "Don't. Move." She mouthed the words.

She frowned. "Why?" she mouthed back, seeing and sensing no danger.

Glory jerked her arm in the air, her face puckered in frustration.

Nothing happened.

Several more heartbeats passed before a cramp bloomed on Grendel's right calf. She'd been standing too awkwardly for too long. She squealed and bent over her spasming leg.

Bugs lit into the air in a whirring explosion.

Grendel, still bent over her leg, tipped onto the ground, her free arm thrown over her head.

The princess shrieked and took off running.

Several footfalls accompanied her, but Grendel was hunched over, unable to clearly see what was happening.

Grendel waited out the chaos, gritting her teeth against the excruciating pain. This close to the ground, the bugs weren't as active, so she dug into her pack for a potion that would help to ease her knotted muscle. Each time she stretched, the muscle tightened, though, which made retrieving the concoction almost impossible. Finally, she found the round vial and slipped it out of her bag. She rolled over so she could dribble a few drops in her mouth and froze, the liquid spilling across her cheek.

A giant child faced her, clutching a sharpened stick to her neck. Dozens of children of differing kinds crowded behind her, the giant being the largest of the group. Similar to Grendel's shrunken size, the child was smaller. The freckles across her nose and the flecks in her eyes were very familiar. "Galumph?"

Her leg tightened, and she gasped. With effort, she tipped the last few drops from the jar into her mouth.

Galumph poked her with the stick and grunted. The others grunted as if in answer. Her sister was filthy, grime caking her orange face and matting her red hair. Her scalp, normally shaved and showcasing her jewels, frizzed out with her flame-red hair, giving her a shaggy appearance. She almost looked as beastly as Grendel had after the hex.

The girl prodded her side with the stick.

"Stop it. I can't move." She hoped Galumph or the others wouldn't decide to attack. It would take a minute for the potion to work on her leg, and she was vulnerable until it did.

Her sister moved as if to swing the limb at her just as the cramp let up.

Grendel scurried backward and collided with a tree trunk. "Galumph, it's me. Grendel."

Several more of the chitterbugs darted around. The bug's susurration rose and fell.

No recognition crossed her sister's face. None of the children responded, either. They all simply stared. What had the Erlking done to her? To them? Tears pricked Grendel's eyes. She'd waited so long to find her little sister, and now she couldn't get through to her.

Grunts and incoherent voices from the other children drew Galumph's attention. She glanced over her shoulder, turned to look at Grendel once more, then spun and darted away from her.

The others ran in front, though her giant sister soon outdistanced them with her longer stride.

"Galumph!" She rose to her feet, her leg still aching despite the cramp loosening. With a heavy sigh, Grendel limped after her sister.

Princess Glory's shrieks echoed in the dark forest. The air

chilled Grendel, though she was covered in a new layer of delicate, cat-like fur. Hustling, she followed her sister in the direction the princess's voice came from. "I'm coming, Princess."

"Well, hurry," she screeched.

Grendel's ankle twinged as she stepped on a hidden limb. She winced at the pain that shot up her leg. Grunting, she yelled at the princess while limping on both legs. "Use your aethrial."

Rounding a corner, Grendel caught sight of the fairy princess surrounded by a throng of children. There had to be hundreds of them. They were of all different races—hobgoblins, goblins, shrunken giants like Galumph, and gnomes. Ten or more bocan children were also in the group. Small and large, they all appeared disheveled and untamed.

Princess Glory positioned a barrier around herself as the children attacked. The lesser magical creatures used sharpened sticks or rocks, and others, like the hobgoblins who had a measure of power, threw snapping spells in her direction. Unaffected, the princess blew into the instrument. For a moment, nothing happened.

Grendel stood on the outer line of mean-looking goblins. They all held large rocks ready to toss at her companion. Then the air changed. The bugs, which had been flittering around, calmed and landed. The children all dropped their weapons and arms at the same moment—a bizarre thing to watch.

"Keep playing, Princess. You're taming them." She limped to where her sister stood hunched, her arms crossed over her head. Galumph quivered and let out a wail, then dropped to her bottom.

Trees rattled around them as the chitterbugs danced to Glory's silent call. The children were no longer bent, ready to strike. They swayed or twirled like normal children often did.

Grendel's heartbeat slowed, calming. Though the forest was dark, it brightened, shedding the fog she'd noticed when they first entered. A befuddlement illusion?

With the thrall gone, the children giggled and played, frolicking with each other.

Grendel's heart twinged at the haggard shape they were in. The Erlking certainly hadn't been caring for them.

Princess Glory shifted, her body moving differently now, and the warm, fuzzy feeling that had eased Grendel's anxiety switched. Tingling, like cold water being poured, rushed over her body in a brisk manner.

Bugs, which had landed on trees, tumbled, most landing on their backs, their legs wiggling in the air. They weren't dead, but they weren't under the Erlking's spell now. The fairy had washed the last dregs of his enchantment from them.

Princess Glory held one last silent note and lowered the aethrial. "It worked? It did, didn't it? My songs broke the spells they were under." The fairy's glow brightened, exuding her excitement.

Grendel stretched her neck. "I think, yes. I feel more awake than I've been in a while now."

"Grendel?" Galumph's wobbly voice rose above the other children's sobbing and muttering. "Is that you?"

~Rowan~

ROWAN'S BARK QUIVERED. The sensation of insects crawling over his body sent waves of alarm through his stem. His sap rushed so that he was dizzy for a moment. He mentally shook himself. Panicking would not help in this situation. He needed to assess and disseminate.

"Well, well. If it isn't the Wilden Land's greatest savior." The Erlking's voice preceded his presence. He stepped from behind a large stringy pine tree wearing a black cloak. The hood was drawn over his head, hiding it.

This was his worst nightmare—caught by his mortal enemy, stuck in a pit while wood-eating bugs crawled all over him, and unable to speak.

Rowan ran through what he knew. This new takeover of Oddar land couldn't have been long established. They'd passed by every inch of western Oddar. They would've come across this bespelled area before now. On the ground, he would've sensed it. Being newly formed, there had to be a way to break through the Erlking's spells.

Though he was loath to do it, he needed to sink his roots in to gather information.

The Erlking clasped bony hands in front of his body. "I'm sure you're wondering how you fell into my trap." His laugh rattled as if he were ill. "Did you really think you had a chance against me? Hmm?" More rattling laughter. A rat plodded over, positioning its head under the evil elf's hand as if it wanted to be petted. It twitched its spotted pink nose at Rowan, its beady eyes glowing orange, reflecting the firelight.

The evil elf hesitated a moment as if waiting for Rowan to respond, then rattle-laughed again. "Oh, that's right. You can't talk." He removed his hood, revealing his bule-tinged bald head. He looked nothing like the regal fairies he'd just met in the blackened Riven. Rowan recalled the fairy princess mentioning he was only part elf. With black veins running under his translucent skin along his skeletal body, he bore no resemblance to any of the other creatures in the Wilden Lands that Rowan knew of.

"Everyone underestimates me." The Erlking pushed the rat away without remorse. It squeaked in protest but plodded to a corner by the children. One of the two hobgoblins turning the spit dug a piece of meat off and threw it at the animal. "Your growth, I'm sure, was a rushed fiasco, thanks to my efforts at thwarting that pesky troll girl." His smile was horrifying. "She doesn't cooperate well with others, does she? Anyway, you weren't supposed to sprout at all. I'll seek revenge on that royal nuisance soon. Don't you worry." He tapped a long, blackened fingernail against his cheek. "Still, I doubt you have a quarter of the knowledge former druids would've started with. It was a shame about your little forgotten forest. Not much of a loss, really, since there was only one inhabitant and only a few stodgy old roods."

Fury boiled inside Rowan. Merrow had been a stellar seedkeeper and the rood's hero even now, working against the Erlking's plots. The Erlking spoke of being underestimated, yet that's exactly what the evil elf was doing to Rowan.

"I see the gears spinning in your head, trying to figure it all out." Crusty laughter bubbled from him. He jerked his head sideways, giving Rowan a good view of the scars where his ears should be. Something below the surface slithered, dark and malignant. "Ah, my pets have your companions on the run. It's only a matter of time before the rest of my plan comes together."

He raised his hands, sending a cloud of magic into the air. "I'm afraid I have to leave. My pets will take good care of you." He waved his hand in the air, and the chitterbugs around him began chittering. Their loud calls rose and fell—an insect melody. The Erlking walked away, the worqs trailing him. The rat snarled at him and ran after the group, leaving Rowan alone with the enthralled children.

CHAPTER 27

~Horra~

Horra debated what to do, what to say. The unkempt children standing before her possessed an air of threat, though none of them moved. What had the Erlking done to them?

"Hello?" she said in her most calm voice. "I'm Queen Bearer Horra Fyd of Oddar."

Several of the more untidy children snarled. Horra had to wonder if they weren't rabid. She'd heard stories of children being lost in forests for too long, becoming untamable wildlings. A hobgoblin boy raised a hand, minor magic sparking across his fingers. Untamed or not, they were still dangerous. The others continued staring, anger twisting their faces in grim ways.

"Not talkative. Got it," she murmured to herself. She glanced around, taking in her surroundings and noting everything she could.

There were no bugs here. She recalled her Defensive Tactics class's lessons. This could be an outer perimeter to a multiple defense strategy. Start with the lesser threat and build to your toughest knights. If that were true and the Erlking was using a target formation—bugs being the first and the children a second line of defense—how many layers would he have built in?

She'd lost count of the different places she'd shifted to in the Riven. This place, however, didn't look like it was nearly so complicated. And the area hadn't shifted yet. That was encouraging.

Her legs ached from remaining poised in one position for too long. The enthralled children were unmoving—a solid blockade. None of the children had major magic, like fairies. The hobgoblins and gnomes could do minor spells—deterrent kinds of magic. The giants and goblins would be the strongest if she were to physically fight them. She hoped she wouldn't have to. It wasn't their fault they were being used. Horra would rather rescue them than battle them.

This ragtag group was the army Glory had spoken of when she'd spilled the Erlking's secret plan in the Conservatory not so long ago. She'd imagined they would be more sophisticated. But they were half-starved, grimy, and haggard. Had the Erlking cared for them at all?

Frustration at the children turned to fury at the Erlking for treating them so callously. It was almost as if he viewed them as dispensable. Something to be used and tossed away. As her mind traveled this train of thought, she grew more agitated and furious. Though she found children to be annoying, they were precious—to their families and to the kingdom. A kingdom could only thrive when the masses were cared for and safe. She clenched her claws.

The children's postures fluctuated. Horra took the moment

to shift her weight, alleviating her strained muscles. If she could tackle the biggest child and break the Erlking's spell, she might save them all.

A screech pierced the laden air.

Pidge?

As one, the children glanced off into the distance to her right.

She glanced that way, keeping her head mainly forward in case they attacked, but didn't see any sign of her pet. She carefully scanned the other direction, but again saw nothing.

Another high-pitched scree sounded, but Horra couldn't tell if it was her pet. The magic-ridden atmosphere dampened the sound. Nor could she tell, besides the children's movements, where the sound came from. It seemed to come from everywhere.

The children, however, had no trouble discerning it. Unified, they sprung into action, rushing toward their new intruder. Though they were emaciated, they moved with focused energy, bounding over fallen logs and dodging bushes.

Within the space of two breaths, they were gone.

Horra hesitated, her stance relaxing now that they'd dispersed. "Gah! What should I do?" Should she run after them, continue her search for Rowan, or try to locate the Erlking and end the madness once and for all?

The tree beside her cracked and popped.

She jumped back, drawing her dagger, fearing another attack.

A familiar face appeared on the bark of the tree she stood by. "Good evening, Your Majesty." Her old instructor's rickety voice sent cold shivers down her spine.

"Woodsly?" Tears gathered in her eyes. "How are you here?"

"The roots here are deep and strong. But the Erlking is

nearby. Be on your guard. Help is on the way." The tree cracked, and the face disappeared.

"Woodsly?" Horra slammed her claw on the tree. "Come back. Woodsly?" She was unashamed of the longing in her voice. "I miss you, my old friend." The rough bark scratched her forehead as she leaned against the tree.

She sniffed, the snot dripping from her nose, and wiped the excess on the woodencloak. The dark forest loomed over her, making her feel younger and more vulnerable than she'd like to admit. "What did you mean, help is on the way?"

Silence.

Her thoughts jumped from Woodsly to his offspring, Rowan. Urgency to find him bloomed in her chest.

Horra glanced back in the direction the children had gone. Only the gloomy forest remained. She adjusted her pack and strode forward, toward what she assumed would be the center.

The farther she traveled, the darker and drearier the forest grew. Strange noises permeated the heavy air, inciting goosebumps along her hide. Things moved, but she couldn't make them out even with her night vision. The heavy air chilled as she moved, ever closer, to the heart of the cursed forest.

Memories of traversing the Erlking's mountain kept flashing through her mind, unsettling her. No wonder the fiend had no trouble traveling through pitch darkness. It was as black as midnight here, though she knew it must only be dinnertime on the outside.

Another dark figure flashed at the edge of her perception. She jerked her head to gain a better view but saw nothing.

Two more steps and a noise forced her to stop. She stayed, awkwardly posed, not desiring to draw any attention.

Squeak.

"Rats," she breathed. Her hide crawled with the thought. Dragon's fire! They weren't what she'd hoped to run into next. Or ever again. She bit her lower lip.

Another murky shape dashed by her other side. "Oh no, you don't," she muttered in a quiet promise.

She turned her attention to the trees. She'd used them to escape the fiends before. Maybe she could do it again if she found one to climb. The first tree—a stringy pine with thin, breakable limbs—wasn't suitable. Trying not to create noise or attract their attention, she scurried to the next one—another pine. It had wide limbs but nothing she could secure a good grasp on. The third and fourth had no low limbs or smooth trunks, proving it impossible to achieve a good grip.

Stupid pine trees. Horra formed a mental note to plant different trees in Oddar's forests.

The shuffling that had started small swelled. Her heart stuttered. Not only one rat but a herd was stalking her like they'd done after she, Torren, and Rowan had left the destroyed Weald.

She spotted an elm with a split trunk and hurried over to it. Elms were solid. Though this one was a bit on the small side. It grew next to a tall oak, however and, though the limbs were farther up, she could switch over when she climbed higher. She clambered up the tree carefully. Thankfully, elms were easy to climb, unlike the stringy pines that grew in abundance here.

She climbed halfway up the elm before the limbs grew too small to bear her weight. Here, though, was a large enough oak branch to transfer onto. Her claws were cold and clammy. The elm limb buckled when she crawled too far out.

Snarls echoed from beneath her.

Her nerves turned her jittery. She shimmied toward an oak on the other side and reached out. This branch was steadier.

Uttering silent prayers, she clutched the thin end of the limb. The elm shook as a rat started climbing it.

It was now or never. Horra braced and jumped onto the oak. The end of the elm limb snapped, the pieces tumbling to the ground. She dangled on the oak limb and held on for dear life. Claw over claw, she dragged herself farther onto the branch until she reached the thicker part near the trunk. With a relieved breath, she flattened herself against the tree.

A squeak sounded from the elm.

She retrieved her dagger, which she'd tucked back into the sheath when she began climbing, and held it in both claws.

This far up, light permeated the branches more easily. This rat was a grungy gray-brown and as large as a small swamp swine. Hair bristling and sharp teeth snapping, it glanced around with beady eyes. After a deep sniff, it looked directly at her.

Horra raised the dagger, ready for battle.

The rat jumped.

~Grendel~

GLADNESS AND RELIEF rushed through Grendel after Galumph called her name. "Yes, it's me," she cried and rushed toward the girl, ready to pull her into a tight embrace and swing her around.

Galumph scurried backward, fear in her eyes. "You're not Grendel. You're a monster."

A child whined.

Another ran.

Grendel's heart crashed to the ground.

Glory rushed to Grendel's side. "No. This is your sister,

Grendel. She's been hexed by that bad man who took you. She's not a monster, just a timid-looking wolf-cat-thing. It's her. Really, it is."

Grendel appreciated the fairy's efforts to convince her sister. But she knew her sister too well. Galumph had a scientific mind like she did—cunning and calculating.

True to her nature, Galumph shook her head. "No. My sister is a giant. Giants are orange and not scary. She's got fangs and paws and everything."

Grendel regretted anew the potion she'd used that changed her coloring . At least her sister would've recognized her if she were orange and furry. "It's me. How else would I know you like to feed your pet bugs your special candy to expand them enough to play with? I read you *Snug as a Bug in a Hug* at night before you went to bed. I'd sneak you turnip snaps when Mom wasn't looking. They're your favorite, remember?" Grendel stepped forward slowly, careful not to spook her sister. Tears stung her eyes. "It's me."

Though she'd gained her sister's attention, Grendel could tell Galumph still didn't fully believe. "Do you remember the dolly you showed me the day I disappeared? That was the troll princess who was lost. She was running from that bad man Princess Glory mentioned, and you found her. I think that's how he found us. And he placed a nasty spell on me that changed me into a beast. Do you remember seeing me in the bathroom mirror? You screamed when you saw me."

"Yes." Her face pinched. "Grendel!" she wailed.

Grendel rushed to her, patting her shoulder and murmuring, "It's okay. I'm here now, and we're together."

They let Galumph cry it out, and she hiccupped at the end.

Grendel finally asked the question she was most worried about. "Did the bad man hurt you?"

Her sister wiped a fist across her damp face. "I don't like his music. It makes me feel all funny. She said he hurted you?" Galumph pointed to Glory.

Grendel sighed. "No, he *hexed* me. You haven't learned about hexes in school yet. He turned me into this." She waved her hand at herself.

Galumph crossed her arms over her chest. "I don't like him. He's not nice."

Grendel laughed, though it wasn't funny. "No, he's not." She stepped closer.

"It's truly you?" Galumph dropped her arms, her eyes wide and innocent.

"It's really me." Grendel reached out.

Her sister flew into her embrace. "I've missed you."

"I've missed you too."

~Torren~

TORREN FOUGHT AGAINST TERROR. His future queen and friend had disappeared in the blink of an eye. He knew an empty meadow among throngs of forest was suspect, but he hadn't thought it would swallow Horra, leaving no trace of her behind. The worqs he spotted didn't ease his fear.

Pidge screeched as they flew around and around, but it was of no use. He didn't spot Horra or Rowan anywhere.

Retracing their steps, he and Pidge ended up back at the carriage. The giant girl and fairy princess were both gone. He thought he'd warned them in time. Had the worqs taken them? "Where in the Wilden Lands did everyone go?" His frustration grew as he and Pidge walked around the wreckage. He swiped his claws through his hair. The king would have his hide if anything happened to Horra, and it would be an international event if Glory went missing again. He shuddered at the thought of a shrieking Princess Misty returning to the castle.

He needed help.

"Let's go secure some backup, Pidge."

CHAPTER 28

~Rowan~

S econds after the Erlking left, Rowan closed his eyes, waiting for the chitterbug's song to lull him into a trance, but nothing happened. He opened his eyes, grateful for the sponges in his ears. The children swayed to the tune, the swine on the spit burning where it no longer turned.

Realization struck him. Since Merrow had instigated his maturation and somehow changed his appearance, his bark had grown almost impermeable—a Ghost Tree, the most miraculous coniferous tree the Creature God had ever created. Impervious to bug infestations, it repelled critters. Hope and relief tingled along his aching body. It was as if his former keeper knew he'd end up here with the Erlking in a pit of writhing critters hungering to devour him.

No longer fearing the bugs, Rowan thrust his roots past the singing pests, digging into the contaminated soil. As he'd thought, the spells were shallow. He worked past the topsoil into a rockier layer before he reached normal soil. From there, he spread out, searching for anything that would help him.

The air filled with smoke, the hunk of swine now aflame. Soon it would be inedible, possibly why the children appeared so gaunt. Still, they stood, transfixed by the natural symphony. Were all the stolen children here? His thoughts spun while his roots bore through the layers of soil, sand, and rock.

Fifty feet down, his roots found something he hadn't expected. An underground pool, like the trapped spirits had found in the Riven. It was small—no larger than a big puddle—but potent. He dipped his appendages in and drank with all his might, extracting pure magic.

The magic was nearly intoxicating. His head grew dizzy, and the world seemed to spin around him. It didn't take long to gain his fill. Too rich to overload on, Rowan extracted his roots. His body buzzed. His arm, which was assuredly broken, stopped hurting. Itchy pinpricks confirmed the magic was healing him.

He waited for the sensation to end, then focused on the ropes. From what the fairy princess had confessed late one evening in the library, it only took a sliver of magic to undo knots. His arms fell to his sides, the ropes dropping to the bottom of the pit. Now to work on the gag.

The gag proved more difficult. It stuck like nothing he'd ever had on his bark before. Venom from the death bringer spider coated the sticky silk, stinging his bark if he worked too quickly. Finally, it, too, fell to the ground. Now all Rowan had to do was climb out and call for help.

He withdrew his roots, having only used a couple drops of the magic to free himself. He leaned against a birch tree and called out to any nearby rood or forest spirit.

A minute later, a voice spoke. *"Hello, dear boy."* Merrow's demeanor was light and giddy. *"You finally made it."*

"Yes," he agreed. "The Erlking thinks he caught me. What would you have me do?"

"Plant the seeds one decibel apart." An equation popped into Rowan's mind, allowing him to see how big that space would be. *"Do not fear contamination, for they are now Ghost Tree seeds. This step is crucial."*

Power, like a gust of wind, rushed through the area, knocking the children back and sending sparks from the fire onto the ground. The hunk of meat fell from the sticks securing it, landing in the flames.

Without thought, a flash of magic leaped from Rowan, extinguishing the whole mess. Startled, Rowan studied the smoking remains. Then he glanced at the children. "Merrow, am I able to free the children?"

No answer. Their link was gone, probably knocked silent from the magical flash.

"Can't hurt to try," he murmured. Raising a hand, he "called" to the three youths.

None of them moved.

He needed an instrument like the fairy princess had. He wished now he would have packed the flute he'd carved, despite what Woodsly had told him about being the instrument, not the maker. However, his first objective was to follow Merrow's instructions. Meditating for a moment to detect the center of the Erlking's hidden forest, he moved over to the fire pit.

Taking calm, measured steps, he worked his way east first.

~Horra~

HORRA HELD THE DAGGER OUT, ready for the rat to pounce. There would be no hope for her if it did, but she'd do her best to take this one out before she fell to the forest floor.

The creature's beady eyes glinted as it crouched to jump. The elm tree's broken limb cracked before it sprung. Wood splintered as the branch broke and the rat dropped, squealing, to the ground below.

Another darker rat, smaller than the first, scrabbled up the elm, digging its claws into the bark and leaving gouge marks behind. It, too, sniffed the air and glanced her way. Irreparably broken, the stub where the limb once grew was a useless splintered hunk. Perceptive enough to know better, the dark rat turned and scraped its way back down the elm, squeaking all the way—probably alerting his rodent friends.

Glory's words about how intelligent the rodents could be flitted through Horra's mind. Were they smart enough to give the oak a try? The bark was rough enough that they could claw a path to the lowest branches. Then it would be easy for them to scramble their way to her.

She needed to sneak out of this tree and away from them. Obviously, she couldn't move back to the tree she'd just escaped from. No other branches were nearby. A stringy pine tree was close, but she knew them to be brittle, and the bark peeled easily.

"Ugh!" she screamed. "How am I going to get out of this stupid tree?"

A wheeze and a click sounded close by.

Horra spun, holding the dagger in front of her. Her heart hammered in her chest. Had another rat come after her already?

A flying figure flickered into view.

The wyvern!

"Well, hello," she said to it. "What're you doing here?"

It snorted, its body curling in the air as its massive bat-like wings held it suspended only feet from her.

The tree shook. A glance down revealed two rats climbing the massive oak.

The wyvern blinked, and its chest rumbled, a sound similar to the one Nimble produced.

Tree limbs around her shook.

"Vinegar and beans!" Horra said, her stomach lurching into her throat. She gulped, but it didn't ease the lump. "Oh please, help me," she prayed.

The wyvern let out a beckoning, braying noise. It hovered closer, moving as near to her as possible.

Horra stared at it for a moment. "I hope this is what you're trying to tell me." She got to her knees on the branch. It creaked as she shifted around. Scratching noises from the rats climbing drew nearer. Tucking her dagger away, she rose to her booted feet and, with a deep breath, Horra vaulted.

The wyvern rose a couple inches to catch her. Its scales weren't as hard as Nimble's and therefore easier to land on. They were, however, slicker, and Horra slipped. Her foot caught the shoulder of the left wing, which steadied her as she scrambled. Without reins or a mane to clutch, Horra clung to the creature's neck.

Two rats scrambled onto the limb she'd just deserted. They chattered at each other. The one nearest the trunk turned, knocking into the second. It teetered before falling.

Horra tapped the wyvern, wishing it would move.

The remaining rat squealed and bounded.

In the blink of an eye, Horra and the wyvern were several trees away, watching the rat join his companion as it, too, dropped. This far away, Horra could see the gang of rats at the base of the oak. Six of them—two of which were injured and one unmoving. Furious squeaking permeated the air. The rats knew they'd lost their mark.

In another flash, they were airborne and sailing through the dark forest.

~Glory~

GLORY WAITED PATIENTLY for a few seconds as the two giant girls had their reunion. "I'm glad you guys are back together," she said, "but we need to either sneak our way out of here or find Horra or Rowan. My magic is almost depleted."

Grendel let her sister go and sent her a fearful glance. "Does that affect your music?"

"Some, yes. I've been adding small bits of magic when I play. But if we run into the wrong people ..."

"I'm scared," a hobgoblin child wailed, reminding Glory their trio wasn't alone.

Glory sighed. "Where is the other troll girl when you need her?" she muttered.

"Can you play something cheery?" Grendel said, taking her sister's hand. "We might as well start walking. Maybe we'll be lucky enough to stumble out of this place."

Glory looked around. "I'm not even sure where we came in from now. I'm all turned around."

"Do you remember much?" Grendel asked Galumph.

The girl shook her head sadly. "I remember music and feeling hungry. It was dark after they took me. Really, really dark." Galumph shivered.

"And we had to walk a lot," a child said.

"It was cold too," another piped up.

"And wet," said an additional voice.

Sniffling spurred Glory on. "It's not going to be that way anymore." She lifted the aethrial and played one of her favorite happy songs.

Within moments, the air lightened and the weeping ended. It took several minutes and playing the song over again before the children's demeanors changed from sad to hopeful. She lowered her instrument. "Now, join hands. We're going to find our way out of here."

She twisted to walk one way, but a hand on her arm stopped her.

"Excuse me, but that's the wrong way." It was a goblin girl. Older than most of the others, her blue cheeks pinked, and she glanced away as if regretting speaking up.

"Thank you—"

"Vorlah." A hint of a smile ticked one side of her mouth.

"Thank you, Vorlah." Glory squeezed her fingers. "Can you show me the way you'd go, then? I'm kind of lost." She hoped if she could lead them to help, it might ease some of their fear.

Grendel smiled approvingly. "Yes! You guys lead the way."

Vorlah took Glory's hand in hers. Her skin was dry and rough. Compassion, a rare emotion for Glory to feel for another creature, blossomed in her chest, warming her. With a nod, she allowed the goblin girl to lead them.

Maybe, just maybe, if Glory worked hard enough on being a better person, her sister and mother—if she ever recovered— would be proud of her. Maybe she could even be proud of herself again.

It was a stretch, she knew. And she didn't seek to do things for show. She'd given up that kind of behavior. Regardless, a sense of rightness settled over Glory, a sensation she'd only ever experienced while composing *Wind's Song*.

Goosebumps bloomed across Glory's skin at the memory of

sitting amid a storm, calmly creating a symphony that reflected its rhythm. And when Maestro Lyrie had bestowed the title of Composer of the Highest Order on her, she'd almost burst with pride.

They drew close to an area with the buzzing bugs again. The rise and fall of the critter's song caught Glory's attention.

She stopped, tugging the child's arm and halting her. "Why didn't I ever notice this before?"

"Notice what?" Grendel said from behind her.

Glory released the child's hand and spun to face the giantess.

"He's using the natural ebb and flow of nature to work his magic." She stared into her friend's flecked eyes. "His songs weren't working. I mean, Horra proved that, right?" Her mind spun faster than she could talk. "And you ... Look at you. He flubbed that one big time, didn't he? You were supposed to be a big terrible monster that would snuff out all the other creatures across the Wilden Lands. But you're a fraidy-cat, scared of your own shadow. No pun intended."

Grendel frowned.

Glory raised her hands. "That's not a bad thing." She snapped her fingers. "Critters, bugs, and animals are instinctual. Creatures like you and I are not. I've found the Erlking to be single-minded. Though he sets many plans into action, they're all for one purpose."

"Control?" Grendel asked.

She shook her head. "Dominance." Her thoughts were a whirlwind, but a theory was gaining traction. "He once said that elves were scientific to a fault. They admire themselves too fully—his words, not mine. Elves are cold and egotistic, thinking they are above any other species. He grew up in a detached society that led him to the wrong conclusions."

"About what?" Grendel said, leaning forward with earnest attention.

"About you. About me. Definitely about Horra. Probably about Rowan as well. The Erlking didn't realize our fickle natures or our empathy for others when he started his war on the Wilden Lands. He doesn't understand it. He only understands dominance."

"So what does all that mean?" Grendel asked.

Glory grabbed Grendel by her shoulders. "It means, my big, beautiful, shadow-caped friend, that he's fallible. And I'm going to work that weakness against him."

CHAPTER 29

~Grendel~

Grendel didn't completely understand everything the fairy princess alluded to about the Erlking. Her excitement was catching, however, as the children grew animated and more energetic. "So, are we trying to get out of here, or—?

Low chitters filled the previously silent background with a murmuring sound. Grendel glanced around, alert.

"Not leaving so fast, are you?" The Erlking stepped out from behind a tree. His corpse-like grayish-blue skin and completely dark eyes gave him a ghoulish bearing.

No wonder Galumph had been so afraid of Grendel. She resembled this fiend with her shadowy appearance.

His dark cloak floated as if he stood on air. But it wasn't air. Chitterbugs scattered from beneath him, spreading out and crawling up the tree. He lowered to the ground, his arms clasped calmly in front of him. The bug's murmuring amplified into a harmonized roar.

The children's shocked cries died instantly as magic filled the noise, choking the atmosphere with its foulness. He was enthralling them again.

For once, the sound didn't affect her. Grendel's heartbeat pounded a rhythm inside her, muting her hearing. Her vision darkened as her fury at the Erlking replaced her fear. She clenched her shaking hands as the rage bubbled through her, boiling her blood.

"Grendel?"

She barely heard the princess's concerned whisper. Her sole focus was on the evil elf. "You"—she pointed an unsteady finger—"will never touch my sister again." Her voice wavered, cracking at the end.

She was changing again. Only this time, she wasn't afraid. She was furious and welcomed the change. Aching pain radiated through every part of her body. Clutching her cape tight, she was surprised when it grew with her. That hadn't happened before. Usually, the fabric split and remained as tight fragments around her.

The Erlking's smiling demeanor changed. He raised his hand as if to signal something.

Out of the corner of her eye, she noticed Glory lift her aethrial.

Hands now clenched, the Erlking glared at the fairy princess. Five rats tottered to join their master, their beady eyes bright and noses twitching. Before she saw them move, Grendel knew their target was Princess Glory.

Grendel embraced the anger and searched for a way to defend her friend. A dead tree stuck out to their left. She tugged at it as if it were a weed. Because it was rotten, the bottom splintered. Dirt flew everywhere as she yanked it free.

The rats surrounded Glory. A bubble of protective magic

kept her safe, but she knew by the way her wings hung limp that Glory's strength was waning.

Grendel swung the mighty trunk, hitting two of the rats and knocking them away. One rose again, but the other limped and fell back to the ground, its leg broken. She readied to swing again, but pressure on the log hindered her.

The children had jumped onto the limb to keep her from defending Princess Glory. She roared, spittle flying from her mouth. They did not react. They were fully under the Erlking's spell.

She shook the trunk, and several of the children fell. Another jerking fling dislodged all but one—Galumph. Grendel dropped the tree, stomped over to her sister, and hauled her off. With another growling roar, she lifted the trunk again and swung, just as the princess's bubble dispersed.

She caught three of the remaining attacking rats and pivoted, drilling the tree with the rats on it into the ground. They didn't rise.

Glory twirled, holding the aethrial in her hand like a weapon, and the attacking rat missed her by mere centimeters. It rallied quickly, digging its sharp teeth into her arm. Sparks crackled on her hands, but her magic died.

Grendel bellowed, dropping the tree. Fear over her friend's fate spurred her on. She grabbed the rat by its scruff and shook it hard. It wriggled, but she had a good grasp on it. It squeaked furiously. She smacked it against an oak tree, and a crunch ended the squeaking critter.

Tossing the lifeless animal, Grendel turned back to Princess Glory. She was bent over, holding her arm to her chest. Silver bloomed across her white outfit. Tingles spread across Grendel's body as she shrank back to her smaller size. In an instant, she grabbed her bag and dug inside for the bandages and potions she'd packed just in case.

The princess cried out when Grendel moved her arm. "I have to tear the fabric to access the wound." With a nod, Grendel did just that. The bite was clean—no shredding or other damage—but wide and fairly deep.

"Where'd the bad man go?" Galumph's timid voice asked from behind her.

Though glad to hear her sister's unenthralled voice, Grendel's hand stilled. She glanced up. The Erlking had disappeared, and so had his pet bugs.

~Horra~

HORRA DISCOVERED she could not steer the wyvern. It snaked through the forest, curling around trees and changing directions often. "Thank you for saving me, but where are we going?"

No answer.

She wished she could communicate with it like the Lady seemed to have done. Sadness pricked Horra's heart at the thought of the late dryad. Horra blew a raspberry. "How many have suffered because of the Erlking? How many more will suffer before we can defeat him?"

The wyvern grunt-bellowed, its nose in the air as if catching a whiff of something.

"What is it?" Horra wasn't sure if the dragon was a boy or a girl, so she didn't even try to address it.

It responded with a low rumbling noise.

Horra sighed. She could jump off, but they were far too high for her to land without breaking several bones. The trees whizzed by, but the arching motion of the wyvern made it difficult to know if she'd actually land where she aimed. Frustration niggled her insides. She needed to find Rowan.

Horra turned her head when she heard voices. She tapped the dragon's neck on the right side. "Over there," she said, hoping it might understand.

It flew straight for another few seconds before dipping.

Horra floundered, trying to find purchase with her claws so she didn't slide down the dragon's long neck. Just as she slid forward, it reared and evened out. "Gah! This is as bad as riding in a carriage with that crazy fairy in control."

Wings flapping, they hovered, then landed.

She could still hear the voices, but they were behind them now. Horra shimmied to the side of the wyvern, clinging to the wing so she wouldn't fall before she was ready. It shook, breaking her grasp, and she tumbled anyway.

Horra landed hard on her behind. "Ow. First you save me, then you rudely knock me off?" She rose, rubbing her backside.

The wyvern flashed and disappeared.

Horra gaped. "Dragon's fire! You're sneakier than Glory, and that's saying something."

"Did I hear my name?"

Horra spun and came face-to-face with Glory, Grendel, and a flock of children. The fairy's white outfit stood out where it wasn't covered in grass, grime, and silver bloodstains.

"What happened to you?" she asked, concerned.

Glory scowled.

"That bad man's rabid rat bit her," said one of the hobgoblins.

"And it might'a been full'n diseases," a dwarf child piped up, emphasizing the last word.

"But Grendel saved her. She smashed it to pieces." A giant girl clutching Grendel's hand dropped it and swung her arms as if she were replaying what the giantess had done. A wide smile creased her orange freckled face.

Horra squinted. The sun had dipped low enough that it was hard to see them. "Galumph?"

The girl nodded like a gulpy, bobbing her head quickly up and down.

Horra finished brushing the debris from her pant legs and joined them. "Okay. Seems I missed a lot. Could someone please fill me in?"

~Rowan~

ROWAN REMOVED the last seed from his crown. Using a shovel he'd magicked from a rock, he dug three feet past the contaminated layers of soil. He placed the seed, bent over, and blinked. Three golden magic-filled tears fell from his eye onto the seed.

He muttered a blessing over the soil he'd removed and pushed it back over the seed. A honeyed glow radiated around the spot. "That is good," he muttered and stood, stretching his back. The magic he'd siphoned from the pool was almost gone. He'd concentrated it into the teardrops, much like the Lady had done when calling the plants to life for her daughter's internment ceremony.

It had fascinated him then. Now experiencing the raw, pure magic, he understood how the dryad had called upon such power. Life itself held power, he now knew. Not that he hadn't been aware of it before. But the unadulterated magic had released new information in his brain stem, and it was exhilarating.

Rowan cleared another spot away for his roots, searching to

access more of the pool. If he could access all the magic, it would only take a thought to purge the Wilden Lands of the Erlking forever.

And after that—the things he could do! He could revitalize the Weald. Reestablish the druid race once his seeds matured. He'd spend his days teaching and his nights communicating with the roods. It would be an ideal life. The euphoria of the magic had him believing everything was possible.

Rowan smelled the worqs—five of them—after his roots sank in and stretched out, seeking the pool. It took effort to drag his roots back in. He rallied the magic, but he didn't have enough to fight off that many brutes. His mistake was letting his guard down in enemy territory. The queen bearer would berate him for it. He berated himself.

An axe came into sight before it hit, digging into his wooden body. Pain radiated through his head. And then ... only darkness.

~Torren~

EVENING HAD FALLEN BEFORE TORREN, Balk, Murda and, unbelievably, the dozen elves arrived at the strange forest. He'd only wished to recruit Balk and Murda, but Torren had to remind Balk of his pledge to Oddar to coerce him into coming. He was not happy to leave the search for his daughter behind.

As the trio left, they ran across the elves who had been sitting down to a meal at the edge of the Riven's border. They'd insisted on coming along.

"No one's here," the elf Belamir said. He seemed to be their leader or the oldest member of their council.

Torren bit back his frustration at the aloof elf. "I know. As I explained, they all disappeared before I left. You said you could help, since it sounded like another Riven."

Murda moved to stand beside him. She'd taken the reins after Pidge's third attempt at chasing a critter in the weeds, allowing Torren to take the lead. "It doesn't look like anything other than a clearing."

He nodded. "It looks stranger when you're flying above it."

The elves murmured to one another in a foreign language. The sounds were familiar to Torren's ears, but the soft consonants and long vowels made no sense to him. And they spoke so swiftly, it was hard to understand where each word started and ended.

Balk jerked his head toward the group. "What do you mean by that?"

Startled by the violent undertone in the bocan's voice, Torren glanced at the elves.

They jumped at Balk's loud demand and stopped talking. Wide-eyed, they glanced back and forth at each other.

Guilt. That's what that expression was. Torren was sure of it.

Balk's glare was sharp as he clenched the sword belted to his side. "I understand lower-caste elven."

It shouldn't have surprised Torren, especially since he now spoke worqish because of the Erlking. However, whatever the elves said bothered the bocan a great deal. He'd rarely seen Balk this worked up—and then only when it pertained to his daughter or the Erlking, who he believed had taken her.

Balk drew the sword out of its hilt. He raised it slowly and held the tip even with the lead elf's throat. The orange sunset glowed on the silver blade like flames. With a start, Torren realized it was fire. Balk used his metalmagic on it. "Out with it."

Belamir lifted his chin at the obvious threat. "Lower your weapon."

The flames on the sword changed from orange to blue. "Not until you explain to me how you know there are children in this forest. And expound on that little detail about the Erlking's oread heritage."

Torren's and Murda's mouths dropped open.

CHAPTER 30

Horra tried not to laugh at Glory's injury. They sat in a circle with the children surrounding the three of them. "You let a rat bite you?"

Glory released a long-suffering breath. "I didn't *let* it do anything. The Erlking sicced them on us. Do I look like a troll knight? I wield magic, not muscle."

Horra's lips twitched. "Then why didn't you engage your magic? I mean, it wouldn't have taken much for a mighty fairy to thwart a rat." She was teasing. The rats could be formidable when there were more than one and no Pidge around to prey on them. But humor was better than letting her fear of not finding Rowan in time overcome her.

"I depleted my magic with the carriage and with the musical spells we've used since entering this dingy place. All I had was the aethrial. I wasn't about to break it. It's one of a kind." She held up the instrument and gasped. A crack ran

257

along the center of the pipes from one end to the other. "That little bugger ruined my aethrial. Ah, my sister is going to kill me." Her voice ended in a high-pitched shriek. Her face crumpled, and she bent over her knees, panting.

Horra patted the fairy on her back. It served the girl right for borrowing the items without permission. "Look on the bright side. We defeat the Erlking, and your sister has no other option but to forgive you."

Glory groaned into her knees.

Grendel wrung her pawed hands together. "But the children. What will we do without the aethrial if the Erlking comes back?"

Horra smirked. "We scare you into your beast form, then you crush him like the rat fink he is." She held her hands up when Grendel opened her mouth. "I'm kidding. Look. If we let fear take over, we'll never form a plan." She glanced over at the children, and the responsibility of having this many lives in their hands—her claws—settled on her shoulders. "And we definitely need a plan."

Something white flickered in the corner of Horra's left eye. She glanced but saw nothing. Fatigue? Horra rubbed her face. "Do any of the children know a way out of this forest?"

Glory sat up, her panic now under control. "They know which direction not to go. But so far, none of them have outright mentioned it."

Another ghostly figure flickered in the depths of the forest behind the outer circle but vanished before Horra could focus on it. Her pulse raced. One flicker she could chalk up to being tired. Two meant they might be in danger. Could she hope to move such a crowd of children if another of the Erlking's surprises showed up?

Shuffling from a different direction distracted Horra.

"Something's happening," she whispered to Glory and Grendel, not desiring to frighten the children.

Grendel glanced into the distance without saying a word. Galumph sat next to her, far enough away she probably didn't hear what Horra said.

Glory swiped a finger across the aethrial. The crack in the wood sewed itself up, leaving behind only a small sliver to show it was still there. "I have enough power for one spell. Plug your ears." She lifted the instrument with her good hand, bending so she could still access her injured arm, and played. This time her fingers didn't fly across the pipes but moved across them in a slow progression.

"What are you doing?" Horra asked, her eyes on the slumping, tired children.

Grendel's eyes were wide as she nodded to her sister.

Glory shook her head.

Yawns broke out. Heads drooped. Children snuggled against each other. In less than two minutes, they were asleep.

Lowering the aethrial, Glory waved.

Horra stared at the fairy. "Why'd you do that?"

She quirked her lip on one side. "I used to play that lullaby for Misty when I wanted to sneak out of our bedroom at night. I added the last of my magic to it. It wasn't much, but they should snooze through the rest of the night and wake feeling refreshed. I wish I could utilize it on myself sometimes."

Glory stood, stretched, then glanced at Horra and Grendel. One wing hung lower than the other, and she cradled her injured arm to her stomach. "Well? What are you waiting for? The children are safe. I doubt the Erlking could wake them since they were already exhausted before we found them."

Grendel gently placed her sister's head—which had ended up in her lap after the lullaby—on the ground and tucked her wild hair behind her ears. "You're sure?"

"Yes. I'd say, have I ever lied to you, but—"

Snores filled the forest. "Well, even the bugs have bedded down. I think it will be okay," Horra said, joining Glory.

Grendel frowned but stood. "Grab the sharpened sticks. We might need weapons other than our hands."

~Rowan~

ROWAN OPENED his eyes to a blurry sight. He blinked, but it didn't help. His head ached and his roots throbbed. What had happened?

He lifted a hand to check a painful spot above his eye, and something held his arm back.

Creak-clack-pop-pop.

Dry grit grated across his eyes, his vision too bleary to know who spoke and what was happening. Rowan turned his head to listen and realized the noises were an ancient forest language used by wood sprites. Whoever they were told him to stay still and don't touch.

He cleared his throat. "Where am I? What is going on?"

Someone tossed liquid in his face.

Rowan jerked backward, scrunching his eyes closed. Incensed, he pushed away whoever they were and swiped his hands across the moisture. But it was too late. He rubbed the stinging sensation away. "What are you doing to me?" He blinked several times. His sight cleared when the pain subsided. He opened his eyes again, and everything came back into focus. "Oh, that's much better. Thank you."

He was still in the dark forest—his roots detected the Erlking's tainted brand in the soil. Before him, however, stood a dozen ghostly tree figures. Pale and skeletal, they were oreads, the counterpart to dryads, though they looked nothing like the more attractive females of the species. Half Ghost Trees as well, their faces were merely marks on their barkish skin. "Oh my." He stared. "That was exceedingly fast."

They creaked and snapped, their mouths not yet formed enough for regular speech. Though Rowan wasn't sure if oreads spoke anything but old woodland tongues. Their feet were actual appendages, not roots, and their arms were barely bigger than their thin trunks. Their fully formed hands ground and mixed ingredients to make a paste in a hollowed hole of a large broken tree limb.

"What is that?" Rowan asked. He listened until he realized they were creating a healing ointment for his head. A vivid memory of a worq hitting him with an axe flashed across his mind. He lifted his hand once more to touch the wound, but three of the little sprigs jumped on his arm. "Oh, dear. Yes. What happened to the worq?"

The group split apart. On the ground lay a dead worq. Drag marks showed they had moved the creature away to work on him. "Did you kill him?"

Knock-creak-pop!

"Ah, good. I'm glad it wasn't you. Possibly this was one of the worqs who agreed to a pact with the queen bearer. That would explain why he collapsed after attacking me. Carry on, then."

They sprang into action—odd-looking miniature halflings running around him, some traveling via trees to other areas to grab something and add it to the lotion. Using a chunk of bark, they scooped the concoction onto the gash, surprising him with their dexterity. It had taken him weeks to grow that steady after he'd unrooted.

Pain flared anew and dizziness threatened. Rowan closed his eyes against the agony and realized his roots were still sunk deep into the ground. He stretched out and found the edge of the pure magic pool before his roots refused to go any farther. It was enough. Between the small amount his roots soaked up and the healing ointment—which his fibers recognized as tingleroot paste—his sapwood was able to sew itself back together. Thankfully, the wound hadn't reached his heartwood, or it would've been more difficult to heal.

Tears formed in Rowan's eyes. When he was a sapling, Merrow had used the tingleroot paste to heal the damage the Erlking inflicted on his seed during the trek to the Weald. How did these creatures know how to create the miraculous salve? He wasn't sure. What was important was that the formula wasn't lost like he'd thought it was after Merrow's death.

Minutes later, the pain lessened. Callus, a natural form of healing tissue, formed over the injury, sealing the open cut with new wood. Rowan let out a relieved breath. He hadn't envisioned the magical blessing gifted from the Lady and Merrow would combine in such an extraordinary way. "Thank you, younglings. Now, let's finish this war."

Snap-snap-creak. Pop.

Rowan grinned at their eagerness.

~Torren~

"Oreads?" Torren's eyes bulged, but he couldn't help it. "They don't exist anymore."

Pidge screeched above them, having broken free while Murda was goggling. Nimble answered her with a distant bellow.

In a flash, the wyvern appeared, scattering them in different directions. It growled at the elves.

Torren stood still as its tail wrapped around him, Murda, and Balk. Its dark eyes gleamed in the dim light of dusk. It opened its mouth, baring its teeth at the Council.

Balk glanced from the tail's protective barrier to the elves, a smile stretching across his white-and-black painted face. "Tell me, gentle elves, what your search for the Erlking, the oreads, missing children, and a gaggle of wyverns have to do with each other?" He patted the scaled tail lightly.

Hostile eyes glared back at the bocan.

An elf lurched, and the wyvern hissed at it. Spittle flew from its mouth.

The elf jerked away from the spit. It sizzled where it landed.

Torren stiffened. He'd fed the wyvern before, brushed it down, all the while never realizing the full extent of the danger he'd been working around. Sweat dotted his brow.

The wyvern turned to glance at him, sniffed, and bellowed a low rumble.

Torren closed his eyes.

"That's a wyvern's way of assuring you, you dimwit," an elf said. "Trolls are so droll."

Torren peeked with one eye. The wyvern returned to glaring at the elves, teeth bared.

"I don't think it approves of your attitude. I have to say, neither do I. So let's get down to some answers before either of us loses our patience." Balk swung his flaming sword in a circle and grinned.

Pidge dove and dropped a trit-trot-sized rat in front of the wyvern. She preened, fluffing her feathers. Then she, too, turned to stare bright-eyed at the elves.

Belamir clenched his jaw, then shrugged. "Fine. Get comfortable. It's a long tale." He sat on the ground, and the other elves followed suit.

The three of them remained standing, as the wyvern's position inhibited them from sitting. The creature tore into the rat and voraciously ate while the elves talked.

"When our kind left the Wilden Lands to create an enlightened empire, we didn't go alone. We took the oreads with us to help us tame the mountainous forest ranges we'd chosen. Some dyrads came, but most of them stayed, not wishing to leave their homes behind. What we didn't realize when we established Endwylde was that others already inhabited it."

Balk grunted. "Who?"

"The drow," Belamir said darkly. "They are a subrace of dark elves created by witches. Disease-ridden and dark magic-wielding, they were almost our undoing. It took several generations, but we conquered them. After that, we established the Riven for the drow loyalists and halfling children they spawned to occupy."

"Was that before or after you experimented on them?" Torren said, recalling what the fairy princess had told them.

The elf's brows rose. "Where did you hear that?"

"Your scientific studies are well-known to the outside kingdoms," Balk said, leaning on the wyvern's wide tail. It had lain down and was dozing now, having fully devoured the rat. Pidge rested beside the dragon, her beak tucked into her wing. "I've met with several elf runaways in the search for my daughter, Floke."

Belamir frowned. "Runaways."

Balk waved a nonchalant hand. "Mongrels, I believe you call them. Elves like the Erlking, whose only offense was being born to the wrong line of elf kind. Do not waste my time trying to portray yourselves as martyrs. You're far from that. And you still haven't explained why you left your lofty kingdom to search for this mongrel."

"Because he defied us," yelled Belamir. His chest heaved.

Torren's head spun. "Wait. Wait. You disappeared from the Wilden Lands to establish a sovereign kingdom free from us lesser creatures and stayed there for how many generations?" He shrugged off Murda's warning claw. "And you don't show your faces until *this* Erlking comes along and defies you? That's it? Did you realize another Erlking existed before him who sent a plague across the Wilden Lands, killing thousands of creatures and starting a war?"

Torren ran his claws through his hair, longing to tear it out. "My father died because of this Erlking. Dozens of trolls died because of him. But you don't rouse yourself to come and fix any of the mess you created until a half-breed monster *defies* you."

"Mongrel," Belamir and Balk said at the same time.

Torren's heart pounded so hard he feared it would come through his chest. The absolute audacity of the elves was beyond his understanding. "I don't care what you call him. The queen bearer might not be here, but let me assure you—I am in charge in her absence. You"—he pointed at Belamir—"agreed to an oath with my queen and our kingdom that you would set right what you put into place. Since you know so much about hidden forests, let's focus on finding this one."

CHAPTER 31

~Horra~

Horra, Glory, and Grendel walked in a close formation through the dark forest. Horra had noticed one or two more of the phantoms, but they disappeared too fast.

"Do you think they're ghosts?" Grendel asked, a quiver in her voice.

Glory tsked. "Ghosts of what? Trees?"

A flicker, closer this time, came from the trunk of one tree and flitted to another. Horra pointed to the tree it disappeared into. "Did you see that?"

Grendel's mouth hung open.

"Huh. And I thought I was being sarcastic," Glory said.

"Could it be a dryad? It glows like one.' Horra creeped closer to the tree. Behind her, Glory yipped.

"It's over there," she said, motioning Horra to go left.

Horra spun around but saw nothing. "Where?"

"Well, it was right there." Glory stomped over to the tree and placed her palm on the trunk.

A twig of a creature stepped out of the tree and ran straight into Glory.

Crack-pop-pop-creak.

It disappeared back inside the tree.

"What was that?" Grendel rushed to Glory's side.

Horra rubbed her eyes. "It looked like a miniature Rowan if he were less tree-ish."

"And white like the Ghost Tree," Glory agreed.

They all looked at each other. "Rowan," they all said at once.

Horra led them, creeping through the forest in search of their woodgoblin druid friend. "Rowan!" she yelled.

"Why are we being sneaky if we're going to yell?" Glory half-whispered.

Horra stopped but then straightened. "I don't know. It just seemed like the thing to do."

The flutter of a thousand wings startled the girls. Horra drew her dagger out and held it in front of her. Grendel and Glory stood with their backs to her in a triangle formation. The small space between them was filled with the fairy's wings.

"Ah, dear. Still here, are we?" The Erlking stepped out of the tree the little ghost twig had emerged from.

Glory was the one who faced him. Horra had to rotate to see the ghoulish elf, who was standing as if he hadn't a care in the world, hands clasped calmly in front of him and dim light gleaming upon his ghastly bald head.

Glory straightened. "Yes. It's too bad about your pet rats, though."

"One would think that after being hexed several times, you'd watch your mouth." He flicked a hand, the spell blending in with the darkness.

"Duck!" Glory yelled, grabbing their clothes and jerking them with her to the ground.

Grendel wasn't fast enough. She staggered as the magic pummeled her. A scream ripped from her chest. Her cry ended in a growl and her body shook, quaking with her change.

Horra grasped her pant leg, but it was ripped away as the girl grew. This was faster than any of her other changes.

She shot up two, three, four times her regular size.

Grendel stood well over the Erlking. He waved his hands, and she roared. He pumped his arms in a strange formation. The noise coming from the chitterbugs rose. Grendel was not amused. She swung her sharp nails at him, knocking him over. Another fierce roar, and she pounced.

The Erlking stretched his leg and touched the tree. In the blink of an eye, he was gone. The chitterbugs fluttered away.

Silence.

"What? Where'd he go?" Horra asked.

Grendel hunched over the spot where the Erlking had disappeared. With a final howl, she shrank and collapsed to the ground.

"Grendel?" Horra rushed to her, breaking her descent. "Are you okay?"

"Tired. So tired." Her head flopped to the side, and a snore broke from her nose.

"Well, I guess it's only you and me," Horra said to Glory. When the fairy didn't answer her, she glanced over. Glory was hunched over and trembling. Horra crawled over to Glory on her knees. "Hey, he's gone."

The fairy shook her head. "I know." Her voice quaked, and she cleared her throat. "I just remember—"

Horra settled a claw on the fairy's knee. "When he hexed you. Do you wish to stay with Grendel? I can go search for Rowan alone."

Glory nodded. "I'm s-sorry."

"Take my dagger. I have two good claws. I can defend myself if I need to." She handed her the bejeweled dagger.

"I won't ruin it. I p-promise." Her wings hung limp, dangling on the ground.

"If you have to brandish it, I don't care if it's left in pieces as long as you survive, okay?"

Glory gave her a tremulous smile. "Okay."

Horra stood to go.

Glory caught her claw, stopping her. "Thank you." Tears glittered in the girl's eyes.

Horra shifted, uncomfortable. "It's only a dagger."

"It's more than that, and you know it. I know it. It's precious. I won't break it."

Horra squeezed her hand and strode away, a lump in her throat. She traveled for several minutes before she found another branchy ghost darting between trees. "Strange. Only dryads can do that," she whispered.

Crunching footsteps sounded on her right. She slipped over to the nearest tree that was big enough to hide behind. Heart hammering, she peeked around the trunk to see what she was hiding from.

Voices spoke but were too dim to distinguish words or who they belonged to. A screech accompanied them.

"Pidge?" Horra said, not too loud.

Screeching answered her.

Horra's heart rate picked up as glee filled her. She waved her hand, still unsure who had spoken. "Here, girl," she mumbled.

In the blink of an eye, the wyvern was beside her. Horra plastered herself to the tree's trunk, her heart racing for a different reason. "Vinegar! You're worse than Pidge and Rowan combined."

"Horra?" Murda called out.

"Over here," she said, trying to catch her breath.

The wyvern rubbed its head on Horra's arm, a gurgling cackle resonating from its chest.

Horra awkwardly patted it on the head. "Good ... wyvern."

Pidge fluttered to the ground beside her. She pecked at Horra's shirt. "Sorry, girl. I don't have a snack for you."

"She feasted on some rats a bit ago," Torren said, stepping around the pudge wudgie. "I think she's happy to see you."

Horra swallowed her relief. "I'm so glad to see you guys."

Balk strode beside the wyvern with no fear of the dragon in his eyes. "What about me?"

"You too." She sniffed. "I left Glory and Grendel not too far from here. Glory's injured, and Grendel's changed so often she's zonked out. Oh, and there are hundreds of children here, so watch out for them."

Balk's gaze sharpened. "Where? Did you see any bocan children?"

"There were some, yes, but I was separated from everyone and spent little time with them. Glory and Grendel can fill you in."

The Sylvan Council stepped into sight, though they stayed well away from them and the wyvern.

"I thought you were cleaning the Riven up." Horra glanced at Balk and Torren, who both frowned.

"There's a lot to catch you up on," Torren said, taking her arm and leading her away from the tree and the wyvern. "First, let's find the others."

~Glory~

Glory's injured arm ached, her wing throbbed, and she was exhausted. She had moved away from the tree, suspicious of whatever else might come out of it, and rested against the snoring giant girl. The dagger was not smooth, so she set it in her lap. But she picked it up every time a small sound echoed across the silent landscape.

She blew out a frustrated breath. "No way am I falling asleep," she said to convince herself to stay awake.

Rustling came from the direction Horra had walked off. Clutching the dagger tight, she lifted it in warning. "Don't come any closer, or you'll regret it."

A screech and a flutter of wings.

"Pidge?" Glory yelled, relief flowing like melted butter through her veins. "Is that you?"

"It's us," Horra called before her shadowed figure came into view.

Murda, Torren, the bocan, and the elven council members all accompanied Horra.

Suddenly, the wyvern stood in front of her.

Glory fell backward over Grendel's body. "What in the Wilden Lands?" She scrambled to rise but bumped her injured arm. "Ow, ow, ow."

The dragon let out a rumbling purr and leaned against her.

She cringed. "Don't let it eat me."

Horra helped her to her feet. "It won't eat you. For some reason, it has decided we are its pack or something."

Glory stepped away from the offending animal. "Yes, well, that makes one of us."

"How's your arm?" Murda asked. "Horra told us a rat bit you? I have some first aid in my bag. Let me check your bandage."

She let the troll knight unwrap Grendel's bandage.

Murda rotated her arm, looking it over. "Ugh. It got you good. This really needs to be stitched up."

"You guys are supposed to be the greatest magic users. Are you able to heal her?" Horra asked the standoffish elves.

Each of them either glanced away, sniffed, or grunted.

Horra pounded a fist on her hip. "The rats are an Erlking problem, which the oath you agreed to included."

The middle elf—the one with the most disgusting long ears—stepped forward. "Of course, Your Majesty." His words were polite, but a scowl opposed what he said. He walked a wide arc around the wyvern's tail. "This might sting a bit."

"Her wing too, if you would. And can you do it so it doesn't hurt?" Horra asked, her contrary haughtiness emerging.

For once, Glory was glad for it. She wasn't sure if she should trust this elf—or any elf, for that matter. Look what the Erlking had done to her.

He frowned. "I'll do my best."

"And you won't sneak a different spell in. Only healing, right?" Glory said, a tinge of hysteria edging her voice.

The elf stopped and bowed. "I will do you no harm—on my honor." He placed his hands on her arm—one above and one below. A spark, then a glow, emanated from his hands.

At first, a warm sensation was all she felt. Then, when the magic finished assessing the injury and targeted the wound itself, pain flared. She bit back a cry, turning her head away and gritting her teeth.

Someone clasped her shoulder gently and squeezed.

When the elf finished and the cut sealed, he worked on her wing. It took less time, since it was a simpler injury.

She could almost taste the relief flowing through her body. Glory glanced at Horra's claw on her shoulder. Dirt crusted beneath her clawnails, and a couple were chipped. If anyone would've told her days ago that she would find comfort from the troll's nasty clawed hand, she would've argued with them. How things had changed. Glory gave her a trembling smile in thanks.

Her torn flesh was now a shiny-white, uneven line. Gently, she touched the skin around the blemish. It would scar, but for once, that didn't bother her. The scar would prove to everyone what she'd survived. Like the cuts on the bocan's arm signifying his vanquished enemies, it was an outward show of a battle—a much more worthy possession than unblemished beauty.

She turned to the elf. "Thank you."

He nodded back, this time without a frown.

"Do you still desire to stay with Grendel?" Horra asked.

"I can stay with her," Murda offered.

Glory considered that. Though fear sparked inside her at the thought of facing the Erlking again, she'd survived the Erlking's and his pets' violent attack twice now. A new sense of courage awakened and inspired her. "I'm going with you. Let's take the Erlking down."

CHAPTER 32

Rowan unrooted after the dip in the pool rejuvenated him, though he vowed not to let the power blind him to the surrounding dangers again. "I need the queen bearer's golden sword. I lost it when I fell." He sent an image to his offspring. "Three of you, spread out and retrieve it. Bring it back to me as soon as you locate it. I am headed for the Erlking's camp."

Obediently, three of the saplings disappeared into different trees.

Satisfied, Rowan turned to his next task. "The rest of you, search for the magical footings and destroy them."

They skittered away into the trees. Quickly following their departure, the first three returned. It took all three of them to carry the heavy golden sword and present it to him.

Rowan accepted the weapon in its leather holder. "Quickly managed. Excellent job, younglings. Now, scatter and hide. I

275

am going to search for my band of companions, but I must do it on foot. I will call if I need you."

The ghostly figures disappeared into different trees. Pride welled inside Rowan. He wondered if he had elicited the same emotion from Woodsly's rood. Why had the comments from the queen bearer about her old instructor always frustrated him so? He pondered this as he walked. A vague notion that he'd yearned to stand on his own merit flitted through his mind. The fact he'd followed such a revered figure also rubbed his bark the wrong way.

He now understood what it meant to produce something so valuable. And his resentment, or whatever emotion he'd held against his forebringer, fell away. He leaned against a tree and closed his eyes. "Forgive my misplaced pride, Woodsly."

It took several moments for the rood to respond. *"Pride is a two-sided coin, young druid. You need a helpful measure if you are to lead and succeed. Your path was perilous from the start and is not over yet. Do not be burdened by what has passed. Focus on your steps ahead. That is burden enough."*

Woodsly's presence faded, leaving Rowan standing alone in the dark forest. No, not alone, he realized. He'd never been alone. Grateful, he continued on toward his friends.

Rowan heard them before he saw them. Pidge's screeches welcomed him first. She landed in front of him and rubbed her head on his trunk, chirruping.

"Yes, yes. I'm glad to see you too." He scratched her favorite spot beneath her chin.

"Rowan? Is that you?" Queen Bearer Fyd called out.

"Yes—" Between one step and the next, the wyvern appeared in front of him. Rowan stumbled, but it drew close and sniffed at the paste covering his wound. It opened its mouth and roared, its hot breath washing over the injured area. A burning sensation lit, traveling along a path from one side of the callus to the other. He touched the area and found it had crusted over and was no longer tender.

"Stop it! It's attacking Rowan," Torren yelled.

Rowan held up a hand to keep them away. "It is not hurting me."

Horra yanked at the dragon's wing. "Allow him some space, you big goon." The wyvern curled its neck around and snorted into the queen bearer's unruly red hair.

A loud guffaw burst out of Torren, and the knight bent over with inelegant, snorting laughter. "You," he chuckled, "have a way with animals."

Princess Glory snickered behind an elegant hand, shrugging when the queen bearer sent her a withering glance. "What? That was funny."

A grin quirked along Rowan's lips as he recalled that Nimble had done the same thing while they'd been on mission to find Princess Glory. Then, she'd had to clean gulgoyle snot out of her hair.

The Sylvan Council hovering behind his three companions stood stoic, unmoved by the event. No, not unmoved. Disgusted, if the appalled looks on their faces read right to Rowan.

Sympathy for the stiff elves and their bereft sense of humor rose inside him. A bubble of laughter escaped his clenched mouth.

The queen bearer slowly turned toward him. "Did you just laugh at me?"

Rowan cleared his throat, still fighting back his laughter. It was wonderful to be in the presence of his friends again, which lightened his mood beyond what he would've imagined. "My apologies, Queen Bearer. That was inappropriate of me."

"Inappropriate!" Emotions played across her expressive green face. "It's not only inappropriate."

Rowan braced himself for her ire.

Instead of anger, she smiled. "It's incredible. Rowan, you've matured. Wit is one of the most complicated emotions, and you just showed you have a sense of humor!" She slapped his arm. "Good for you, old friend."

Warmth caught in his heartwood and spread out. "That is true, isn't it?"

Torren, still snickering, chucked him on his shoulder. "It is."

Rowan basked in their praise. "Yes, well. Be that as it may, there is still much to do." He steepled his fingers in front of him.

"You have a plan, don't you?" the queen bearer asked.

"I do. But first, where is Grendel?"

~Horra~

HORRA AND GLORY took turns informing Rowan of what had happened since they'd been separated. Rowan, in turn, filled them in on his experiences since being dragged into the forest after his fall.

Pidge darted around the area, devouring errant chitterbugs flying about. The wyvern had settled between them like a cat, its barbed tail over its nose, napping.

When the druid finished, Horra gaped at him, then glanced at his bare, broken crown. "You—what?" The dragon opened its golden eyes, darted between them, then shut them once again.

Rowan clacked and swept an arm wide. Two ghoulish twig creatures stepped out of separate trees. They snapped and popped in a very woodgoblin way.

The dragon jumped up, its tail banging against the ground

excitedly. It sniffed the two Ghost Tree oreads, licking one of them.

Horra jumped away from the twiggish creatures, pointing at them. "That's what we saw. Grendel thought they were ghosts. I knew they looked like you."

His eyebrows rose, though the one he'd injured stretched tight.

She narrowed her glance at the wound. "You could've been killed." She automatically reached out her claw to inspect the gash.

He leaned away from her. "Personal space, please, Queen Bearer."

She pursed her lips.

Behind her, Glory and Torren snickered.

"All right. I may have deserved that. Now, what's your plan?"

"We check on Grendel and the children. The Erlking travels via tree, so he could pop up anywhere in this forest, like my saplings." Rowan crackled at the ghostly twigs. "Does anyone volunteer to go with them?"

Balk lifted his arm. "I need to see if my Floke is with the children."

"I'll go," Murda offered.

"Very well. The rest of us will travel to the center where the Erlking has placed his camp. We'll find him there," Rowan assured them.

They split up. Rowan led her, Glory, Torren, and the elves. Pidge and the wyvern followed, flying or winking in and out of sight next to someone. It was unnerving, but Horra didn't wish to leave them or tie them up, if one could tie a wyvern up. It would simply disappear before she could even begin to try. And Pidge would always come back to her.

One question burned in Horra's mind. "How is the Erlking able to travel through trees?" she asked.

"I don't understand myself," Rowan said.

Torren grunted. "The elves can help you understand that."

Horra, Glory, and Rowan stopped to stare at the elves. If not for her oath covenant with them, they could easily overpower her right now. "Speak."

Belamir's lips thinned. He explained about the witches creating the drow elves, their efforts to eradicate them, and then the creation of the Riven.

"That still doesn't explain why he can utilize trees to move. Is it a magical thing like fairy paths?" Horra's brow crinkled, then twitched. Exhaustion would soon overtake her.

Glory tsked but didn't argue with her assessment. "I'd like to know this myself. It would explain how he can show up unexpectantly in different places."

Rowan held up a finger. "The only creatures known to do that are oreads and dryads. And dryads cannot travel far from their home trees."

The elf shuffled his feet. "It is a long tale."

Impatience bit at Horra's gut. "Break it down so us inferior creatures can understand."

The elf let out a quick puff of breath. "The drows were dangerous. They had to be eradicated."

"But you left the worqs behind after the Witching Wars," Torren pointed out.

He sniffed. "The worqs were dumb animals when we migrated. The drows posed a greater threat. Their magic equaled our own. Drows lived like pigs, in an uncivilized manner. They also carried many diseases we were not previously exposed to. They posed a lethal threat to our numbers. There was no question about what we had to do."

"Kill them," Horra muttered, her anger ramping up inside her.

Rowan clacked a cough. "Which you obviously did a splendid job of, since two of the most reckless ones escaped your imprisonment."

The elf ignored Rowan's pointed observation. "When it was apparent that we could not eliminate the drow menace, either by force or magic, we used the last weapon in our arsenal: gene modification. The drows were powerful, yes, but uneducated. Together with the oreads—with their permission, I might add—we experimented on those we captured. Oreads are beneficial creatures—in tune with nature, peaceful. Our magical genetic manipulations rehabilitated ninety percent of our prisoners. Sadly, eight percent didn't survive. And two percent were irreparable. We exiled them to the Riven, far enough away from Endwylde that they could not intermingle and cause more problems."

Glory gasped. "He was telling the truth. You did experiment on him, then when he didn't measure up, you tortured him by removing his magic and his ears—fat lot of good that did, since he can obviously access them. Then you threw him out."

Pidge scree'd in the distance, the only sound in the silent forest.

Heat traveled up Horra's chest and tingled along her scalp as the information sunk in. "That's unconscionable."

Belamir nodded. "Yes. They were irredeemable."

Horra pointed a claw at him. "Not them. You. Tell me, great and mighty Sylvan, did they attack you first?"

The elf clenched his hands. "Witches created them. Their very existence was blasphemous."

Disbelief clouded Horra's mind for a moment. She shook it off. "You're as awful as all the tales I've heard. No wonder my foremother attacked your kind. I never thought I'd say it, but I almost feel sorry for the Erlking. He never stood a chance in your treacherous kingdom."

Belamir's lips thinned.

"What did the drow look like?" Rowan asked as they started walking again.

"Pale skin, dark veins, and no hair. They are usually gaunt. with bony, witch-like fingers and feet."

Princess Glory's wings tittered, then stilled. She pushed a tangled lock of hair behind her ear. "That's the Erlking in a nutshell. What happened to the oread?"

"They were our keepers of the Riven. That is, until after we placed the second Erlking there. We weren't concerned, until one day, an elven guard went to check on the prisoners and vanished. Other guards sent to find him could not get in. We realized he'd changed the foundational spells. When we breached a boundary, we found the bones and uniform of our missing guard. He'd been dead for quite some time. Then the Riven sealed itself again."

"So what did you do then?" Glory asked, her gaze intent on Belamir's face.

"As we stated, witches created the drow race. They're malevolent by nature. We feared for our lives."

Glory pointed a finger at him. "So you did nothing! How many people stumbled into the Riven from the Wilden Lands and lost their lives?"

Horra sent the fairy a side glance. Since when had the girl become a defender of other creatures?

"Elves live long, but we do not have many children. The Sylvan Council could not risk elf lives by trying to infiltrate the Riven to reset the spells. We came as soon as the dryad queen destroyed the Erlking's spells. On reflection, we should've granted the Conductor—or second Erlking, as you call him—

the mercy he didn't deserve by ending his life instead of placing him in solitary confinement."

"Ah, but you didn't." The Erlking stepped out of a tree. In his hand, he held an elaborate pan flute. Shadowing him was the dryad it must've belonged to. Three worqs accompanied them, one of which held Pidge. "And you will die regretting that decision."

CHAPTER 33

~Rowan~

R owan dug his roots into the ground. "Let the bird go," he demanded.

The queen bearer shrieked and leaped at the worq, her dagger catching it in the shoulder. It roared as Pidge fluttered off.

"Hide, Pidge!" she shouted.

Rowan sent a pulse to the bird, telling her to take cover until the danger was over. Knowing the pudge wudgie, there was only a fifty percent chance she'd actually listen.

His attention returned to the gathering. He witnessed the elves stumbling around in a stupor, running into each other and the trees. It was as if the off-key notes made them blind, mindless, and frantic. This was not the usual spell the Erlking used to gather the children. This was a chaos spell, meant to drive its hearers mad.

Before Rowan could act, a cloud of chitterbugs flooded the

air. Frenzied children came next, weapons in hand and magic flying from their hands.

"I thought you put them to sleep?" The queen bearer's voice rose in alarm as rocks flew through the group. She dove to avoid a large stone.

With an arm over her head, the fairy princess dodged the sticks and snapping spells the children sent out. She bumped into Torren, knocking him sideways and out of the way of the sharpened end of an accurately tossed stick. They tumbled to the ground, Glory tucking her wings as she rolled.

Horra helped them both up and, together with Torren, worked on disarming the magic-less children while dodging the spells from the magic wielders.

Rocks pelted Rowan's crown, snapping more of his outer branches. Chitterbugs fell eagerly upon his splintered flesh. A spell snapped at his trunk, tearing the smooth bark. It held more power than what the children should possess. Though the pure magic he'd ingested earlier was shielding him, the strength behind the spell had him believing the Erlking was siphoning his magic into the song he played.

He thought he would have sensed the Erlking coming, but he hadn't. Somehow, the evil elf accessed the same sigils Rowan had been given by the roods, hiding him effectively when necessary. Even if he hadn't sensed him, he should've known the worqs were close by.

Glory drew out the aethrial and played, her fingers flying over the holes. She moved as furiously as the Erlking, and their magic warred against each other.

"Princess, let me help." Rowan formed a silver ball of magic and tossed it to her, aiming for her hand. It struck her shoulder hard.

The princess shuddered, glaring at him, but his magic settled and she played faster.

With the others occupied, Rowan turned his attention back to the Erlking, who was distracted by the fairy. If only he knew a disarming spell, he could knock the pan flute away from his enemy.

"Galumph! Come back." Grendel's voice leaked into the melee. Larger than normal, but still half the size of a giant, the children's attacks didn't seem to faze her. The younglings went flying as she crawled on her hands and knees, tossing them aside while she searched for her sister. Balk accompanied her from a distance. They worked their way through the children, snapping the sharpened stick weapons in half as they moved through the massive crowd.

By now, chitterbugs crawled all over him, tangling in his branches and digging furiously at the callus. His saplings had disappeared and, though he didn't blame them, he was disappointed.

Then, he saw them in the tree above the Erlking. Four of them hung off a low limb, dangling in a line while precariously holding onto each other, reaching for the Erlking's pan flute. Focused on his tune, the Erlking didn't see them.

But the dryad did. Emotion crossed her barkish face. She reached a hand toward them, and Rowan feared she was going to swat them away. His roots broke through the ground, ready to knock her back. Instead, she bowed her head and stepped away.

Children surrounded the queen bearer and Torren. Horra swung her dagger at the sharpened sticks with some success, but more rocks and magic spells dominated both of them. It wouldn't be long before the children overwhelmed them.

Rowan sent his roots down and farther out. They popped up at the Erlking's feet, and he grabbed the creature's leg. The saplings used that as their opportunity to steal the pan flute. The Erlking jerked the instrument back, breaking the spell momentarily, but the sapling held on. Rowan sent out another root, but the Erlking was ready this time.

Flames erupted from his palm. He touched Rowan's roots, and they instantly caught fire and spread across his rooty flesh.

With a squeal, Rowan drew them back into the ground, but the pain remained even after he doused them with the pool's pure magic.

"Rowan," Grendel said, digging in her bag. She tossed him a vial. "My super-secret special potion incoming."

He snapped it out of the air. Sticking a finger into the sweet liquid, he realized what it was. He tipped it to his mouth and drank. Warmth followed the liquid's path down his throat. It soaked in easier than water, and in an instant, it exploded inside of him, ripping and shredding. A dizzying sensation spread as he expanded, growing in every direction. Then a strange tearing occurred, as if being towed through a too-small hole and carried along on a current. The sensation wasn't good or bad, merely odd.

He blinked and found himself sitting atop a large silvery branch, gazing down at the other trees like they were weeds at his feet. No, that wasn't quite true. He moved and realized he was separate from the tree he rested upon. His offspring joined him in the tree's crown, bouncing from limb to limb, clattering in excited bursts.

And it occurred to him: This was what he had been created to do. All the magic he'd siphoned from the pool brought the immense Ghost Tree to life.

Two saplings took his hands and dragged him off his limb. Then he was inside the tree. Music and voices erupted as roods and dryad spirits crowded in beside them. The tree was large enough, the roots he'd spread out securing it. Light blazed in Rowan's eyes as the tree sparked to life—a sentient being. A sense of rightness clicked into place. This was supposed to happen. This was his sacrifice. It was time for him to finish his divine mission. He stepped out of the light and back into the dark forest.

HORRA SCREAMED as something big bumped into her. It knocked her to the ground, sending her rolling head over feet. "What in dragon's fire?" she said around flying dirt and leaves, glancing at the largest tree she'd ever seen in her life. It towered into the sky.

Pidge's singsong cackle came from above. A gruff roar from the wyvern joined her song.

Torren, lying on the ground several feet from her, glanced at it as well. His mouth hung open and his eyes gaped at the sight before them. "What is that?"

Grendel, now in her regular shrunken size, rushed by. "It's Rowan. I giantized him."

Horra couldn't see around the tree, which now took up an incredible amount of space. Shaken, she placed her claw on the tree to help her stand, and light ignited in her sight.

"*Queen Bearer, it is good to speak with you again,*" a golden figure with Woodsly's voice spoke into her mind.

"Woodsly, how are you here inside ..." She hesitated.

"*This is no longer the home for your druid woodgoblin companion. It is now a holy tree, like the Great Yew tree in the Weald. You have witnessed the birth of a new Weald forest.*"

Horra's heart sank to her feet. "Does that mean Rowan's dead?"

More golden ghost-like figures floated around Woodsly. The tree glowed with an eternal light. "*No. He is very much alive, as are his seedling sprouts. You, however, need to return to the fight. The Erlking needs defeating. Go. Help Rowan finish this battle."*

A pulse shoved Horra's claw off the trunk. She fell into Torren, who had his claws on her shoulder, shaking her.

"Whoa." Horra stared dumbfounded at the tree. "That was intense."

"Are you all right? You went deathly still, and I was afraid something dire had happened to you." Torren swiped his hands through his hair, which was filled with dirt and chitterbugs.

"I hardly know what to say." A rock pelted her backside, snapping her out of her wonder. "Ow." She found the goblin boy who threw the rock and tackled him.

Balk strolled over, carrying a stone. "Let me help." He took the stone and, with his metalmagic, formed cuffs from the metals in the rock to grip the goblin's wrists. "There. That will keep him for a short time."

"Thanks," she said as the bocan rushed back into the crowd.

Torren had already returned to subduing the children.

"Rowan," she called out. "Where are you?"

A slim tree creature stepped from the tree in front of her. "Queen Bearer?" Rowan's voice was younger-sounding, his body much thinner and shorter than before.

She rushed to him. "Rowan, are you all right?"

"Right as rain, Queen Bearer." The high-pitched tone of his voice denoted a younger tree. "Let's finish this," he said, a devious smile creasing his smooth face.

The ground rumbled like the far-off roiling sound of thunder, shaking the area.

Horra windmilled her arms out to keep from falling. "What's happening?"

The bugs whipped around them, frenetic. Three worqs

dashed off to their left, away from the epicenter of the action. The cowards.

Rowan clapped his hands. "My saplings have deconstructed the Erlking's spells at last."

Her eyes widened at his proclamation. The surrounding darkness dissipated, though it was still night out. The thick, fog-like magic vanished.

Children stopped attacking, dropping their hands and weapons. Bugs, followed by the Sylvan Council, dropped to the ground.

No music played. The hushed silence sent chills across Horra's hide.

Horra glanced at Rowan. As one, they both raced around opposite ends of the tree to find the Erlking.

Princess Glory's fingers shifted speeds again, and she loped over to the Erlking. He had fallen to the ground and now sat huddled like a scared child. His keening whines joined the children's sniffles.

"Wait for me." Murda rushed into the throng. Red stained her green hair. She skidded to a stop and stared. "What happened?"

Horra glanced her way. "I think we defeated the Erlking."

Rowan cleared his throat but, instead of two dry sticks rubbing together, it sounded more like a snap and crackle of a wood fire. "Princess, what did you do to the Erlking?"

"The 'Disgrace of the Music Man' song." The fairy produced a torn sheet of paper out of her aethrial bag. "This is the song that took the Music Man down after he lured the children away from the villages. I used his fable against him."

"Yes. Finally!" Horra pumped her arm in the air. "You're pure genius."

Glory shrugged. "I wasn't sure it would work. It's a

children's fable, after all. But by the time I played it, we had nothing to lose."

Torren strode over and picked up the fairy, spinning her around. "Amazing!"

Her wings flicked back and forth, and her face flushed when he set her back on the ground. "Well, I am a musical savant."

In a flash, the Erlking stood, startling them all. "Curses on all of—"

Glory lifted her aethrial.

Horra, her dagger still in hand, pounced on him. The air thickened around him and grew silent as Glory suspended him with her song's spell for a prolonged moment. Horra positioned the blade on the Erlking's throat. "Don't say anything else, or it will be the very last thing you do."

Glory's spell ended, and the Erlking's neck bobbed as he gulped. Her blade dug into the skin but didn't break it.

Thwip.

Something flew by Horra's hair.

She blinked. A web covered the Erlking's mouth. She eased her grasp on the elf and rotated to see where it had come from.

Galumph stood with the large death bringer spider in her arms. Glee lit the girl's face, and she jumped up and down, throttling the deadly critter she hugged like a pillow. "Grendel, I found a new pet." Giggling, the girl ran off, searching for her sister.

Fear wrapped itself around Horra's heart. "Torren, go warn Grendel that the spider Galumph possesses is dangerous. Very, very dangerous."

With a salute, her knight took off running.

Rowan dug the magicuffs from a hidden pocket in his bark. He glided over to the Erlking and snapped the golden restraints over his bony wrists. They shrank to fit tight.

The Erlking jerked, trying to break free from Horra's grip. "Oh no. You're not disappearing this time." She shoved him to sit on the ground. "Stay put."

Balk strode over to her, his hard eyes raking across the Erlking. "I told you one day that dagger would be held to his neck." He patted her on the shoulder. "Job well done, Queen Bearer." He thumped a fist to his chest and bowed in reverence.

Pride filled Horra. "So you did say. Thank you, my friend."

CHAPTER 34

Horra rubbed at a throbbing spot where a rock had struck her side. She would be black and blue for days after this.

"Has anyone seen a bocan child? About yea high?" Balk stepped around the children. "Her name is Floke?"

"I'm Floke," a girl called from behind him.

He spun around, searching. "Where are you? Come to Papa."

A child, taller and older than the rest, stood unsteadily. She was thin. Too thin.

"Floke!" Balk cried. They ran toward each other, children scooting out of their way. He swept her into his arms. "My daughter. I've missed you so."

Floke cried against his shoulder, murmuring "Papa" repeatedly.

Horra's heart swelled, and joy rocked her. Her bocan ally

had not forsaken his cause and had finally found his long-lost daughter.

Moonlight shone across the forest, and the Ghost Tree glowed, giving the area the illusion of sunlight. The chitterbugs, having recovered from their frenzied flight, crawled away, clearing the ground. Children gathered around them. The dryad she'd spied earlier peeked from around a tree. One sapling handed her the pan flute, which she cradled to her chest. Like a ghost, the dryad fled into the night.

Horra scanned the rest of the crowd, looked past the jittery elves, and settled her gaze back on the Erlking. She stowed her dagger away. "What do we do now?"

Rowan dragged the Erlking to his feet. The elf's muffled cries leaked from the webbing across his mouth. "We serve justice." His gaze was steady and sharp. He removed the sword from the scabbard and plunged it into the ground.

The Erlking's eyes widened, and he jerked as if to run away, but vines shot out of the ground, wrapping around him like a cage.

Belamir stood on shaky legs. "Good. It's time he paid for his crimes." The other elves rose, their legs trembling, and joined their leader.

Horra realized they didn't even see their own hypocrisy.

Rowan cleared his throat. "What are his charges?"

Horra straightened, shifting into a more official stance. "Treason against Oddar in the highest degree, false imprisonment of a royal, conspiracy to maim, murder, or otherwise harm creatures from across the Wilden Lands, theft in the first degree for utilizing stolen Oddar land for nefarious reasons, magical and musical manipulation of creatures and critters far and wide, infringement upon every creature heretofore, and … I could go on. Is that enough, or shall I continue?"

"No need." Rowan spun in a half circle. "I call upon you all to aid in this endeavor. As the defendant cannot speak for himself, I must ask you all to bear fair and truthful witness. Is he guilty of the aforementioned charges, and possibly others we did not mention?"

A great cry rose in affirmation.

Rowan gripped the golden hilt. "Are we all in agreement that the first Erlking's curse ends here with the sentencing of the second Erlking, as he has fulfilled that curse? No other curses that he has placed here or across the Wilden Lands shall be loosed or remain. And do we also consent that his magic, musical or otherwise, is removed from this moment forward so that no others shall suffer under his power?"

If the children were confused, none showed it. More calls of agreement answered Rowan's question.

"Then the balance of good and evil, as it pertains to the Erlking, is now restored." Piercing his free hand with the blade, he left a line of sap on the sword.

A resounding crack filled the air as the druid's magic oath sealed his proclamation.

The Erlking whimpered, his dark eyes draining as his power left him. Ice-blue eyes drilled Horra with a furious glare. His chest heaved as his sentence settled.

"Is that it?" Belamir blustered. He stepped toward Rowan, but Torren stopped him.

"We're not finished," Horra sneered. "May I?" she asked Rowan.

"Of course, Queen Bearer." He thumped a hand to his chest and bowed, moving back by the gigantic glowing Ghost Tree.

"I relinquish command of the Erlking into the care of the Sylvan Council—"

"What?" Belamir howled. "He deserves death." The other elves raised their voices, supporting the death penalty.

"Should I have Galumph return with her new pet, Queen Bearer?" Rowan asked, shutting down the elves' complaints.

They fumed in silence, angry eyes boring into Horra.

"Thank you, Rowan. I see that won't be necessary. The Erlking shall be allowed no pets, musical instruments, or books he could apply to manipulate anything. He will live the life he planned to provide for the stolen children, but his jailers will not misuse or abuse him, or those who inflict violence upon him will suffer death. Oddar will send a knight assembly to check on his treatment and condition until he is no more. So I have spoken, and so it shall be."

Horra looked at Glory, communicating an unspoken question to the fairy.

"And he has to remove the hexes he's placed on all of his victims, including on me and my mother." Glory's lips curled into a satisfied grin.

"Oh. Me too," Grendel said as she hustled to Horra's side, Galumph's hand in hers. The spider was nowhere in sight.

The elves recoiled from the giantess, who no longer looked like a great shadow in a cape. Her beastly fangs stood out against her fox-like face. She looked almost as ghastly as the Erlking.

Horra smiled sincerely at Grendel and Galumph, liking the sharp animalistic features her friend's curse had left her with. Timid as she was, she would look right at home in Oddar's Hall of Monstrosity. Taking her dagger, she sliced her palm and rubbed it alongside Rowan's sap. Taking the hilt, she nodded. "So be it."

The hum of the oath settling drowned out the Erlking's shriek.

Rumbles rocked the ground, shaking the trees.

Horra turned to the Sylvan Council. "What are their charges?" she asked Rowan.

Shouts of anger burst from the elves. Torren held onto an enraged Belamir as Glory placed a bubble around the others to keep them from attacking anyone. They pounded uselessly against the invisible barrier.

Horra turned to her, surprised. "I thought you were depleted?"

She shrugged. "I snuck a thread or five of magic from the elf when he healed me."

Rowan lifted a finger. "Carrying on with their charges. Magical medical crimes against the drows and the oreads. Mishandling of the Erlkings—plural, two known dangerous creatures—and carelessly monitoring them. The Sylvan Council and, by extension, all elves, also violated the sovereignty of Oddar by taking possession of the Riven. There may be other charges, but these should suffice."

"Now, just a minute. The oreads agreed to the experiments," Belamir raged, his pale cheeks darkening with his anger. He twisted to get away, but her knight was easily double the elf's size.

"Did they survive the testing?" Horra asked, knowing the answer before he responded. It was as obvious as the lobes on the ancient elf's ears.

"Well, no, but it wasn't our fault. They caught the crud from the drows. There's no cure for that. There was nothing we could do about it."

She flinched at the mention of the crud. Visions of her mother danced in her mind's eye. She pinned him with controlled hostility. "You could've left the mountains to the drows. But you couldn't do that, could you? You'd fled the Wilden Lands, and to return would've been a disgrace." Horra curled her lip. "Especially since the trolls had already taken control of the Iron Mountains you'd deserted. When all of your actions to eliminate the drows didn't work, you stole Oddar land to form the Riven to rid yourselves of your problems. But you failed in that as well." She waved her free arm at the Erlking. Her blood rushed through her body, fury hot in her veins.

She took a fortifying breath, allowing her ire to cool before speaking again. "So, without having to read through those charges again, what is your plea? Is anything I said untrue? Speak now before I continue."

Belamir clenched his jaw. The other elves did the same.

"I'll take that as a no. What is your plea?" She held her fury in check.

"We refuse to answer to any charges you contrive against us. We are not your subjects and therefore not burdened by your judgment." Belamir's smile was savage.

Horra bared her tusks and lowered her voice. "You have been our subjects since the day my grandmother, Oddar's first queen, forged a deal with your kind. Therefore, considering your obstinance, your sentence will be less gracious."

She clenched the sword's hilt tighter, digging it farther into the ground. "Your borders will no longer remain closed to the rest of the Wilden Lands. You've proven to be corrupt and duplicitous by nature. Therefore, you will no longer have unbridled rein to do as you will. You will accept our ambassadors, and we will allow representatives from Endwylde, via restricted travel, through our lands."

She took a breath and continued. "Last, and for clarification, you are now, and until his death, the Erlking's custodians. You will treat him respectfully, but he will be your prisoner in every sense of the word. You will ensure he and any other violent elf from now until forever does not escape and harm any other creature, or you forfeit your coveted kingdom to Oddar. The balance of good and evil in Endwylde is restored."

Boom! Crack!

The elves shrank, unrestrained terror on their faces.

Glory staggered, a hand clutched to her chest. Light burst from her.

Grendel cried out and crumpled to the ground.

CHAPTER 35

Grendel twisted to sit, her body trembling. Her head hurt and she was queasy. She'd felt this before—the first time she'd changed. Alarm blared inside her head.

The queen bearer dropped to her side and grabbed one of her hands. "Grendel, don't move. Rowan, take the Erlking over to the elves. Torren, see to Glory."

"What happened?" Grendel asked, confusion muddling her mind.

"You collapsed after I removed your curse." The troll royal handed her a water canister. "Take a drink. It might help. I don't know if you're dehydrated, or if reversing your hex caused you to pass out." The Ghost Tree shone on them, the air clear and crisp. Were they still in that horrible dark forest?

"The hex is gone?" Grendel checked her arms. The dark fur and tint on her skin were gone. "I'm back to normal?" She reached out and felt her face and hair. She had jewels on her

303

skull again. Bringing her arm down, she smiled to see it was a natural orange hue again.

The queen bearer chuckled. "Well, you have one black streak in your hair." She rubbed a claw over it. "But otherwise, you're your natural, beautiful giant self again."

"Grendel? You okay?" Galumph climbed onto her sister's lap. It was almost like old times.

"She's going to be fine. Have her take a sip," Horra instructed the girl. "I have to check on the others."

The queen bearer left in a rush, and Galumph wrapped her arms around Grendel's neck. "I was afraid something happened to you."

"Kkk—choking." Her sister loosened her grip. "Thanks. I don't know what it was. One minute I was clasping your hand, and the next I'm sitting up and my brain is all jumbled." Her head pounded a rhythm. She lifted a hand to a sore spot and found a lump. "Someone struck me with a rock."

Galumph shrugged. "What's going to happen to the bad man?"

"He's going away. You don't have to worry about him anymore." It felt good to smile again.

Crashing footsteps thundered against the forest floor.

They glanced at each other. "Giants."

Galumph hustled off Grendel's lap.

Grendel stood, but her knees were weak. She leaned against her sister, who didn't seem to mind. A group of giants ran through the trees, directly toward them.

All the children scattered except for the giants, who eagerly awaited the newcomers.

Grendel hugged her sister tight, hoping to see if their parents were among the group.

A squeal sounded, and a girl ran to her mother. Another

boy ran to his parents. Grendel craned her neck, hoping against hope.

Finally, she saw them. "Mummy! Poppy!" she shrieked at the same time as her sister. They took off running. Their parents bent low, tears streaming down their faces.

"Our girls!" Her mother gathered them into a tight embrace.

"We've missed you so!" Her father enveloped them in his big strong arms.

Grendel soaked in her parent's love and concern, wondering why she had been so afraid to reveal herself before.

Galumph wiggled out of their grasp. "Mummy, Poppy, I have a new pet."

"Of course you do, my little carrot." Their mother dragged her back into their embrace.

Grendel's heart almost burst. She'd taken her family for granted before. She vowed never to do so again.

~Glory~

PAIN RIPPED through Glory's body as the hexes unraveled inside her. She gladly welcomed the agony, knowing it wasn't the end of her this time but the beginning of a renewed life. Lightness replaced the heavy weight the Erlking's magic had left in every cell of her being. Her wings quivered, stretching to their glorious full length.

Her mind instantly turned to her mother. Would she awaken from the debilitating curse the Erlking placed on her? If so, would her sister rejoice while having to give up her position, or would she resent Glory for restoring the queen's health?

Light coalesced around her, glowing like a beacon. Magic flowed freely in her veins, and she basked in it. She lifted her arm. Her puckered wound was still there. Good. It was a symbol of what she'd gone through. A lesson she wouldn't quickly forget.

Horra grabbed her wrist. "Help us with the children, please? Some parents have shown up." She waved at Grendel and her family. "But most are still under our care. They're half-starved and unbelievably grimy."

"What do I do?" she asked, surprising herself by wishing to help.

"Food. Not flowers." Horra quickly modified the request. She sniffed the air. "It smells as if something is cooking already. Please check on it and make sure they get something to drink also. If we head back to the castle on foot, they'll need to be physically able to travel." She strode off.

Glory spun in a circle, feeling lighter than she had in far too long. Her wings fluttered, uninhibited. The muted purple tinge they'd adopted was gone, replaced by a healthier pearl hue. Fully restored, they weighed nothing at all. If only she'd realized the easiest way to remove the hex was to work with the troll, Glory could've saved herself a lot of trouble.

She moved into the center of the children and whistled.

The children quieted and focused on her. It was almost like old times when creatures would stop and admire her. An uplifting thought, but she set it aside. She had work to do.

Calliope thundered into the forest, her eyes ablaze and her dark mane flowing. The kelpie landed beside Glory, jerked her head up and down, and nickered. "It feels good to be free, doesn't it, girl?" She laid her forehead between the animal's eyes and scratched her neck. "Help me one last time?"

~Rowan~

ROWAN GATHERED his seedlings at the base of the giant Ghost Tree. "We need to establish this forest as the new Weald. That means placing new, stronger foundation spells."

They clattered back at him, understanding the task he'd offered. "Good. Now go and make me proud."

After they disappeared, Rowan laid his hand on the tree's trunk.

"Very well done, my boy!" Merrow crowed above the rest of the voices. Hundreds of spirits crowded the tree. Though it could possess that many phantoms, it wouldn't take his offspring a long time to establish the new perimeters and seal the forest. Then everyone—roods, dryads, oread souls, the essence of the fray folk—could scatter into the safety of the trees, finding new homes again.

"Will you stay to help establish a new druid race?" Woodsly's voice reverberated through the noise.

"Yes. I believe that is my next mission," he replied, a rightness in the declaration filling his fibers.

"What is your next mission?" The queen bearer stepped around the tree next to him.

He glanced into the canopy's dark silhouette against the sparkling night sky. He never realized how many stars glittered from the heavens above them. "I will stay to establish another round of druids to help usher the Wilden Lands into a time of peace and prosperity."

A smirk crinkled the royal's green lips. "That was such a mature response from a middling's mouth."

"I may look like a pre-adolescent now, but we both know I've matured beyond my physique." His voice did not reflect the stern authority it had once held. He clasped his thin hands together behind his back.

Several emotions crossed the queen bearer's expressive face. She squeezed his shoulder. "It's okay, Rowan. I failed to grow for three years. If anyone understands, it's me. Look at it this way. You've been gifted a second chance to grow and do it in the proper way now. No more expanding pastries rushing you on your way or roods accelerating your growth to confront a terrible evil invading the Wilden Lands. You took on the Erlking and won. Balance has been restored. You're a hero."

He bowed. "As are you, Queen Bearer."

In a rush, she swept him into a tight embrace. "But I'll miss you, you big stick in the mud."

He awkwardly patted her back, enduring the hug. "If you need me, employ the Yew tree in the Conservatory."

Her thick, unruly hair scratched across the soft bark of his face as she nodded.

Finally, she let him go. "Take care of those saplings. I'll come visit you when everything settles down."

He quirked an eyebrow.

She lifted a claw to his face where the worq had injured him with the axe. "It's still there," she assured him. "Don't forget about me."

A creaking laugh bubbled up in his chest. "I will always think of you when I hear something slurp."

They shared a smile.

THE END

EPILOGUE

~Horra~
Eighteen months later

Horra stretched the neckline of the silky red dress poking her hide. She stood in the middle of her bedroom—enlarged to include Woodsly's old room when she'd requested more space. Without a druid instructor, the room wasn't needed. Grendel Largeness—apothecary owner—and Princess Glory Toppenbottom tittered around her, readying her for her coronation.

"Did you sneak prickly powder in this?" she asked Glory—beauty consultant extraordinaire, as the fairy now boasted. The princess had offered to create her an epic dress for her special day. Preferring it over her stiff Oddar uniform, Horra had agreed. Now, she wasn't so sure.

"You're not used to wearing fine fabrics, and if you would've used the lotion I provided, it wouldn't be prickling you right now." Glory grumbled as she adjusted the hemline to reflect the inch she'd grown since she'd taken her last measurement. Her flittering wings added a soft breeze to the room, swirling her sweet perfume around. "Seriously, did Rowan or Grendel send you some mysterious expanding powder or something?"

"Our girl be making up for lost time," Sageel said as she cleared the dirty clothes from Horra's bedroom floor. "'Sides, trolls always be growth spurting at this age."

"Well, it would've been nice if someone would've told me that the last time I was here." Sparkles clouded the air as she sent one last spell into the fabric. "There. That should do it." Glory stood.

"I was in the middle of my trials. I didn't think about it," Horra grumbled, scratching the itchy spot again.

"It's a good thing we arrived early," Glory said, stowing her brushes. "I didn't realize how much time it would take to create troll beauty."

Horra made a face. Once, she would've taken that as an insult. Now, after a year of friendship and correspondence, it was the natural form of teasing they'd fallen into.

"Stop itching," Grendel said, digging in her bag. "Use this." She took out a bottle of paste and handed it to Horra. "It's from the tingleroot recipe Rowan sent me. It works amazingly. My apothecary sells out of it as soon as I assemble a new batch."

"Speaking of Rowan, is he going to come?" Horra asked the giantess while she applied a dab of the coveted concoction to her hide. Though Horra had communicated with Rowan often, Grendel and Rowan talked nearly every day.

"He said he has a surprise for you, so he'll be here. When is he never on time?" Grendel joked.

Glory, brush in hand, adjusted the curls she'd forced Horra to endure earlier that morning. "Don't move. I almost have this perfect." She sprayed something in the air.

Horra gagged at the uber-sweet scent. "That's awful. What is it?"

"Botanical hair spray. It's the newest product in my beauty line." She took a deep breath. "Sweetsuckle. Mmm."

Horra formed a gag face. "I'm not a flower."

"No, you're not. You're more like a weed," Glory said as she packed the rest of her cases full of makeup, hair products, and clothing swatches.

A knock came at the door, and the girls froze. It couldn't be Sageel. The hobgoblin hadn't had enough time to scuttle to the laundry room and return.

Glory waved Horra away from the door and opened it. She left it ajar and whispered under her arm, "It's Torren."

Torren, her knight escort, had arrived to take her to the front courtyard, where they were holding the coronation. Normally performed inside the castle, they'd received so many RSVPs that they'd had to move it outside. Thankfully, it was a lovely late Falltide day with plenty of sunshine and no rain clouds in sight.

When Glory was sure Horra was ready, she opened the door wide.

The heeled shoes she wore clicked against the stone floor. Horra determined to ditch them after the ceremony and go bare-clawed. She stepped in front of the door and blushed when Torren's mouth dropped open.

"Y—you're lovely," her knight stammered, his face darkening.

"That's all me," Glory said, pushing Horra out the door and following behind her, almost knocking her over with her wings.

It took all Horra's concentration not to tip over in the confounding shoes, but Torren's arm shot out to steady her. "Thank you," she told him, ignoring her fluttering fairy friend.

They strolled down the stairway and out of the throne

room. A gulpy herald halted them, waiting for the crowd to settle down. He bobbed his lolling head, punched a fist to his chest, and bowed, ushering them outside.

The front courtyard was full beyond capacity, with standing room along the edges. Dignitaries and heads of kingdoms, including Queen Stella Toppenbottom—looking regal and healthy—sat on the chairs, which were carved and gifted by the Sylvan Council—a peace offering. Others, such as hobgoblins, gnomes, goblins, and other creatures from across the Wilden Lands, stood where space allowed.

Horra hesitated, her claws growing clammy. "What if I forget the words?"

"You won't," Grendel whispered as she skittered away, taking her seat among the throng.

Torren led her to the far end, where a red runner carpet ran the length of the aisle and potted plants lined the path. Dryads stood among the trees, blending in to form a formidable barrier. "I can't believe so many people showed up."

Torren squeezed her claw. "You saved the Wilden Lands. I would expect no less."

He let her arm go, and she sent him a startled glance.

A woodgoblin stepped from a row of dryads.

Rowan. His brown bark was clear and polished. He wore a bark suit, coattails included, but no shoes. A bow tie bobbed at his throat.

"You made it." A wide smile broke across Horra's face.

He held out a branchy arm for her to take. "I wouldn't have missed it for the world."

He led her across the path, where he presented her to her father. The king held a royal-red pillow with Oddar's formal crown—her crown. Jewels along the golden frame winked in the sunlight.

Balk, with his daughter, Floke, smiled and nodded as she

passed. She recognized several faces in the crowd, which buoyed her.

Stepping over to the newly carved marble thrones, Rowan thumped his fist to his chest and bowed, moving to the side.

Pidge chirruped from a tree at the edge of the courtyard.

The king handed the pillow and crown to another gulpy. He placed the golden blade on her shoulder and passed it to her other shoulder before sinking the blade into the ground. "My daughter. It is with great honor I present this crown to you. No longer will you be queen bearer. You are Queen Horra Fyd of Oddar. May you rule with a mighty claw, like your foremothers before you." He placed the crown on her head, careful not to snag it in the perfect coif Glory had created.

"And my father before me," she said clearly.

Her father faltered, then grinned. "Indeed. May you take this honor in full knowledge of the sacrifice required to rule and be true. Hard work is the bounty of a kingdom, and providence is its guide."

Horra repeated the new motto she'd changed as soon as they'd returned from the Extermination of the Evil, as they now referred to the events. "I shall serve Oddar faithfully and fully with the knowledge of the sacrifice I make. May it be so."

The ground beneath them trembled, sealing her spoken oath.

Cheers erupted from the crowd.

Horra spun, her silky red skirt flowing around her feet. With a claw on her crown, she kicked the shoes off, much to the delight of the crowd, and took her place on her new throne.

ACKNOWLEDGMENTS

I thank God for the gift of seeing stories in my mind, and then giving me the courage to figure out how to write those visions down and make a book out of them. And to my husband and family who root for me, lift me up on those dark days, and help me brainstorm when I need help, I will always love you more. For my friends who have supported me even when my writing was cringe-worthy, thank you and I love you for it. Thank you Scrivenings Press and ScrivKids, I'm so blessed to know each and every one of you. To my readers, I want you to know how much it means that you take precious time out of your lives to read this story. I hope it doesn't disappoint.

About the Author

Winner of the 2016 ACFW Genesis Award and Finalist in the 2023 Carol awards and the 2024 Realm Makers Realm awards, Dawn has been recognized for her published and unpublished works.

As a child, Dawn often had her head in the clouds, creating scenes and stories for anything and everything she came across. She believed there was magic everywhere, a sentiment she has never outgrown. Nature inspires her, and her love for the underdog and the unlikely hero colors much of what she writes.

Dawn adores anything Steampunk, is often distracted by shiny, pretty things, and her obsession with purses and shoes borders on hoarding. Dawn lives in Iowa with her husband, a chef and food service business owner.

ALSO BY DAWN FORD

Woodencloak

The Band of Unlikely Heroes—Book One

Thirteen-year-old troll princess Horra Fyd's life changes forever after an unexpected visit from the fairy queen and her two daughters. Tales of fairies gave Horra nightmares as a young troll. Before evening falls, however, a real nightmare unfolds. Horra's father, King Fyd, goes missing. Her woodgoblin instructor is poisoned and uses his magic to revert to a seed. And a mysterious, gaunt man wearing a cape and playing a panflute joins the fairies in trying to capture her.

Horra flees but is instantly lost in a world she's never had to travel alone. A letter hidden in her knapsack from her late instructor informs her that a power-hungry Erlking seeks revenge against her kingdom and their allies for a two-generation old war. She is tasked with getting his seed to the Weald, a magical forest. There it can regenerate into a druid, the only creature with the power to hold the balance between good and evil, and who is able to defeat the Erlking.

However, the Erlking is always one step behind her. Horra must fight to protect herself, but she has no magic. She accepts a gift from a dead druid spirit of a charmed woodencloak to disguise her. But magic failed her mother, how can she possibly trust it?

Can Horra have faith and courage enough to trust a power she can't see, and become a warrior heroine her foremothers can be proud of? Or will she allow fear to rule over her and lose everything that matters —including her life?

Get your copy here:

https://scrivenings.link/woodencloak

Mossycoat

The Band of Unlikely Heroes—Book Two

Troll Princess Horra Fyd may have succeeded in getting the druid seed to the magical Weald forest in time to sprout, but she's finding that getting her kingdom back in order is not as easy as she hoped. Oddar's subjects are rebelling and trolls are mysteriously disappearing without a trace. Horra and her father King Divitri are at a loss on what's happening, but they know who's behind it all.

When Horra's summoned back to the Weald to meet Rowan, the new druid warrior, she finds the woodgoblin a know-it-all stick in the mud. Rowan's not impressed with the troll princess, either. However, after a suspicious magical fire destroys the Weald, they're forced to rely on each other to venture out in a kingdom that's becoming more dangerous by the day.

Will Horra and Rowan be able to set their differences aside to become a strong team? Or will they fall into the Erlking's traps, stopping their mission before it even gets started?

Get your copy here:

https://scrivenings.link/mossycoat

Tatterhood

The Band of Unlikely Heroes—Book Three

Troll Princess Horra Fyd and young druid Rowan team up to reverse the evil Erlking's spells and save the creatures across the Wilden Lands. However, Fairy Princess Glory Toppenbottom is still a thorn in Horra's side. After Horra and Glory have a heated fight, Glory sneaks out of the castle. She is bent on finding the Erlking to reverse the hex he cast on her. This creates a political disaster when Glory's sister announces she's coming to retrieve Glory.

Angered by Horra's treatment of a royal guest, King Fyd proclaims Horra to be Queen Bearer. She becomes the ad hoc ruler, freeing her father from the scandal. Shocked, Horra assents. Her first move is to find the missing fairy princess before it becomes an interkingdom war. They form a search party and leave.

The Erlking stalks their every move. When the only choice points them toward the Riven, a cursed hidden land, they don't hesitate. They find Glory is already there, but are immediately separated. The trio finds that the Riven is nothing like anyone imagined. Will they survive the Erlking's magical traps, or will they, like everyone else, perish within its borders?

Get your copy here:

https://scrivenings.link/tatterhood

The Girl with Stars in Her Eyes

Firebird Series—Book One

Eighteen-year-old servant girl Tambrynn is haunted by more than her unusual silver hair and the star-shaped pupils in her eyes. Her uncontrollable ability to call objects leads the wolves who savagely murdered her mother right to her door.

When she's fired and outcast during a snowstorm, her carriage wrecks and she's forced to find refuge in an abandoned cottage. There, her life is upended when the magpie who's stalked her for ten years transforms into a man, Lucas. He's her Watcher and they're from a different kingdom. His job is to keep her safe from her father, an evil mage, who wants to steal her abilities, turn her into one of his undead beasts, and become immortal himself

Can they make it to the magical passageway and get to their home kingdom in time for Tambrynn to thwart her father's malicious plans? Or will Tambrynn's unique magic doom them ?

Get your copy here:

https://scrivenings.link/thegirlwithstarsinhereyes

The Girl with Fire in Her Veins

Firebird Series—Book Two

Former servant girl Tambrynn struggles with her new firebird abilities, especially the internal fire she cannot control. So, she, along with her Watcher Lucas, and her grandfather Bennett journey to a hidden mountain keep to find the answers she seeks before she sets the kingdom aflame.

But there's a new dragon who's targeting Tambrynn, a mergirl who wishes to manipulate her, and the froggen king, Siltworth, who hasn't forgotten that Tambrynn destroyed his watery reign. When her father, the evil mage Thoron, attacks someone she loves, Tambrynn's group is separated and she has to face another powerful foe alone.

Is she strong enough to withstand the deluge? Or will she drown in the fire and the flood?

Get your copy here:

https://scrivenings.link/thegirlwithfireinherveins

The Girl with a Dragon's Heart

Firebird Series—Book Three

After being injured while reversing the froggen's flood on Anavrin, Tambrynn travels to the depths of the mysterious Bloodthorn Forest for a cure. There she finds what she's looking for, but she also finds more trouble than she can handle. Thoron, her dark mage father, has found her and he's brought the Hulda, a villainous spirit Guardian, along as well. Tragedy strikes during the ensuing magical battle, leaving Tambrynn reeling from one loss closely followed by the death of a loved one. Shaken, Tambrynn barely manages to escape to her grandfather's mountain sanctuary to hide.

Burgeoning with power siphoned from dragon bones, Thoron is only a few steps behind her, making that sanctuary a prison. When unrest spreads across Anavrin, threatening all the Anavrinians again, Tambrynn must race to unlock the hidden power of her firebird abilities in order to defeat her evil father. But time is of the essence, and there's no way out of the mountain in sight.

With time running out, and hidden dangers around every corner, will a fairy tale and a secret pathway lead Tambrynn to find a true dragon's heart, the only power pure enough to take on Thoron's enhanced malevolent magic? Or will her father do what he set out to do since she was born—steal her abilities and destroy all that the Kinsman has created?

Get your copy here:

https://scrivenings.link/thegirlwithadragonsheart

ScrivKids.com is an imprint of Scrivenings Press LLC.

Stay up-to-date on your favorite books and authors with our free e-newsletters.

https://scriveningspress.com/join-our-email-community/